THE

GOD

DAMN

DEAD

BY

COLT SKINNER

D & T
PUBLISHING

To my brothers, Darryl "Death Mask" H., and Fast-Eddy B. Thanks for all the wild times!

I would like to thank everyone who helped with this book, inspired me to write it, and provided their knowledge to the world so I could do research for it.

Thank you to Dawn and Tim Shea from D&T Publishing for taking a chance on me. To Tasha Schiedel for the edits, Ash Ericmore for the awesome cover, and Ruthann Jagge-who encouraged me to submit to the Emerge Series when I was first starting.

Thank you to Johnathan Davis, Cliff Matias, Danny D-Low and everyone else on "bikertok" for sharing your community. Thank you to Chris Yellowbird, Ira Timothy, Vanessa the Resilient Inuk, and the scores of other indigenous creators who share the knowledge of their culture with the world.

Thank you to my grandmother for always encouraging me, you will always be with me. To my uncles, aunts and cousins, who read my work even though it scares them. And thank you to my mother who makes me feel seen and valued. Who moved us to a farmhouse with mummified spiders in the basement. A place where the coyotes howled at night, the owls stared, and the barn cats followed us through the fields. It was the best place to grow up that a young creative and creepy mind could have possibly asked for.

And thank you to my family; my beautiful children, and my incredible wife, who allow me to be who I really am, and love me for it.

THE

GOD

DAMN

DEAD

W I L L I A M

Bill McConnell looked down the gravel path that led into the quarry and smiled. Spiraling down the algae-green stained walls of the open mine, the old service road led into a murky cesspool of brown stagnant water. There were rumors that a great and evil thing lurked within those depths; a monstrous thing that slithered along the silt bottom and hunted any children who dared to venture close to the edge. Bill knew that those were just stories though, fibs grown-ups told to keep their kids away from the quarry, and that there was nothing to fear down inside that pit.

"I'm not sure this is a good idea, Billy," proclaimed a timid voice behind him.

Bill looked over his shoulder at a small boy with dark ringlets wearing a long sleeve spiderman shirt. "If yer scared Patrick, then don't come."

Patrick kicked a patch of dirt, sending it high into the air. "I'm not scared of that stupid quarry Bill, but when dad finds out you stole that bike, he's gonna beat you worse than he did that time you made a Molotov cocktail."

The wind picked up, and the skeletal motorcycle Bill clenched in his hands rocked gently. Just before dawn, Bill and Pat had crept out of their house, snatched the bike from where it had been left to rot behind their father's mechanic shop, and took turns rolling it the six kilometers between their house and the quarry. The bike had no fairings, nor fenders, the gas tank was gone, and the engine had been removed. Now, a rusted chassis, two bald tires, and a busted-up seat were all that remained of the 60s era Harley-Davidson Sportster. For years, the brothers had taken turns sitting on the bike and racing down the gravel driveway that separated the tiny McConnell house from their father's shop. Sometimes they would fall off and hurt themselves, other times their father would become enraged by the noise they were making and give whichever one of them happened to be sitting on the bike at the time a smack to the head. Patrick never seemed particularly interested in the Sportster, except for using it for the occasional joyride, but Bill saw the motorcycle for what it could be; not just a heap of metal and rubber to ride around the dirt roads of Bastard Township on, but a gateway into manhood.

The only other thing that had ever made Bill feel "manly," were the girls in his sixth-grade class. The warm smell of lip balm or the wave of flowing hair easily caused Bill to feel light-headed, and made the words that came out of his mouth to fumble over themselves. In contrast, when Bill gripped the handlebars of the Sportster, he felt in control of something wild and dangerous, and ultimately, he felt powerful.

"I don't give a shit about that," Bill said, defiantly. "Dad's gonna hit us the next time he gets drunk anyway. All taking this bike has done is give him a reason to beat on us."

"What if he gets mad at mama?" asked Patrick in a mousy tone.

Bill glared at his little brother. The mention of their mother sent heat into the boy's cheeks and riled him up more than he'd hoped to be that morning. "She had nothing to do with us taking the bike!" Bill hissed. "If anything, maybe dad'll get worked up over this and leave her alone for a while. Shit, I'd take a beating or two for mama, anytime."

"I don't get why he's always hittin' her. All she does is try to help him." Patrick bent over and collected a stone from the ground. The younger McConnell brother threw his arm back, and then launched the rock high into the air with a grunt. Together, the brothers watched the stone rise and come down into the cesspool with a plop. "She's so nice to everyone."

The heat in Bill's cheeks cooled a little bit. "That's why he beats on her," Bill huffed. "He can't stand kindness. It reminds him of how horrible he is. The only thing good about him is that Wide Glide of his, and even that's getting old."

Bill looked at his brother, and as soon as their eyes met, Patrick turned away. Tears dripped out of the younger boy's eyes, leaving steaks along his face. Patrick was about to walk away when Bill caught him by the shoulder and pulled him in close. They said nothing to one another, but silently looked out over the quarry and watched the last traces of the morning's yellows and pinks disappear into the blue of the day. In the nearby forest, critters scurried through the underbrush and songbirds chimed out warm melodies.

The moment lingered, but after a while Bill released his little brother and walked over to the Sportster. On the precipice of the gravel path, Bill felt gravity tug the motorcycle forward, reminding the machine of its birthright to go fast.

With a wild eagerness, Bill threw a leg over the rusted frame and grabbed the handlebars. "Yer already my accomplice, Pat. So, you might as well hop on, unless yer chickenshit. Either way, I'm going down this hill."

Patrick took a final look around the quarry with his hands laced together pensively. He scanned the tree line for signs that some adult was about to pop out and drag them both back to their father to be dealt with, but he saw nothing except branches rustling in the wind. Then, with a sudden wave of courage, Patrick scurried over to the motorcycle and leapt onto the back.

"There's no footrests on this thing, Billy!"

"Probably better that way, one less thing for you to break your legs on." Bill looked down the uneven terrain before him, and for the first time that morning the idea that he could be hurt while riding a scrap-heap motorcycle down a dangerous hill crystalized in his mind. The thought only made Bill angry though, so without giving it any more consideration he pushed the Sportster forward.

Speed came on slowly, but only a moment later Bill felt the morning air rushing over his face. The sensation electrified his skin. He propelled the bike with both feet, pushing once, twice, but on his third push, the ground caught his right foot and shot it backward. The

Sportster was in free fall now and there was nothing more Bill could do except lift both of his rubber boot covered feet into the air, lean forward, and try his best to steer the bike away from the jagged rocks that lined the side of the quarry.

A third of the way down the path, Bill felt a pain beginning to form in his cheeks. He thought it was the cold winds at first, but soon realized that the sensation had nothing to do with the air. For the first time in his young life, Bill McConnell was smiling so hard that it hurt.

Without warning, something crashed into Bill's shoulder. For a moment, the boy was confused, but then he realized that he could hear his brother screaming; "Slow down! SLOW DOWN!" But Bill didn't pay Patrick any mind, he couldn't. All of his fears and frustrations had disappeared into a gray and green blur that looked like a smeared oil painting. Nothing existed outside of that blur. The pounding on his shoulder and the terrified screams of his little brother were distant and vague, like an echo bouncing off a rockface. The brakes were gone anyways, but even if they weren't, Bill wasn't going to slow down, not now, not ever again.

The pounding on Bill's back came to an abrupt end, and the bike was suddenly lighter. Bill took a quick glance over his shoulder and saw Patrick tumbling ass-over-apple cart by the side of the path. He let out a single and wicked "Ha!", then leaned back and stretched out both of his arms like he was Christ crucified. His shirt fluttered and his lips flapped. Bill closed his eyes and relished the sensations of wind and motion and courage.

Then, the bike bounced. Both wheels came off the ground, and when the Sportster came back to earth, it did so like a thousand-pound weight. Bill grabbed the handlebars tightly and made the first mistake of his riding career; he tried to turn out of the crash. Like a bullet from a gun, the front wheel spun to the side and dug into the gravel. Bill felt weightless and the next thing he saw was blue sky, then gravel, then sky again. The boy landed hard on his shoulder, and a flash of lightning white pain ignited there. The road under him rumbled, then ripped away his shirt and flayed some of the skin on his back. The Sportster rolled beside him and continued to tumble even after Bill came to a stop by the water's edge. With a splash, the bike crashed into the stagnant pool and sent droplets of murky water flying through the air.

Bill rested on the edge of the cesspool. His shoulder throbbed and his back ached, but in truth, the sensation was oddly comforting. As he stared up at the blue sky above, with a face full of smelly water, he felt incredibly calm.

A moment later, two weak hands grabbed Bill's arm, and pulled him upwards. "Oh my god! Are you alright?" It was Patrick, who was wide eyed and trembling. "I thought you were gonna die!"

"I'm alright," said Bill, as he struggled to his feet. The older brother dusted off his pants, and then touched his back. His fingers ran slick with red blood.

"That looks painful," Patrick offered. "We should get mama to look at that."

Bill shook his head and grinned. "It's not so bad."

The Sportster was lodged in the mud at the end of the path, and its rear wheel stuck out of the water like a duck's bum. Bill stared at the bike for a moment and then started walking towards it.

"Where are you going?" Patrick asked. "We can just leave the bike, Billy. If we're lucky, dad'll probably think it was the O'Riley brothers that took it. Don't go in there Bill, you know there's some monster living there!"

Bill was about to go into the waters when his brother's words stopped him. The image of a vile, bloodthirsty creature flashed in his brain and Bill wondered if there was any chance that the stories he had heard were true. His heart quickened. But when Bill looked up and saw the wreckage of the Sportster, he remembered the feeling of wind against his cheeks. The boy reminded himself that the only thing he had to fear in that pit was a bunch of leeches and nothing more. Bill closed his eyes, pushed the thought of the quarry monster out of his mind, then boldly stepped into the water and walked over to the bike. Nothing attacked him. Even the leeches left him alone. The pain of the crash was already dimming as he reached the Sportster, and as he began pulling the motorcycle out of the mud, Bill turned to his little brother and said, "Are you kidding me? I'm gonna do that again."

CALEB

On a balmy summer day, with the scent of gasoline and rubber permeating the air, Caleb Driscoll and his Uncle Gordon sauntered through the streets of Port Dover, Ontario. Just as it was every Friday the Thirteenth, the small beach-front town had transformed into a midway of two-wheeled-suicide-machines that glistened with chrome and glossy paint. A hundred thousand people, dressed in leather and high-density nylon, invaded the meager downtown area of the city. With ice cream dripping over stainless steel rings, visitors purchased motorcycle themed t-shirts, orange and black fudge, and tiny chopper figurines, with cash pulled out of authentic Harley-Davidson wallets. The local Kinsmen, who sponsored the massive motorcycle gathering and always had a stage set up for speeches and performances, blasted classic rock anthems out of two enormous speakers.

One of Geddy Lee's iconic baselines trickled into Caleb's fourteen-year-old ears and helped his mind drift vacantly. The angst-ridden teenager felt a jab in his ribs, and after dusting off the cobwebs of his brain, he saw that his uncle was pointing towards a sparse looking antique motorcycle.

"Check out that knucklehead over there!" Gordon said, as he raised and lowered his eyebrows like a lecherous cartoon character.

The bike was a post-world-war-two era Harley-Davidson, the kind with a springboard seat and white rimmed tires. It was painted candy-apple red, with luxurious cream trim. The owner was sitting on the seat in a cavalier fashion, revving the engine, and allowing the v-twin to hum the signature *potato-potato* melody that only Harleys offer.

Caleb gave the bike a quick once over, nodded and said, "Yeah man, it's gorgeous."

The boy's response lacked the vigor and enthusiasm it usually held in the presence of such a magnificent machine though. Gordon picked up on his nephew's downtrodden reaction and playfully tried to continue the conversation. "Don't get me wrong, I love my Electra Glide, but it would be a lot of fun to putter around on something like that! You know how many heads you'd turn?"

A sly grin came over Caleb's face. "You'd turn heads, but they'd belong to a bunch of old dudes."

The good-natured teasing gave Gordon a small degree of hope that the day wouldn't be entirely filled with doom and gloom. "Oh, my young apprentice, you have a lot to learn bud. When you get a little older, you're gonna find out that refined ladies dig a guy who has himself a refined pallet, even if that pallet is directed towards motorcycles."

"So, that's why you ride that grandpa bike of yours?" As soon as he made the comment, Caleb put both hands up in a jokingly defensive stance.

"Hey!" Gordon snapped, while smirking and playing into the levity of Caleb's jab by raising a pretend fist. "That Electra Glide is a fine machine! And, chicks feel comfortable on it. Makes them want to snuggle up, not just hold on for their lives. Besides, if I had some crotch rocket, or a chopper, your mom would never have let you ride down here with me."

Caleb's face immediately turned grim. The mention of his mother brought a plague of melancholy to the boy. It reminded him of how troubling the last few weeks had been, and the strains that had been placed on his already tense home life. A sense of confusion also came with that melancholy. Not that he was complaining, but Caleb did wonder why he had been allowed to make the journey with his uncle all the way from his home in the Leslieville area of Toronto to Port Dover.

Strained and frustrated, the boy clenched his fist and tapped his thigh. "How did you talk her into letting me come with you?"

Gordon blew air out of his nostrils. It made a whooshing sound, like a heavy-breathing bull. "Ah shit, she knows this is important. A boy's gotta have a chance to hang out and learn how to be a man every now and again. She's pissed off, don't get me wrong, but that doesn't mean she's looking to fuck over your whole life."

The pair walked over to a nearby bench and sat down. Gordon took a cigarette out of a small metal case and lit it. Briefly, the boy thought about asking to bum a smoke, but quickly realized how terrible that idea was. There was at least a fifty-fifty chance that his uncle would pelt him over the request, or even worse, drive his ass right back to Toronto. Instead of pressing his already razor-thin luck, Caleb suppressed the muted pangs of an addiction that was just beginning to form and sat in silence.

"Did the school make a decision about you coming back this fall?" Gordon asked while taking a drag.

Caleb shook his head and looked down at the grass. "Nope. Honestly, I doubt they're gonna let me come back."

"The school board can't deny you an education. They'll just ship you to some *alternative* school with the rest of the hard luck cases." As Gordon said the word "alternative," he raised his hands and bobbed his middle and index fingers up and down making air-quotes.

"Jeez man!" Caleb spat onto the ground, and leaned back in his seat.

"Hey, that's what you get for clocking your teacher buddy." Gordon took another drag of his smoke, tilted his head to the side and chuckled. Caleb's uncle was a man of small stature, barely five-foot-five-inches tall and slim in frame. The pair shared a body type, as well as a tenacious and quick temper.

"He fucking deserved it," Caleb said through gritted teeth.

Gordon nodded. "No doubt. And, if I'd been there and his punk ass had said what he said about your mom I'd have put him six feet under. That being said, I'd have at least waited to do it, man. Found him walking around after school, you know, heading back to his car or something. I'm not telling you to do that, but it would have been smarter than throwing down in front of everyone else in your class. I know you got a temper, like me and your mom do, but you gotta learn to control that shit."

Caleb stared at a cigarette butt on the ground in front of him and scowled. "You know what really pisses me off?"

"What's that little man?"

"When I was sitting in the vice-principal's office, that jerk kept talking about how he knew what I was *going through*, and that he *empathized* with me. Said he understood how tough I had it at home.

I know he knows about my mom and all her troubles, so I was thinking that maybe he did understand. And then, just as I was feeling like there was someone in my corner, he says that I gotta put all that aside though and figure out how to act right at school. Otherwise, the next time I *get out of line* he'd call the cops on me and have my ass taken to jail."

"Sounds about right."

"I mean, this prick knows what I went through with Children's Aid. He says he's trying to help me, but then tells me he's gonna call the cops on me if I strap up again? FUCK THAT!" Briefly, Caleb looked at his uncle to see if the man was going to correct him for his choice of swear words, but Gordon didn't seem at all interested in reprimanding the boy, so Caleb continued. "So, I suddenly realized that this punk doesn't give a shit about me. He's just blowing smoke up my ass, trying to get me to simmer down and be yet another quiet little drone who doesn't rattle the cage."

"For sure."

"And you know what else? He never once mentioned that my teacher was wrong for saying what he said about my mom. It's bullshit man! School, the cops, Children's Aid, everything, it's all bullshit."

Gordon took a long haul of his cigarette and then blew out the smoke slowly. He looked into the crowd and seemed to ponder. Just as Caleb was feeling worried about what his uncle was thinking, Gordon began to speak. "You know what Caleb, you're not wrong." Gordon leaned in towards his nephew, like he was about to tell him a secret. "Hell, you're figuring out a sad truth about the world, and early too. I guess that's a good thing. Look, none of those fuckers are gonna be there for you, bud. Don't you *ever* think they will. The only people in this world who you can truly rely on are your family and your friends, your *real* friends. You take your time figuring out who the people you can trust are, and once you do, you stick to them like glue. Because *nobody* who works in the system is your friend. Not your teachers, not your vice-principal not the jag-offs at Children's Aid, and especially not the fucking cops."

Caleb nodded and looked over at a nearby intersection where a police officer wearing a bright neon green vest was directing traffic. The boy thought about what his vice-principal had said, about calling the cops on him, and felt the sudden urge to walk over to the intersection and punch that cop right in his face. But, as the first riff of the Guess Who's "American Woman" blasted out of the nearby speakers, Caleb's reckless urge subsided.

Gordon leaned back on the bench, and while looking out over the crowd asked, "I know you decked him because of what he called your mom, but before that, what did that old bastard of a teacher say that got you so riled up?"

Caleb chuckled. "I was talking about the HMCS Haida."

"The World War Two destroyer?" Gordon raised an eyebrow and looked puzzled.

"Yeah. I mentioned in class that it was named after the Haida people. My teacher said that he didn't think that was true, that he'd never heard of the Haida people. I was dumb-founded. I asked him where he thought they got the name from, and he got flustered, 'cause clearly he didn't know. So, I told him that it *was* named after the Haida people and that's why it was part of the Tribal class of destroyers. All of sudden this old bastard yells "WRONG" at the top of his lungs and says I'm making things up. Basically, calling me a liar in front of my whole class. He got all uppity about how he's a teacher, and he ought to know things like that. So, I said that he *should* know things like that. I said that if he didn't know simple facts, then he was probably just a stupid mother fucker. He got red in the face, and it all went downhill from there."

Gordon burst out laughing, slapped both knees with his hands and then clapped his nephew on the back. "Good for you, man! Fuck him! Even if you gotta go to some alternative school, pay it no mind kid. You're gonna do just fine in life. Shit, yer smarter than I am. Mind ya, that ain't saying much." Gordon stood, threw his smoke on the ground and stamped it out with his riding boot. With a quick jab of the chin, he motioned for Caleb to follow him towards the main drag.

As they approached the street, Caleb noticed the swell of a rumbling sound. At first it was distant, like popcorn being made in the next room, but the deep pitter-patter rose like an approaching thunderstorm and soon became guttural and violently loud. Suddenly, the entire downtown screamed like it was filled with fireworks and cannon blasts.

As if Moses had commanded them to do so, the crowd on the street parted and a caravan of shiny metal horses paraded through. The procession was filled with big-engine North American made motorcycles that had dazzling paint jobs, and were adorned with matching decals. The riders were a motley crew of desperados. Most of the men wore faded blue jeans and t-shirts, but a small contingent had massive sombreros fastened to their helmets, while others wore clothing so stylish that it could have only come from the trendy Queen-West area in Toronto or Rue Sainte-Catherine in Montreal. As varied as their garb was, every rider had one thing in common; a black leather vest with matching patchwork on the back. Front and center in the patchwork was a skeleton dressed in a full Mariachi outfit riding a long-fork chopper. With a guitar strung over his back, the cartoonishly dead musician fired a pistol into the air with one hand while gripping the chopper's throttle with the other. Below the skeleton, written in black horror-show letters on a blood-red background were the names of various areas. Most riders appeared to be from Ontario, but Manitoba, Saskatchewan, Nova Scotia, and British Columbia were also claimed. At the top of each cut, clinging to the rider's shoulder in the same beautiful black and red club colors, was the name "Dead Mariachis."

As the caravan passed by, Caleb felt a smile light up his face. Ever since he was little, his favorite part of coming to the Port Dover Rally had always been watching the Dead Mariachis Motorcycle Club arrive en masse. The Parade of the Dead was a tradition in Port Dover, and the Dead Mariachis were always greeted with cheers and applause so loud and wild that it rivaled any hockey game or concert. Today was no different, the excitement of the crowd drowned out the sound of the Kinsmen's P.A. system, silencing the Guess Who.

Across the street from him, Caleb watched a buxom red-headed woman pull out a pair of panties from her pocket and throw them at the bikers. The panties landed on the helmet of a gruff-looking older Dead Mariachi, who snatched them off his head, took a long sniff, and laughed heartily.

"Jesus!" Gordon exclaimed with a radiantly warm smile. "Imagine being one of those guys? You'd be a fucking king."

"How come you never tried to become a Dead Mariachi?" Caleb asked.

Gordon chuckled nervously. "That's not me kid. Those guys are professional riders, man. You're looking at the equivalent of a major league sports team right there. Like the Maple Leafs, if the Leafs could actually win something. You see that vest they have on? It's called a cut. A lot of people think it's just some patches on leather, but it means a hell of a lot to them. Each and every one of those guys would die for that cut. Hell, they'd kill for it if they needed to. People think that makes them criminals, but that ain't what it's about. That club has its own rules, its own values, and its members follow those rules because they *choose* to. Those guys live outside of the law, in a world where a man is expected to be a man, to *control himself*, to stand on his own two feet and, if need be, to do whatever is necessary to protect the people he cares about. Maybe I'm not saying it right, but it's a big deal to be one of those guys. There are expectations that go beyond just being good on your bike, although that's important. You wanna be one of them, you have to be made from the same material. A lot of guys think they have what it takes to live that way, but you gotta be a real man to actually make it happen."

Just as Gordon finished saying all of that, a Dead Mariachi wearing a sombrero, and riding an obscenely gaudy-looking Road-King, caught Caleb's eye and tipped his oversized hat towards the youngster. Caleb smirked, and with two fingers saluted the biker. The parade finished passing by, and the Dead Mariachis took their place along the main drag, in a spot that had been reserved and kept empty for them all morning. Immediately, the members of the Dead Mariachis were surrounded by well-wishers, admirers, and wannabes.

For the rest of the day, Caleb's mind raced with thoughts of motorcycles and manhood. On the ride home, sitting on the back of his uncle's touring bike, Caleb dreamed about being in control of his own motorcycle while wearing a leather vest adorned with the three-piece patch of the Dead Mariachis. Lying in bed later that night, he thought of the rumbling sound of v-twin engines and about panties flying through the air. As he drifted off to sleep, he fantasized about the way the crowd had parted, and the words his uncle said rang in his ears; "A lot of guys think they have what it takes to live that way, but you gotta be a real man to actually make it happen." When he awoke the next day, all of Caleb's thoughts were tinted in the black and red colors of the Dead Mariachis Motorcycle Club, and for years they would remain that way.

D A N I E L

Daniel heard the knocking, but it wasn't until he registered his mother's voice that he was able to pull himself out of the deep waters of sleep and back into the waking world. She was speaking rapidly and in a halting manner that was unusual for her. Daniel knew right away that something was wrong. Below his bedroom, near the back of the house, a door slammed against the wall. Large work boots trotted through the porch and into the kitchen. Finally, a low baritone joined the clamor. There was a man in the house, at a time when a man had no business being there.

The boy slipped his feet out from underneath his covers and swung them over the side of his bed, guiding them down until they found the macrame rug on the floor. As he stood, Daniel's bones popped. First it was his knees that snapped, and then his spine crackled like a percussionist dragging a drumstick over a xylophone. His cracking bones were something Daniel was always sensitive about. It was the insecurity that his classmates noticed in him, and teased him mercilessly about.

When he told his mother about the teasing, she smiled with a good heart and laughed. "You're an old soul," she told him once. "Your bones simply remember what it's like to ache!" Even though he viewed his mother's superstitions as a quirk, the thought of being an old-soul made Daniel feel better. It gave him the sense that he was worth a little more than the other children.

Carefully, the boy crept across his bedroom, past piles of dirty clothing and stacks of comic books. He knelt beside his door and turned the handle gently, it opened with a pop. He heard chaos happening below and listened to the hushed voices drifting up the stairs.

"When did this happen?" asked Daniel's mother.

A snarling deep voice, which Daniel thought he recognized, answered. "An hour ago! What does it matter, woman?"

"It matters because I need to know how strong to make the tincture. The more recent, the less diluted it should be, but if you drink too much, or if the mix isn't right, it'll kill ya."

"JUST MAKE THE FUCKING THING!" barked the angry man.

Daniel frowned. Hearing a man scream at his mother brought on grim feelings, and reminded him of a memory that was buried deep, yet still skimmed the surface of his psyche. The boy recalled the smell of cologne, sweet alcohol and cooked meat, as well as the sound of screaming and the feeling of being cold.

"Keep your voice down!" Daniel's mother shot back. "This is my home, and my boy is sleeping upstairs. I'll not have you wake him up just because you played the fool and got nicked by some hooker. You *will* keep a civil tongue in here, a quiet tongue. Do you hear me?"

A chair scraped across the kitchen floor, and heavy footsteps crossed the room. "Do you know who yer speaking to, WITCH? I'll use whatever FUCKING tone I want!" Pots and pans rattled and then fell to the floor. "You fix ME up, cunt, or I'll fix YOU. It'll be the last goddamn thing I do before I die."

The sharp sound of flesh smacking against flesh came next, and Daniel's mother screamed. "Get out of my house! Die in the fields for all I care, but I'll not mend you, thinking you can talk to me like that!" More utensils fell to the floor and then another volley of fleshy collisions, but these were lower in tone, deeper. Daniel heard grunting and tussling, then to his horror a wet-gagging sound replaced the voices drifting up the stairs. Black sickness invaded Daniel's stomach. The boy reached into the closet beside him, and without looking grabbed something solid and smooth. The baseball bat he pulled from the closet was lighter than he remembered it being, but it would have to do. With a burst of righteous fury, the young man threw open his door and left the safety of his bedroom behind.

The staircase was dark, illuminated only by a dull amber hue from the bottom. Daniel raced downward like a runaway train, and with each step he took the stairs groaned like a wounded old man. When he reached the bottom, the light from the kitchen nearly blinded him. As his eyes adjusted to the brightness, he finally saw the intruder in his home. The man was enormous. He wore saggy work clothes, which had a glistening crimson circle on one side. Lodged between the man and the kitchen counter was Daniel's mother.

Her head was pressed against the cupboards at an unnatural angle, and her legs flailed wildly, searching in equal parts for something to gain leverage on and something to kick. When the man tried to head butt her, Daniel's mother used a free hand to rack her nails across his face. The man howled, then reached up to grab her wrist, but Daniel's mother lunged forward and bit his knuckles instead. The intruder tried to backhand her then, but she ducked, and the man's open hand collided with the cupboard. This gave Daniel's mother the space she needed for her foot to find the man's groin. With a yelp, the intruder bent forward.

With an intensity that he had never felt before, Daniel crossed the room in three quick steps. The young man raised the baseball bat high over his head, and just before he brought it down, the intruder looked up. Daniel recognized the man immediately; his name was Curtis Parker, and he was a bastard. Curtis was a half-crook gin-drunk farmer with a violent reputation. His oldest daughter had left town as soon as she was sixteen, and no one ever heard from her again. Curtis' youngest child was in the same remedial classes as Daniel, and it wasn't uncommon for her to show up to school with bruises and cuts. Everyone knew that these injuries were the handiwork of Curtis Parker, but no one in their small-town bothered to do a damn thing about it.

The bat came down hard, and just before the moment of impact Curtis recognized what was about to happen and his eyes went wide. Daniel was surprised with how much he enjoyed the look he saw in Curtis' eyes. The sound of the collision was hollow and deep, like a pumpkin thrown out of a moving car. Blood exploded from the intruder's nose and drenched the front of Daniel's t-shirt. Curtis fell to his knees, and Daniel raised the bat again. This time he brought it down on the back of the intruder's head, and there was a satisfying crack. The bloodied farmer toppled to the floor, and splayed out. Then, like he was swinging a golf club, Daniel drew the bat back and smashed it into the side of Curtis' head. A chunk of flesh flew through the air and splattered on the kitchen wall. It stayed in the spot where it landed for a moment and then slowly peeled away, finally falling to the floor with a *thwack*. Still caught in the moment, Daniel raised the bat over his head once again, intending to bring it down with every ounce of strength he had, but before he could deliver a death blow, something grabbed him gently by the shoulder. It was his mother.

Calmly, the woman guided Daniel's hands downward until the bat was at his side. She cupped Daniel's face, and smiled with watery eyes. "No! No, no, no, no! Danny Boy, no! Don't do that. We're not like that. We're not *that* sort of people, my love."

"Ma!" Daniel cried. "He was… he was hurting you…"

Daniel's mother slipped a shaking hand over her son's and squeezed. "But, that part is over now. Just look at him." At first the young man's gaze remained fixed on the woman who had given him life. Then, with iron forged grit, she commanded, "Look at him, Daniel!"

He looked down and saw a pathetic thing on the floor. Cutis Parker was a spasming heap, foaming at the mouth and oozing blood from the scarlet gash on the side of his head. Clear fluids seeped from Curtis' ears and nose, and a puddle had formed by his crotch. Urine pooled on the floor, and Daniel had to take a step back to avoid the slow-moving yellow tide and approached him.

"He ain't hurtin' anyone anymore," said Daniel's mother, calmly. "Now, help me pick him up."

Together they lifted Curtis until he was seated on his arse, and propped up against the cupboards. He breathed like a sleeping mastiff, and drooled like a bottle-drunk infant. His left eye was swollen shut, but his right eye remained open and fixed on some unknowable point on the floor. A few times Curtis' head swiveled and noises escaped him that were, maybe, attempts at regaining consciousness, but they were all failed attempts.

As she checked Curtis's eyes and ears, Daniel's mother told her son, "Go get your sled."

"Why?" the young man asked.

"Just get it!" she snapped. "It's in the garage, above your grandfather's workbench. I put it in the rafters years ago, but you can reach it."

Curtis moaned, and Daniel's mother placed a delicate hand on his forehead. "Shhhhh, just stay awake for a little while longer, Curt."

Daniel didn't understand why his mother appeared to be caring for her attacker, but like the good son he was, the young man left the kitchen and went to fetch his old sled. On his way through the back porch, he put on a pair of rubber boots and a coat, and then stepped out into the night. It was cold outside and pissing rain that was nearly ice. The winds howled and stank like damp leaves. As Daniel walked across the driveway, he felt Curtis' blood begin to freeze against his skin.

He was shaking by the time he reached the garage, as much from the cold as from the shock of all that had happened. Daniel pushed the side door open and stepped into the garage. It was frigid and dark inside, but there was no wind, so he felt warmer. The young man prodded the wall, found the light switch, and turned it on, revealing a cavernous single room cluttered with boxes and small broken-down machines. The entire place was dusty, and it stank like mildew and motor oil.

On the far side of the room, sitting beside the workbench, was a 1958 Panhead Chopper, which had belonged to Daniel's grandfather. Both of the bike's wheels were flat, and its blue paint was now dull and covered in dust. Daniel had a vague memory from when he was very young of sitting in front of his grandfather on the bike and holding onto the old man's forearms as they took a quick joyride down the street. Every time he saw the bike, he was reminded of that good feeling that meant he belonged and that he was loved. It was a stark contrast to the feeling he had when he thought about his own father, who was everything violent and angry and filthy in the world. Tonight, however, he barely registered the bike. He looked past the defining possession of his grandfather to the workbench on the other side, and then up to the rafters where the sled had been stored and forgotten.

The young man raced across the floor and leapt up onto the bench. From there, he reached out towards the sled, but was barely able to touch the dangling string attached to the front of it. After failing in his first attempt to dislodge the toy, Daniel jumped carefully, caught the sled by the corner, and batted it out of the rafters. The plastic sled flew backwards and tumbled down onto the Panhead. A lightning bolt of guilt reverberated through Daniel for having allowed the sled to touch his grandfather's bike, but he quickly shook off the feeling. The young man hopped off the workbench, landed on the floor with the thud, then swept up the sled and raced out of the garage and back across the driveway.

When he was safely back inside the farmhouse, Daniel let out a breath which he had been holding in since he left the garage. He stumbled into the kitchen and saw that his mother had been busy in his absence. There were two blankets with intricate needlework on the dining table, and a gym-bag stuffed to the gills resting on the floor. Daniel's mother had on her rubber boots and a thick winter coat.

"Bring that thing over here, and help me put Curt on it," she said.

Daniel brought the sled over to where Curtis was seated, and with a great deal of effort the pair rolled him onto it. Then, Daniel's mother tossed the folded blankets on top of Curtis Parker in an unceremonious manner ,which did nothing to cover the man. With Daniel pulling and his mother finessing, they maneuvered the sled out of the kitchen, through the porch, and out into the backyard. Thankfully, the winds had died down a little bit and the rains were gone, which made dragging Curtis across the yard all the more easier. When they reached the fence that led into the back fields, Daniel's mother handed him the gym-bag.

"Come on," she said, "we need to take him to the orchard." Daniel's mother unlatched the gate and allowed it to swing open. Her curly black hair fluttered gently as she did, and Daniel noticed that her cheeks had taken on a ruddy complexion which contrasted her alabaster skin.

On a good day, the walk to the Orchard took ten minutes, but on that cold night, dragging an enormous heap of a man by sled across the grassy fields, it took the Church family almost a half an hour to make the trek. The grove was filled with row after row of twisted dark trees that had been barren since the end of the picking season. Caught somewhere between moonlight and wind, the shadows of the trees danced, threatening to reveal the horrors of the night, but always shying away from doing so. Owls cried and vermin scurried. The ground crunched and sloshed beneath their feet. Daniel's arms and legs burned from work and exhaustion, but finally they came to a spot surrounded by crooked branches and broken stones, and he was able to stop pulling. In the middle of the ground, covered by a plywood board that had been camouflaged with leaves and hay, was a deep pit.

Daniel knew the pit existed, and he had vague memories of sitting around it while waiting for something awful to happen, but the pit was something his mother never discussed with him. It was the type of secret that plagued families and burdened everyone that knew about it. Without being asked, the young man removed the plywood board and rested it on one of the nearby trees. Meanwhile, the matriarch of the Church family cleared a patch of grass and placed one of the blankets down neatly, like they were about to have a picnic. When they had both finished their tasks, Daniel and his mother returned to the sled.

"Help me tip him in there," she said, as she bent over and began lifting one side of the sled. Daniel grabbed the spot near Curtis' head, and together they toppled the heavy-set man and sent him tumbling into the pit. He landed with a wet *thump*.

"Is he dead?" Daniel asked, as he looked down into the pit at the mud-covered intruder. Curtis wasn't moving.

"No," was his mother's simple reply. She sat down in the spot she had made for them and began unraveling the other blanket. "Come and sit, Danny."

The young man did as he was told and sat down beside his mother. The winds began to pick up, and they carried with them the earthy scent of fallen leaves and decay. From the gym-bag she had brought with them, Daniel's mother pulled out a robe that was covered in black feathers. She draped the garment over her shoulders, then took off all of the clothing she wore beneath the robe until she was completely naked underneath. She took out a bundle of kindling and some newspaper from the bag, and in a clear spot set up the sticks in a cone shape with the newspaper inside. Using a flint rock and a scrapper, she lit the newspaper, and within minutes the kindling was burning bright orange.

"Fetch some more wood," she commanded as she stared at the flames.

Daniel took a short walk and collected every dried stick he could find in the area. His mother smiled when he returned, and as he sat down she kissed his cheek. Her lips lingered and Daniel enjoyed the sensation of her warm breath on his skin. She used the wood that Daniel had collected to grow the flames, and then took out a cast-iron bowl, like a small cauldron, from the bag. She jabbed a metal hook into the ground, and placed the cauldron over the fire. Reaching back into the gym-bag, she took out a small leather pouch and a bottle of brandy. She poured a healthy swig of liquor into the cauldron first and then began adding items from the pouch. Daniel recognized the pinches of Wormwood and Yellow Dock that his mother added, but a number of other items that went into the mixture were unknown or seemed very strange. Besides the botanicals, there were several powders, a bone of some sort that still had marrow in it, two shriveled mushrooms, and shavings from the bill of a large black bird. The elixir smelled sweet and good, it reminded Daniel of the last time he had seen his father, on the night the man disappeared.

After a while, the bowl began to glow red and the face of Daniel's mother took on a waxy quality. Soon, she looked three decades older than she really was. Daniel's mother bowed her head, held both hands out in front of her, and in a language that Daniel recognized as belonging to the "old country," began an incantation. When she was done with her spell, Daniel's mother blew a kiss towards the cauldron and said, "Thank you, Dian Cécht, my love."

A few moments passed. Daniel's mother placed a hand on his knee and squeezed. "When he wakes up you'll need to drink that," she pointed to the liquid in the pot, "and listen to what I tell you to do afterwards."

"I will," Daniel replied.

"Will you?" asked his mother, raising an eyebrow, but still staring into the cauldron. "Will you do what I tell you to do? No matter what it is?"

Daniel felt a weight between them. "Yes. I'll do whatever you tell me."

They didn't speak again for hours until the first speckles of dawn were begging to dust the horizon. It was then that Daniel heard a voice coming from the pit. Curtis Parker was awake.

"Hew-oh? Whare za fug am I? Hew-oh?"

In one furious motion, Daniel's mother tossed the blankets off of herself and stood. She took a ladle from out of the bag, dipped it into the elixir and drank. Then she covered her head with the feathered hood of her cowl and strode towards the pit. When she reached the edge, she glared downward and with a ferocity that Daniel had never heard before, and spoke in a commanding voice.

"Can you see me, Curtis Parker?"

"Whosh zchaid zzat," Curtis replied as he slumped against the wall of the pit.

"I did!" Her voice thundered in the pale light of the coming day. "And you will look at me when I am speaking to you!"

Curtis looked up but was unable to focus on the woman standing above him.

"Do you know who you are speaking to?" Daniel's mother asked.

Curtis swayed forward and then fell back against the wall. "Whaaaat ish hapnin. WIDTCH, izzs zat oooo?"

Daniel's mother went red with fury, and screamed into the pit. "I am the Nemain, the Macha, the Badb! I am not yours to call a witch, as if it were some scarlet letter! I am the CROW! I am Morrigan Church and you will die SCREAMING my name!"

Morrigan pulled out something that had been hidden within the cloak, it was bright and even in the dark morning light it sparkled. She turned to her son and calmly said, "Drink the potion now and then come down into the pit with me."

She leapt down into the pit, and as soon as she landed, Curtis screamed. "No Morrigan! Stop!"

Daniel stumbled to his knees, pulled the bowl from the hook, raised the cauldron to his lips, and tipped the tonic down his throat. The red-hot metal burned his lips, and the mixture scalded his esophagus as it went down. It tasted vile and sloshed in his belly worse than any liquor he had ever tried. His vision blurred a moment later, then his heart slowed and a tingle moved throughout his body until he felt like he was bathed in rainbow flames.

There were more screams from down in the pit. Daniel floated over to the edge. He looked down and saw his mother dragging a knife across Curtis' forehead. Blood poured over the man's face, his eyes bugged out, and his mouth grimaced. Curtis slapped at his own head, trying to stop the knife from scalping him, but he missed entirely. Morrigan pressed her fingers into the wound, grabbed a hunk of flesh, and then stretched back the skin like it was taffy and peeled it away from Curtis's skull. The intruder let out the hellish scream of an animal caught in a snare, and Daniel felt the warm glow of the elixir mix with the terribly hot and damp sensation of a new trauma forming.

As the sounds of agony echoed through the fields, Morrigan looked up at her son. Her face was serious, wretched, and covered in blood. "Do you see this, Danny-Boy?"

Daniel nodded, his mind was focused on the violence below but was somehow adrift and calm at the same time.

"THIS is who *we* are. We don't kill like we are slaughtering a fattened Christmas pig. When we kill, son, we make them die screaming! That's the only way the magic works, boy. That's how you will get to live forever, my precious son." Morrigan smiled and licked Curtis' blood off her knife. "Now, come down here and become a man."

Suddenly, Daniel saw his mother fully, for the first time as a complete woman, and he realized what was happening. It was the name Dian Cécht that put everything together for the young man. That was the name of a God who worked his magic through healing pits that were dug into the earth. Morrigan had told her son about the Great Healer, she said his powers were so profound that some people believed he could even give back a life after it had been snuffed out. He remembered that Morrigan had told him once about ripping open a hole between the spirit world and ours, and that she had forced Dian Cécht to become her lover and to share with her his divine secrets. He had always thought this was a tall-tale, an allegory for Morrigan's feminine prowess, but now he knew differently. Daniel knew that all of his mother's stories were true; that his bones cracked not because they were brittle, but because he was an old soul, that he was more than some poor farm boy from the country, and that his Scum-Fuck of a father had never run away, but was still a part of him, kept safe in the warmth of his belly and his blood. Daniel smiled. The fresh day bathed him in glory and graced him with the promise of prosperity. With hope in his heart, Daniel Church dropped down into the pit, and with his mother, consumed the flesh of the bastard Curtis Parker.

PART 1: A LITTLE WAYS DOWN THE
ROAD

CHAPTER 1

Snow drifted across Highway 401 in sheets, turning the expressway into a slow-moving boulevard, and causing the pavement to sometimes vanish altogether. William "Hellbilly" McConnell gripped the steering wheel of his Chevy Colorado and cursed. The biker leaned forward, squinted, and looked through the static in his front window to the exit sign up ahead. To Hellbilly's relief, a gust of wind caused a break in the snowfall and Bill was finally able to see that he was looking at the exit for Highway 26. The Chevy skidded a little as Bill veered to the right and followed the path off the highway towards the industrial area of Oshawa, a city on the outskirts of Toronto. As Bill arrived at the first stoplight off the highway, the sound of the Tragically Hip's *The Darkest Ones* faded away and was replaced by a deep and soothingly generic male voice.

"Hello, I'm Vince Harper and you're listening to Good Mornings on CKRG. In today's news; the snow that has incapacitated much of the Southern Ontario area will continue, at least for the time being. Our meteorologist, Cindy Lee, says that we can expect the storm to taper off in the afternoon, but that it will likely return with a vengeance this evening. Here's Cindy with more…"

A perky voice explained how the storm would pass through the area, dumping another mountain of fresh powder before finally petering out. Bill's grip on the steering wheel tightened throughout the weather segment, and by the end of it his jaw was tense. Hellbilly disliked driving anywhere on four wheels, it made him feel confined, and he loathed driving in the snow. Ever since he had stolen his father's dilapidated Sportster as a kid, Bill preferred the feeling of having two wheels beneath him and the sensation of being in total control of a machine. The riding season was over for the year though, and if he was destined to travel on a day like this, Bill took some comfort in knowing that the Chevy, with its all-wheel drive and high visibility, was built for it. There was a natural turn in the road, which Hellbilly followed, bringing him eastbound. As he completed the change in course, the perky Cindy Lee signed off and the monotonous sounding voice of Vince Harper returned.

"In other news, the search for eleven-year-old Oscar Delaronde, who went missing from the Cataraqui Town Center last month, entered its third week this morning. Oscar's mother, Renee Delaronde, gave a statement last night during a council meeting in Tyendinaga Mohawk Territory, where community members, Elders, and Healers from various First Nations, Inuit and Metis peoples, held yet another vigil for the boy."

Hellbilly came to a mostly vacant business complex, where half the units had boarded up windows, and the parking lot was filled with cavernous potholes. Bill wondered when the last time someone had made a serious repair to the complex was and figured it must have been a decade ago at least. On the radio, Renee Delaronde began addressing the media.

"It is clear to me now that the police have no leads on the disappearance of my son, and that the reporters who came here like locusts when Oscar first went missing, have moved on as well. Three weeks ago, I couldn't see the back wall of this meeting room because there were so many cameras, but tonight I only see one lonely reporter back there. I know what people are saying; that my boy ran away, or that he is already dead. Oscar left my side for ten minutes! He walked away from the table where we were having lunch to go visit a store he had been to a thousand times. Somewhere between the food court and that store he went missing. He did NOT run away, he is a little boy and he was TAKEN! I know something else, too. I know he is alive. That he is somewhere, scared and crying for his mom, but he's alive. Someone knows where he is, someone knows what has happened to him, and by god I am going to find out exactly what is going on!"

Hellbilly pulled into the parking lot slowly and scanned the place for signs of covert law enforcement; such as Ford Expeditions with tinted windows, Crown Victorias with longer than usual antennae, or groups of homeless men hanging around doorways in the dead of winter. He saw nothing in the lot, except a lone black Dodge Charger with red racing stripes down the middle. Bill parked beside the Charger and noticed that the number of stripes on the car was four, and that there was a decal of the number thirteen beside them. The biker chuckled to himself at the subtle nod to the Dead Mariachis, whose club colors were black and red and who often abbreviated themselves numerically as "4-13"; with "4" representing the letter "D" in "Dead" and "13" representing the "M" in "Mariachis." Bill looked down at his passenger seat and stole a quick glance at the black leather vest resting there. In the center of the vest was an embroidered skeleton mariachi riding a motorcycle. Red banners with black horrorshow font encircled the dead musician, and stitched on the left breast was Bill's road-name, "Hellbilly."

The unit Hellbilly now found himself parked in front of was an automotive garage at the very end of the complex. Like the rest of the place, the garage looked sleepy and worn out, as though a strong enough wind could topple it. Bill cut the engine to the Colorado just as the shaking voice of Renee Delaronde was replaced by Vince Harper's prattling drone.

"The Ontario Provincial Police have faced increased criticism over their handling of the Delaronde case, and just yesterday, during a media scrum, the Prime Minister said that he believed it may be time for the federal government to step in."

Hellbilly removed the keys from the ignition and the radio fell silent. He tucked them into the front pocket of his jeans, closed his eyes, and took a moment to enjoy the stillness of his truck. The sound of wet snow clunking against the windshield calmed Bill's nerves, and the cold air that had seeped into the cabin through the cracked weatherstripping ignited his skin. Hellbilly breathed in for four seconds, held his breath and counted to four, then slowly allowed the grimy-smelling air to escape his lungs. This mindful-breathing technique was one of the few positive things Bill had taken from his time in group therapy at Collins Bay Penitentiary. In the relatively short time he had been back in the outside world, he found that he used the technique regularly. Slowly, Hellbilly's jaw unclenched and the tension in his hands released. Except for the tightness of his chest, which had been there since the night before, Bill felt mostly calm. Around ten o'clock last night, Bill received a call from his current chapter president, informing him that his old boss, the now great and powerful Paulo "The Paulbearer" Renaud, had asked for Hellbilly to personally see to a matter of great importance.

Back when he was twenty-one, impressionable, and first thinking about joining the Dead Mariachis, Bill had worked for Paulo at one of the more upscale strip clubs in Windsor, Ontario. Paulo was nothing more than an ambitious club president back then, but he filled the coffers of the right people and bolstered the club's reputation with charity events and publicity stunts. Now, fifteen years later, Paulo had become the President of the Nomad's Chapter, making him the de facto leader of the entire club nationwide. Bill, on the other hand, was an ex-convict with a beat-up Chevy.

After a few more deep breaths, Bill opened his eyes. The windshield was now a blanket of white, and the cabin was filled with condensation. Hellbilly looked around and caught sight of his sunken eyes in the rearview mirror. Framed by long dark hair and olive-coloured skin, Bill felt that those eyes looked old and tired. His beard was the next thing that caught his attention. It was long, peppered with gray strands, and ran all the way down to his chest. Scribbled just below his beard, on the left side of his neck, was a tattoo of his road-name in black script. That tattoo was now a bluish-gray, and much lighter than it had been when he first got it as a reward to himself for becoming a full patch member of the Dead Mariachis.

Below the rearview mirror dangled two three-inch laminate flags; one being the green, white, and orange flag of Ireland, and the other a red flag with a bright yellow star bursting out from the middle and the profile of a Haudenosaunee man in the center. The flag of the Rotisken'rakéhte, the Mohawk Warrior Society of Kahnawake, was a symbol of unity for indigenous people everywhere, and for Bill it represented the missing half of his heritage, which he had been trying to learn about and embrace over the past decade.

Jangling beside the flags was a picture of a small boy with wild brown curls and a baseball bat slung over his shoulder. Bill couldn't recall exactly how old his son had been when that picture was taken, but he knew this image belonged to a happy memory filled with cake and outside games, grass stains and muddy faces. Then it came to him; the picture had been taken at his ex-wife's birthday, the fall before he had been arrested. That meant that Emmitt had been four. Bill thought about the shaking voice of Renee Delaronde, and realized that if Emmit went missing he would have no idea the boy was gone until Gloria finally decided to call him, if she even had his number still. Lost in a moment of melancholy, Hellbilly did a quick calculation and came up with a sad figure, which was fifteen. Emmitt was fifteen years old now, and they hadn't seen each other since Hellbilly went to prison. Bill wondered if he would recognize the boy if they walked by each other on the street. He doubted it. More likely than not, they would simply pass as ships in the night, never realizing how close they had come to one another.

Bill shook the sorrow-filled thought out of his head. He reached over to the passenger seat, grabbed his cut, and threw it over his winter coat as he stepped out of his truck. Briskly, the biker made his way to the sidewalk and then to the front door of the garage. When Hellbilly opened the door, he was greeted by a familiar round face which belonged to a man he hadn't seen much of since getting out of prison.

"Hey-ya Dom, how ya been doing?"

Dominic Di Forno, who had once sponsored Bill's prospective membership into the Dead Mariachis, looked up from the Carver Pike novel he was reading and scowled. "Hey Bill, you look like a dog's ass. How's Malton been treating you? You getting plenty of rest there?"

Dom, who was now the Sergeant at Arms for Paulo Renaud's

Nomads, was referring to the chapter Hellbilly had transferred to when he got out of prison. The Malton Chapter had been founded in the nineties during the first war between the Dead Mariachis and the Scum Fucks MC. Back then, the biker war was tearing apart entire communities in Quebec and Eastern Ontario, and some of the older members of the 4-13 elected to distance themselves from the raucous by forming a new chapter in a working class community near the Toronto Airport. When Bill got out of prison, the guys in the Malton chapter hooked him up as the security manager for one of their stripclubs, and Hellbilly took to it nicely. Within a year he was managing the security for all three of the clubs owned by the Malton Dead Mariachis. Not that the Malton chapter couldn't hold its own, all outlaw clubs can hold their own, but the Malton chapter was in some ways considered a quiet chapter to be a part of, and there was a running joke amongst the other Mariachis that Malton was where the Dead went when they were ready to retire.

"It's been great Dom. A little slower pace, but I don't mind that."

Dom nodded and looked nonplussed. "You been out for like two years now, right?"

"Three in March," Hellbilly affirmed.

"You did your whole bit, I heard. Never took parole?"

"Yeah man, all seven years. I didn't want to have some P.O. looking over my shoulder while I pissed, just so I could sit at home on Friday nights."

Dom's chin went up and down, and his nose crinkled. "Probably would have gotten more time if you'd been wearing your cut that night eh?"

Hellbilly felt his chest tighten. Dom was slapping Bill in the face with a point of shame that the biker hadn't been unable to shake during his entire stay in prison, and it made Bill feel like a mouse; tiny and small and squishable.

"It's cool you did your whole bit, though," Dom continued. "That's old school man. Not a lot of guys do that anymore."

"Used to be the way everyone did it," Hellbilly countered.

Dom's eyebrows went up in a look of agreement. "Anyways, Paulo ain't here just yet, what with the weather and all. Go wait in the office. It's about half way down the hall, on the left. We'll come get ya when it's time to talk."

Hellbilly left the front foyer and walked down a decrepit looking hallway. The walls were stained amber and had drips of old nicotine running down them. At his feet, a checkered linoleum floor had faded from what was once probably white and black into charcoal and gray. In some spots the floor felt spongey, in others it seemed brittle. Halfway down the hall, Hellbilly came to a door covered in chipping green paint. The window on the door said "office," so Hellbilly opened it and stepped inside.

The room was saturated with moist air. It stank like mildew and old urine, as if someone had pissed in the corner six months ago and no one had bothered to clean it up. The same checkered flooring that had been in the hallway was there as well, but here the white squares were what could best be described as hemorrhage-brown.

Sitting on the other side of the room, in the only good chair, was a short and ugly man who played with a silver ring on his index finger. The man looked up as Hellbilly entered the room. He had crooked teeth, a bent nose, cauliflower ears, a giant scar on his cheek, and a hairline that was desperately retreating away from his face. Like Hellbilly, he wore a leather vest stitched with an intricate patchwork of red and black flashes, and although they had never spoken before, Bill recognized the man immediately. His road-name was Death Mask, and amongst the members of the Dead Mariachi's Motorcycle Club, he was famous.

Death Mask nodded slowly as Hellbilly walked in, and Bill returned the gesture. The long-haired biker looked around for a place to sit but saw only a wrecked looking chair with a rust coloured stain on the seat, and a battered looking desk. Hellbilly figured the stain on the chair was either blood or some toxic chemical, and didn't feel confident that the desk would hold his massive frame, so he elected to stand instead.

"You're Death Mask, right?" Hellbilly asked with a gruff chin wag. "From the Leslieville Chapter, in Toronto?"

The small man tapped a flash on the left breast of his cut, which read "Death Mask." Just below his road-name, Hellbilly noticed a "Sgt. At Arms" officer patch, which made him tense up a bit. However, as much as being around an officer made Bill feel on guard, it was the badge on the other side of Death Mask's cut, just above his "Dead Mariachis" flash, that Bill found truly ominous. In inverse colors to their other flashes, black background and red lettering, Death Mask sported the numbers "1313." Members who were granted the "1313" patch were considered to have proven their loyalty to the Dead Mariachis twice over, and were now "Double Mariachis." With few exceptions, the only way to get a "1313" patch was to kill someone while defending the club. It was a special honor to have been awarded this flash, one that Hellbilly understood well, for he too wore the numbers "1313" on the right side of his cut.

"Well, I'm Hellbilly. I ride out of Malton. I seen you around a few times. You were at Ohsweken Race Track this year, right? When we rented the place out for the day.

The small man in the corner nodded, but his expression remained steeled.

Hellbilly felt awkward with the silence and continued talking. "You had that fine ass looking Dyna Low Rider, right? With the buckhorn handlebars. That a CVO?"

"Sure is," said Death Mask in a graveled voice, "From oh-eight."

"Screaming Eagle!" Bill smiled. "Nice. Looked like you did a *lot* of work on that thing. Love whatever it was you did to the pipes. Vance and Hines, but modified right? They sounded tight."

Death Mask tilted his head to the side and a hint of a smile touched his lips. "Thanks man. I've turned every bolt on that thing at this point. She's my baby."

"So, you like the Dynas? I had a Fat Bob for a hot minute after I got out of the can, but I took a tumble out by Wasaga Beach and I figured it didn't bode well for the thing, so I sold it to some Prospect out in Barrie."

Death Mask raised an eyebrow. "It's good for a guy my size. Nimble. I do a lot of dumb shit, so I need a bike that's spry."

Hellbilly chuckled. "Yeah I bet. I seen you doing wheelies and front spins, and all that shit. Takes some balls to do that on a v-twin. I'm pretty sure that every single person at Ohsweken was watching you. Whole crowd gob smacked. You should think about taking that show on the road brother, could make some money out of it."

Death Mask shook his head, but raised his other eyebrow in a friendly expression. "Nah, I just like fucking around." Then, in a gesture that was sharp and quick, he looked up and directly into Hellbilly's eyes. "Someone told me you had a Rune?" The last word, "rune," lingered like molasses.

Hellbilly smirked, but his guts tensed. He recognized the question for exactly what it was, a test. Dead Mariachis, for the most part, were supposed to ride North American made motorcycles with giant engines, and it was odd to find a member who blatantly embraced something else. Death Mask was asking for the reason behind Bill's choice to own the Rune, and the way Bill answered would matter.

"The Honda!" Bill beamed. "Hellz yeah! Great bike man!"

"She ride's well then?"

"Like she was forged by Thor's Hammer." Hellbilly had scrapped, bartered, and hustled just enough to purchase the ostentatious 1800cc, six-cylinder behemoth of a motorcycle, secondhand from a lawyer in Atlanta. When he first presented it to his fellow Mariachis they chided him for spending such a large sum on the Japanese bike, but Hellbilly just laughed off the comments until a hang-around called it a piece of "jap-junk," and said that only a traitor would buy something like that. The young man's jaw took four months to fuse back together, and he never ended up finding a sponsor for membership.

Death Mask leaned forward in his chair, his elbows rested on his knees and he laced his fingers together in front of his wildly unattractive face. His look became more severe, almost predatory, and in a tone that was nearly a growl he said, "A lot of guys wouldn't touch something that wasn't made *here*."

Hellbilly adjusted his smile into a single sided smirk, and straightened his back a little. "Ahh hell, I'm too old to give a shit about that. A man likes what he likes. I only take the Rune to the track, or when I'm fucking around by myself. And, I have a Road Glide too, and a shovelhead chopper, so what are they gonna do? Take my cut? Besides, the Runes were built in Ohio, man."

Death Mask nodded once again, this time a gesture of approval. Hellbilly had stood his ground on the matter of the Honda, and it was respected.

"It's funny, you know," Hellbilly said as he walked over to the desk and took the risk of sitting on it. "There's only a city between my chapter and yours, but I see the boys from Thunder Bay and Manitoba far more often than I see you guys."

Death Mask looked Hellbilly over, searching for breaches in etiquette. "It's nothing personal. Our business is all out east, so we don't head west very often, even just to go to the other side of the city. I spend half my life riding between here and Halifax, checking up on shipments and following transport trucks around."

"Oh, hell I know that man!" Hellbilly exclaimed. "I got a lot of respect for you guys. I know how hard ya'll work. I prospected in Windsor myself, spent my first few years there."

Finally, Death Mask's expression lightened. "Woof! You're a regular business man then eh?"

Hellbilly puffed out a hot breath of air. "Hardly man! I like the speed in Malton nowadays. It's a nice balance of business and tomfoolery. I'm just saying, I get what it's like to ride with a chapter that's focused on hustlin'."

"No worries man," said Death Mask with a dismissive wave. "I get that. Hell, I could probably use a little more tomfoolery myself some days."

Hellbilly reckoned that the man sitting in front of him couldn't stand any more than five foot five, and probably didn't weigh an ounce over a hundred and fifty pounds, but Death Mask was wired in a scrappy sort of way that had just enough muscle to be dangerous. Stories about how the tiny man had received his road-name floated through the club like fables and were dangerously close to becoming legend. Rumour had it that some of the higher-ranking Nomads, Paulo included, were even feeling intimidated by the attention and notoriety that Death Mask had garnered.

The story that was becoming more and more dangerous was this; during the second war between the Dead Mariachis and the Scum Fucks, Death Mask had been part of a raid on the Scum Fucks' Toronto clubhouse. The purpose of the raid was to get revenge against the President of the Scum Fucks, who had tried to overthrow the power dynamic in Ontario by killing several high-ranking Dead Mariachis and attacking their families. Though it may not seem like it to outsiders, outlaw-bikers do live by a code, and attacking families is something that is considered wholly unforgivable. Hellbilly had been in jail for most of the war, but he had a close friend named Fast-Eddy who had been active the entire time, and had been part of the same hit-squad as Death Mask during the raid. Supposedly, Death Mask had gotten separated from their squad and when the other members finally found him, his face was covered in the blood and bone of the Scum Fuck's President. Somehow, the small man had beaten to death a legendary biker-king, renowned for his capacity for violence, using only his bare hands and his face.

Bill couldn't resist himself. The chance to confirm such a harrowing story was too tempting, so he took a chance and asked, "I hope this isn't rude of me, but I heard about how you got your name and all. Buddy of mine, Fast-Eddy, he was at the Scum Fuck raid with ya," Hellbilly calmly stated while studying Death Mask for cues suggesting this line of conversation was unwanted. The mention of Fast-Eddy seemed to have piqued an interest in Death Mask, so Bill continued. "Pretty gnarly man. Did you really do that to their President? I mean, did you actually beat Daniel Church to death with your own face?"

Death Mask grinned so wide that his broken teeth popped out of his crooked mouth. "It was my forehead really. I didn't have any more weapons on me, and old Danny-Boy had both my hands wrapped up."

Hellbilly let out a long whistle. "Dang brother! So, that's how you got your name eh?"

Death Mask's face was plastered in a sly grin, but his eyes were hollow. He was always proud of the role he'd played in eradicating the leader of the Dead Mariachi's rival club, but whenever he thought of that night, he was reminded that it wasn't just the blood of Daniel Church he had on his hands.

"What about you?" Death Mask asked. "How'd you get the name Hellbilly?"

"Well…" Hellbilly said, as his cheeks turned red. "My name's Bill, I'm a goddamn hillbilly, and I'm going to hell. Not really anything special there."

With a reserved laugh, Death Mask said, "And here I thought maybe you was just a big Rob Zombie fan or something."

Now it was Hellbilly who laughed. He bent over, rolled up the right side of his jeans, and with a small struggle pushed his pant leg over his large calf revealing a greenish-gray face framed by black dreadlocks. In the center of the tattoo's forehead was a red "X," and if you squinted and tilted your head at just the right angle, you might be able to make out that the face belonged to one Robert "Rob Zombie" Cummings, that or you'd probably think it was an emaciated Charles Manson.

Hellbilly beamed through his bearded face, and said, "The first album I ever bought with my own money was Tubthumper by Chumbawamba, but the second album I bought was Rob's Hellbilly Deluxe. I don't fuck around."

Death Mask's face lit up. In a warm tone he exclaimed, "Mother Fuckers Forever Man."

Bill felt pride swell in his cheeks. He brought his left hand to his stomach and ran his thumb over his knuckles; first over the M on his index finger, then across the two F's on his middle and ring fingers, and finally over the M on his pinky. This was a small ritual he often performed whenever one of his brothers recited the mantra which Death Mask had just spoken. If you were a supporter, a fan, or just someone who paid attention to the club, you might recognize MFFM plastered on the bikes, cuts, and bodies of the Dead Mariachis. If so, you probably read an article in the papers or heard a brother say publicly that MFFM meant *Mariachis Forever Forever Mariachis*. However, if you were a full-patch member, then you knew damn well that MFFM stood for a sacred mantra that could only be said from one brother to another, because only another Dead Mariachi could get away with calling a member a Mother Fucker.

"Yeah brother, Mother Fuckers Forever Man," Hellbilly replied.

An affirmation had occurred. The brothers had sized up one another, and for now, found themselves on level ground.

Death Mask leaned over, smiled broadly, and stuck out his hand. "My name's Caleb by the way, Caleb Driscoll."

C H A P T E R   2

————|————

Death Mask and Hellbilly passed the time by swapping war stories about good runs, bad spills, and idiot-moments with shared friends. As it turned out, they had quite a few mutual acquaintances, and were both especially close with the wildest man from the Etobicoke Chapter, Fast-Eddy. Hellbilly, it turned out, had known Eddy the longest, and regaled Death Mask with a story about a time in Thunder Bay when Eddy had fallen asleep while getting a blow job. Awakened by a slight pinch on his dick, Eddy, who had forgotten about the act he was engaged in, became startled. The wildly blonde biker yelped, which scared the girl on his crotch and caused her to bite down instinctively. Startled even more than he had been, Eddy stood up and in doing so caught his penis on one of the girl's teeth. His foreskin was torn open like a paper bag. Hellbilly was in the middle of describing the way Fast-Eddy had run through the hotel lobby, naked as a jaybird with a trail of blood following him, when Paulo Renaud burst into the room.

"Look at these Mother Fuckers right here!" bellowed the gigantic Paulo as he strutted across the floor. The biker-king raced over to Hellbilly and embraced him in a titanic bear hug. He lifted Bill straight up off the floor and planted a kiss directly onto his lips. Bill felt his stomach lurch as his enormous frame was carried into the air, and for a moment, he panicked at the sudden loss of control he experienced. Then, without warning, Paulo let go and Hellbilly crashed down onto the floor. Bill's feet touched the linoleum first, then slipped out from underneath him. Desperate to maintain his footing and not touch a vile floor below, Hellbilly flailed out. Fortunately, his left hand caught the corner of the rusted metal desk, and he was able to prevent his fall.

Then, Paulo turned to Death Mask and slapped him square in the balls with the back of his hand. Caleb absorbed the blow, and barely flinched.

"Balls of brass, eh brother! You always did have a giant set of cajones on ya!" Paulo stood a head taller than Death Mask, but half a head shorter than Hellbilly. He was built like a battering-ram though, barrel chested with legs like tree trunks and arms like telephone poles. Paulo made a point of telling people that whenever he was arrested it took the police two sets of handcuffs to immobilize his unyielding frame. Adorning the Nomad President's flesh were expensive tattoos and custom gold jewelry, most of which had something to do with the Dead Mariachis. His long black hair gave him the appearance of a grease monkey, but he smelled like orchids and his soft pink hands betrayed him to be the man of leisure that he really was.

"Either of you going to Dawson City this year?" screamed Paulo, like a wildebeest. "I think I'm gonna take some time and actually go up. You know, it's the only run I've never made."

Hellbilly grinned in a hollow kind of way while trying to hide the contempt he had for the crowned ruler standing before him. Bill despised men like Paulo, who were really just criminals who used the club to cloak their atrocities. Paulo was a fraud, and Bill knew damn well that if the biker-king actually did make it all that way up to the Yukon that summer, that he would have flown first class across the country to Vancouver, where he would have met the motorcycle he shipped there, and then taken a leisurely stroll up the west-coast of Canada. Men like Paulo Renaud didn't ride across the country. They were too busy for that, too important.

Hellbilly explained that he wouldn't be able to make it this year, but had been once already. Death Mask just shook his head.

"Well, shit! Guess I'll have to find someone else to give me a rim job while I'm up there," shouted Paulo, just before he erupted into laughter. The way the biker-king chuckled was unfettered to the point of abandon. His eyes bugged out from his skull and they screamed with black dilation. Paulo slammed a hand into Hellbilly's back, then grabbed his own stomach and bent over till his face was almost into his knees. Hellbilly glanced over at Death Mask, who was still seated.

The pair shared a brief look of concern. Paulo's fit lasted too long, it was unsettling, and when the king of the Dead Mariachis finally regained his composure, his eyes remained bloodshot and frantic. Hellbilly was used to a fair amount of violent insanity, but Paulo's brand of off-kilter made the hairs on the back of his neck stand up and left a rotten feeling in his stomach.

"I have an errand for you two," said Paulo through strained giggles. "And I only trust my doubles for something like this."

"Is someone riding into the night?" Death Mask asked in a voice which Hellbilly thought sounded uneasy.

Another set of giggles came from Paulo, but this time with more impishness than violence. "Nothing like that tiger, but *if* things get hectic, I need some level heads. You feel me?" Paulo walked over to Death Mask and knocked on the top of his balding head like it was a ripening melon. "Seems level enough to me."

The President sat down in the crumbling and stained chair opposite Death Mask and lit a cigarette. Hellbilly noticed that all of Paulo's fingernails were painted different colours, and that he had a faint trace of black dust around his eyelids. "The thing is, I need some discretion here boys. I have my hands in a lot of different cookie jars, and most of the time that's just fine and dandy. Usually, the oatmeal cookies don't mind if my fingers have a few chocolate chips on 'em, but sometimes I dip my hands into something other than cookies, you see. Like, maybe I want a brownie or an eclair. Shit, maybe I want some fucking jet-fuel!" Paulo ran the back of his hand over his forehead, leaned backwards, and rolled his eyes into his skull. "QUELLE DAMAGE!" He flipped himself to an upright position and grinned like a maniac. "So, my boys, on those occasions I have to be discreet. You following along?"

Hellbilly stole a glance at Death Mask, whose gaze remained fixed on Paulo. Both men nodded.

"Okay, good," said Paulo, as his eyes danced from Hellbilly to Death Mak, and back again. "It's a run, just a run. Quick, easy, no nonsense. I *hate* nonsense," said Paulo, as he pulled out a fake flower from his pocket and threw it directly into Death Mask's face. The flower hit Caleb softly and then fell lazily to the floor. "Well, maybe a little nonsense is okay." Paulo smiled like a jackal and glowered at Death Mask, daring him to do anything except sit quietly. Death Mask took a deep and controlled breath. His face never changed. Silence saturated the air like a humid August afternoon, and then, like a thunderclap, Paulo brought both hands together and cackled. "Alright boys! Outside there's a car. Once you're ready to go, I am gonna tell you an address, which you will memorize, not write down. You get in the car and drive straight there. Feel free to take a piss or a breather if you need, but otherwise don't make any fucking stops, and don't leave the car alone, okay?"

Again, Death Mask and Hellbilly nodded in unison.

"Once you get to the address, you leave the car there and walk away. That's all you gotta do," said Paulo. "Nice and simple."

"Easy enough," said Hellbilly, calmly, but underneath his words his voice bubbled with anxiety.

Death Mask nodded in agreement, but said nothing.

The left side of Paulo's lips raised, just a hair, and his eyes sparkled. He could see the trepidation he had instilled in his subordinates, and he loved it. "Fuckin' alright! Let's go see the new ride, shall we!"

Paulo led the way out of the office and down the grimy hallway. Hellbilly thought his boss moved like Johnny Depp in *Fear and Loathing in Las Vegas*, with large comical steps that were liquid and wobbly and with a hint of menace. At the end of the hallway, a single brown door with a wire-mesh window was held open by a cinder block. The trio passed through the door and found themselves inside a large garage with several car lifts. The windows at the top of the room were boarded up, and only the white fluorescent lights illuminated the space.

In the center of the room, clouded in a haze of tobacco smoke, was a red Ford Taurus, the old kind that had those strange grooves along the sides. Sitting around the car were three men, two of whom Hellbilly recognized immediately. The first was Dom, who had evidently migrated from the front door, the other was an older Nomad named Cliff whom Hellbilly had never held much esteem for. Both men were long time bootlickers of Paulo's and had followed him from the Windsor chapter during his ascension. The third man, who was sitting on the far side of the Taurus, was an unknown. The stranger had short red hair and old scars all over his face that looked like boils or pockmarks. His lips bore the worst scars, they had been badly damaged and had healed atrociously. The man reminded Hellbilly of a story his mother read to him as a child, about a golem that came to life and when rejected in love, tried to murder an entire town. As Hellbilly came through the door, he saw the red-golem lower the sleeve of his black hoodie, and Hellbilly couldn't be sure but he thought he saw the man covering up a tattoo of four paws and a pile of shit buzzing with flies. Bill knew that wasn't possible though, the only people who had tattoos like that belonged to the now extinct Scum Fucks Motorcycle Club. And despite his feelings about Paulo. he knew that the Nomad President wouldn't have anything to do with a former enemy like that.

Paulo placed a firm hand on Hellbilly's shoulder, and with the other, motioned towards the Taurus as if it were a thing worthy of admiration. "Ain't she a beaut! A classic really. And she's all yours boys! Hell, I'll even pay you to take her off the lot!"

The Nomads laughed in an eerily quiet manner. The red-golem did not.

Hellbilly thought the car looked feeble, and he doubted that it could do anything more than reach and maintain highway speed.

"Does she have any troubles?" Death Mask asked.

"We all have troubles," Paulo responded in a flippant tone.

"She'll get you where you need to go," said the red-golem.

"We ain't gonna get pulled over cause our taillight is out, is what I mean," Death Mask clarified, with just a hint of agitation.

Paulo stepped in between Death Mask and the unknown man, and crossed his heart using his middle finger. "Criss Cross applesauce, little brother. I promise you this horse is saddle-up right proper." Then a vacant, but serious look came over Paulo's face. "That being said, if you do find yourself in a jackpot with the piggly-wigglies, I suggest you do everything in your power to make sure they don't search that car."

Another uncomfortable silence befell the room. Hellbilly scanned the Nomads and realized that they were not making eye contact with either Death Mask or himself, and hadn't since they'd entered the garage. On the other side of the Taurus though, Hellbilly saw the Red-golem staring at Death Mask with a look of near carnal intensity. If Death Mask noticed the golem's gaze though, he paid it no mind.

"Straight to Ottawa, no stops, except for maybe a piss break," Death Mask said. The confirmation of orders seemed to cut through the tension in the room, and it made Paulo smile.

"Straight to Ottawa. You get an A-plus D-D-D-Death Mask. Check in with the Parliament Chapter when you're done, they'll square ya away with a ride home." Paulo's tone lightened, and he nodded away like a corporate yes-man, rather than the violently deviant criminal that he was.

"Welp, daylight's wasting, so to speak," Death Mask said as he tapped Hellbilly on the shoulder. "Unless there's something else we need to know about this job, I'd say it's time my compadre and I hit the road."

Paulo kept his eyes fixed on Death Mask and continued to nod. "Make sure you're in Ottawa by nightfall. The shipment is time sensitive. And, I know that you two don't need to be told this, but don't look in the fucking trunk."

"It's for your own good," said the Golem.

Hellbilly tried to see through the smoky haze and get a better look at the red-headed menace sitting across from him but couldn't make out the man's face through the gloom. Death Mask tugged gently on Bill's arm and Hellbilly acquiesced to his partner. Together, the pair walked towards the Taurus, but just before they reached the vehicle Paulo yelled.

"You're cuts!"

Hellbilly turned. He felt confused.

Paulo rolled his eyes. "If you two noodle heads do get pulled over, I'd rather you look like a couple of roughnecks rather than full blown outlaw bikers. Take off your cuts, and give 'em to Dom here. He'll drive 'em over to your respective clubhouses and you can pick 'em up when you get back."

Dom stood up and stretched his hand out, ready to receive the sacred garments. Hellbilly looked over at Death Mask, who raised his eyebrows and tilted his head to one side, a gesture which seemed to say, "*what the hell?*" So, Hellbilly nodded in agreement and took off his cut. Death Mask did the same and both men gently folded their vests in half and carried them over to Dom.

Relieved of their hard earned rockers, Hellbilly and Death Mask climbed into the dark red Taurus. Hellbilly took the wheel and Death Mask rode shotgun. As soon as they were settled in their seats, Paulo stuck his grinning head through the driver's window. For the first time that day, Hellbilly smelled the man's breath, it stank of onions and rancid leather.

"4206 Fenly Way," said Paulo. "Technically, it's in Osgoode, not Ottawa. And boys, I mean it when I say you better not look in that trunk and you better not let anybody else look in there either."

The pair nodded, and without another word Hellbilly started the car, pulled out of the garage and headed towards the dark clouds that were spread out over the horizon.

———————————

Winston watched the Taurus pull out of the garage and felt a sudden urge to kill all the remaining Dead Mariachis in the room. The red-headed Scum Fuck thought about how much blood coursed through Paulo Renaud's fat body, and how the biker-king's warm flesh would feel in his mouth. The thought made Winston's teeth tingle and sent a gush of lusciously warm saliva into his mouth.

"My friends will be ready whenever you make the call," Paulo said as he watched the snow falling through the wide open garage door. Winston stood up from his seat and joined the Dead Mariachi king by the door. "You just gotta tail those boys till they stop for a bite to eat, or, god forbid, make it to Ottawa."

Winston stared at a throbbing vein in Paulo's neck. Each pulse of blood that widened and then retracted the vein sent a shiver down the golem's spine. "I've got what's left of our Montreal Chapter coming down. They're bringing the others as well, just in case. If those bastards make it all the way up to Ottawa, they'll regret it. Is there anything at that address you gave 'em? Anything that can be linked back to you?"

Paulo shook his head. "Nah, I just picked it at random. If they make it there, it'll be a hell of a show for the neighborhood though!"

Dom and Cliff shared an uneasy laugh while Winston sneered. The Scum Fuck crossed the garage to the far corner where a shrouded motorcycle waited quietly. He ripped away a blue tarp that covered the bike, revealing a road-worn but well maintained Harley-Davidson Electra Glide Ultra Classic. The green bike shimmered in the fluorescent glow of the shop. "They won't make it to Ottawa. They'll get lazy and stop. When they do, I'll call you. You just better have your fools ready to go."

"Don't you worry about my guys. They'll be right on your ass, okay!" Paulo scowled. "Dom and Cliff are gonna follow you too, just in case you need some help down the road."

Winston put on a black motorcycle jacket, and a pair of gloves, then he threw a leg over the Electra Glide and hissed, "I don't need your sidekicks!"

"Too bad! They're going with you. I want them to see it."

"I'll tell you when it's done!" Winston barked, as he placed a full-face helmet over his head and pulled it into place.

"Thanks, sweety," Paulo smirked, "but I don't really give a shit about what you see. I want *them* to see it."

Winston pushed in the starter button on his touring bike and the Harley roared. He revved the engine, let go of the clutch, and lunged towards Paulo. When he was only a few feet away from the king of the Dead Mariachis, Winston pulled the brakes. The Ultra Limited's back tire hopped off the ground and then bounced back to earth. Paulo and Winston stared at each other, not saying a word, as the Harley sputtered its gentle *potato-potato* sound. Paulo raised his middle finger daring the Scum Fuck to press on. Then, in a mocking tone, filled with disdain and venom, he said, "You better be careful out on the road. It's a snowy day, I'd hate for you to get hurt, Winston."

The Scum Fuck laughed into his helmet, which damped the sound of his cackle. Winston returned Paulo's middle finger, pulled back on the throttle, and followed the Taurus out of the garage and into the blizzard.

CHAPTER 3

————|————

Death Mask stared out the passenger side window of the Taurus while the sluggish jalopy chugged along the expressway. The sedan's engine howled like a thirty-year-old golf cart going up a hill, and every now and again the car traveled over one of the patches of black ice that peppered the asphalt and its bald tires spun wildly. Whenever this happened, the car would lunge forward, sending her passenger rocking from side to side and causing Hellbilly to curse and grip the steering wheel a little tighter. Outside, great cyclones of snow drifted across the highway and ended their journey by folding into one of the crisp white mountains that had formed against the edge. As he watched the dancing snow, Death Mask thought about his performance at Ohsweken Race Track that summer, which Hellbilly had reminded him of earlier.

There were nearly a thousand people at the race track that day. The crowd consisted of Dead Mariachis and their families, and support clubs like the Skeleton Crew and the Waheguru Riders. Drag racing and trick competitions had been the order of business so far, and Caleb had already won the first cruiser race and helped a kid win the prospect games by dragging him around the centre field on an old tire. Suddenly, the crowd began to chant his name, "DEATH-MASK! DEATH-MASK! DEATH-MASK!" Caleb had been expecting this, a command performance. The legend of how he received his "1313" flash was reserved only for club members and few of the more trusted old ladies, but trick riding had made him a star amongst the friends and family of the Dead Mariachis– and they always demanded a show. His routine started with Caleb gunning it across the blacktop on his Dyna, then spring-boarding into a frontside wheely. Using all the muscle he had in his small frame, he spun the bike around until he faced the other direction, planted both wheels on the ground, and bounced into a rear wheely. Looking like the Lone Ranger screaming atop his gray stallion, Silver, Caleb waved to the crowd. As the bike tipped forward, Death Mask pumped the clutch, pulled back on the throttle, and bunny hopped back the way he came. The rest of the show was mostly Caleb standing on the seat of his Dyna in various yoga poses and doing burnouts while riding the lowrider like a skateboard. For the finale, Caleb gunned it towards a limbo pole— which had been used for one of the prospect games earlier — and jumped over the bar while his bike passed underneath. He landed back on the Dyna with both feet on the seat and maintained perfect control of the bike until finally plopping himself down properly, and giving a final wave as he rode away from the audience.

Trick riding was something Caleb had done since he was a little boy on his blue mountain bike. It helped him garner the respect and confidence from his peers that his small frame refused to provide. And when he finally worked up the courage to knock on the front door of the Dead Mariachi's Leslieville clubhouse, it was what cemented his potential as a member.

"We ain't buying any girl scout cookies. Fuck off!" said a rough voice from behind a reinforced steel door.

Caleb looked into a pair of fierce eyes that glared at him through a one-inch-wide slat which had opened when the young man knocked on the door only moments earlier. "I was just hoping to introduce myself. I grew up in the neighborhood, I ride an XL883 and I really admire everything about this club."

The eyes furrowed. "If you want to support us you can buy some merch at the shop on Eastern. Otherwise, we always sell support gear when we're at rallies. Come to Port Dover this fall, we'll be there."

"I appreciate that sir, but I been buying support gear since I was sixteen." Caleb stepped back and opened his jacket revealing a black and red t-shirt with "RED AND BLACK, I GOT YOUR BACK!" written on the chest, and "SUPPORT 4-13" across the belly.

"So, that means what?" asked the eyes. "You been buying merch for six months? You even old enough to drink?"

Caleb's face went flush with embarrassment. "I turned twenty-three last week. I'd have come by sooner, but I went to college in Afghanistan and just got back a few months ago."

The eyes nodded up and down and a chuckle bubbled. The slat closed with a shlucking sound and a series of chains and deadbolts were unhooked and turned. The dark-skinned man who opened the door was tall and muscular. He had a large jet-black afro and a thick salt and pepper beard. Like a caricature from a 1970s disco movie, he wore a red and black silk shirt that was opened nearly to his belly button revealing a forest of course gray chest hair and a battalion of gold and platinum chains. The man looked Caleb over from the top of his head to the bottom of his feet, and then back up again.

"What'd you do in Afghanistan? Besides take college classes, apparently?"

With a nervous grin Caleb promptly answered. "Infantry, sir. Walked around half the country with a C7 under my arm."

"You ever fire that weapon?" the man asked, while raising an eyebrow.

Caleb felt a disgusting pit form in his stomach. He heard the sound of bullets ricocheting against armor plating and caught the stench of charred flesh wafting into his brain. "Yeah, I did."

The man nodded, but studied Caleb's face intensely. "We had the C7 when I was in Bosnia, but that was the old version. It had different scopes than what you were probably used to."

Caleb felt his confidence return. "No doubt."

"You doing okay with everything since you got home?" The man inquired with a suspicious look. "Hell of a thing, to have been through the kind of shit guys like you and me have been through."

Caleb swallowed a dry lump of nothing. He flashed to an image of a burned-out room with a smoldering heap of people in the corner of it; a dead man, with his blackened wife, clenched tightly in his burned arms. One of the Privates in his squad cheered; "FUCKING HELL C-MONEY, YOU GOT EM!" Meanwhile, Caleb watched the women's frantic eyes dart around the room and try to make sense of what had just happened. She looked confused and more terrified than any person Caleb had ever seen before. Eventually, her eyes stopped moving, and dimmed into opaque glass.

"Yeah man," Caleb lied. "I'm managing."

The Dead Mariachi took a deep breath and let it out slowly. "Bueno chico! An eight eighty-three is a girl's bike. You gotta be riding something with at least twelve hundred cc's to it. We have rules about that sort of thing. If you were ready to join, you'd know that already."

Caleb looked down at his feet and scuffed them along the front step. The man was right, and the wannabe biker worried now that he might have jumped the gun on presenting himself to the club.

"Look, I appreciate what you're doing here kid, but this ain't how it happens," the man continued. "We sort of approach you, not the other way around."

"Oh, I didn't realize that. I just wanted to introduce myself and let ya'all know I was interested."

The man nodded in a way that suggested finality. "Okay, noted. Next time you see one of us at a rally, come on up and say hi. If I'm there, I'm pretty sure I'll remember you."

"Okay then."

"I'm Bruno by the way. You can call me The Rose, or Rosey, that's my road name." And then, just as Caleb was beginning to feel good about how the interaction was going, Bruno added; "You know we got a height requirement, too?"

Caleb's heart sank. He looked at the menacing biker before him, but saw nothing to comfort him in the man's face. Bruno was deadpan. Caleb's dreams were about to crumble into oblivion when a smile exploded across The Rose's aging mug. "I'm just fucking with ya kid."

"Oh right. No doubt," Caleb said as a spark of hope returned to his soul.

"Adiós!"

The young man returned Bruno's goodbye and walked away. His trip down the front steps and across the street felt painful. He had taken his shot, and although this was not the worst outcome that could have occurred, Caleb assumed a bullet to the back of the head would be the ending of a truly disastrous first meeting, he couldn't help but feel deflated by what seemed like total rejection.

Caleb mounted his sportster and stroked the cherry-red gas tank lovingly, then plopped a half shell helmet on top of his head and started the engine. The bike purred right away and the rumble tickled Caleb's balls and reverberated through his entire body. As he lifted the kickstand, the young man looked back at the clubhouse entrance and noticed that Bruno the Rose was still standing on the front porch watching him.

Caleb pulled back on the throttle, leaned to the right, and spun the bike around into a cloud of smoke. Then he tore down the street until he reached a dead end. In a seamless motion, he turned the bike around and gunned it back down the street. As he approached the clubhouse, Caleb pulled back on the clutch handle, revved the throttle, then dumped the clutch completely, a maneuver which caused his front tire to levitate.

Caleb leaned back, caught the sportster in a balancing act, and allowed his hand to glide along the warm asphalt. When he was almost parallel with the front door, Caleb shot forward, planted the front wheel firmly on the road and hopped into a standing position on the front seat. He stood up quickly, let go of the handle bars, spread out both arms, and waved at Bruno as he passed by. From his perch on top of the bike, Caleb saw the Rose smile.

"This fucking car is a hunk of junk!" shouted Hellbilly as he slammed his fist into the steering wheel. "I should have had Paulo load whatever is in the trunk, into the back of my Colorado. If we're not gonna be on two wheels, we should at least be driving something that's built for this weather."

Death Mask nodded and then returned his attention to the window. The first vigorous fiddle strokes of the *Devil Went Down to Georgia* hummed out of the speakers. Hellbilly released the steering wheel from his iron grip and allowed his right hand to fall to his knee, where it began bouncing up and down in rhythm to the song.

"You like Charlie Daniels?" Hellbilly asked.

"Love him," Death Mask replied. "Just wish the radio would play more than Devil."

"I knew there was a reason I liked you," Hellbilly grinned.

Death Mask looked over and gave Hellbilly a half smile. "I prefer *Simple Man* myself."

"I've always been partial to *Long Hair Country Boy*," Hellbilly offered in return. The car fell silent for another minute and Death Mask saw Hellbilly look over at him a few times with an eager expression. "So, what are you carrying?"

Death Mask's left eyebrow shot upwards. "Pardon?"

"I usually bring my Beretta for these things, it's an M9A3." Hellbilly grinned like a basset hound. "I like the grip, and it has enough kick that you can feel it, but she's still manageable with one hand. If shit really goes to pot, I like to know that I can still reach for my knife at the same time as I am firing my pistol."

Death Mask's other eyebrow raised now, joining the first. The bravado of Hellbilly's statement was wildly shocking to the otherwise reserved Caleb. "That's a pretty tactical weapon. Not a bad choice. You can take the front sight off those, right?"

Hellbilly smiled, seemingly happy to find that his compatriot knew about guns. "Yup, but I keep it on though. You lose a little on the draw, but I like to line up when I shoot."

"I have a .45 ACP," Death Mask said with a stoic face.

"That's a classic!" Hellbilly beamed.

Death Mask smiled a crooked, yet charming, smile. "My uncle has a dubya dubya two model from '43. Son of a bitch still works."

Hellbilly looked out the front window. Sitting just off to the right, nestled behind a bridge, was a black and white Chevy Tahoe. "Shiiiiit…" he sighed. "That's gotta be the fifth copper I've seen since we left the Dirty 'Shwa."

Death Mask looked out his window and caught sight of the Ontario Provincial Police cruiser as they passed by it. "It's a rough day. Probably just keeping an eye out for stranded drivers."

"Probably," Hellbilly agreed hesitantly. "But it's a Thursday. Seems like a lot of coppers for a weekday afternoon in the middle of winter."

The sun finally broke through the clouds, lighting up the crystal white piles of snow. A few minutes later, as they passed through Napanee and made their way towards Kingston, Death Mask looked over from his window and asked, "So, you've known Paulo for a while, it seemed like."

Hellbilly nodded. "Yeah, we go way back. Me and Dom, too. They were Pres and Sergeant of the Windsor chapter when I was there. Dom was my sponsor when I prospected, actually. I know Cliff too, but not so well." Hellbilly paused, and seemed to hesitate before adding the next part. "As it were, when I got pinched, I was protecting Paulo's old lady."

Death Mask slapped his knee and pointed at Hellbilly. "Oh, shit man! I didn't realize that was you! So, you saved Olivia Renaud eh? And even did a bit for it. Shit brother, I was feeling iffy about this gig, but knowing that, I feel much better. I mean, Paulo owes you big time right."

Hellbilly gave an uneasy grin. "Nah, not really man. I was just doing what you're supposed to do."

Death Mask put both hands up and bowed. "True, true brother. I meant nothing by it."

After a moment, Hellbilly's eyes furrowed. He shook his head, like he was shaking off a nasty thought, then turned to Death Mask and asked, "Why were you feeling iffy about this job?"

"Not trying to start anything man," said Death Mask, as he pulled out a cigarette and lit it.

"I didn't think you were. I'm just curious. If you don't mind telling me what you meant, I promise it won't blow back on you, whatever you tell me."

Death Mask took a long pull of his smoke, then took survey of his partner. Hellbilly seemed eager, maybe even a little scared. Caleb figured that since he had been the one to open the flood gate in the first place, he should also be the one to step through it. "Paulo and I have never really seen eye to eye. As you know, I have a reputation within the club. I guess I keep it going with all the stunts and shit, and the fact that the boys from my chapter do well financially just adds to things. I've heard rumours that Paulo resents me a bit, specifically the attention I draw away from him."

"He did seem a little hostile towards you back there." Hellbilly pulled out his own cigarette and lit it while using his wrists to steer. After his smoke was lit, Hellbilly snapped his zippo lighter shut, and tossed it back into his coat pocket. "Let me ask you something. Have you ever seen that red-haired goon before?"

Death Mask shook his head. "Can't say I have, but he did look familiar. Couldn't tell you where from though."

"I missed a few years there, but I've been neck deep in the club since I got out. He didn't look like anyone I'd seen around." Hellbilly fidgeted with his smoke, then looked over at Death Mask quizzically, and seemed to ponder a question that had been nagging at him. "Any chance you saw his forearm as we were coming into the garage?"

Death Mask stopped mid-pull from his cigarette and lowered the smoke thoughtfully to his knee. "With the tattoo of a pile of shit, and some paws around it?"

Hellbilly nodded. "That's what I saw, too."

"The only guys I ever knew who had a tattoo of a dog shitting were Scum Fucks." Death Mask scowled. "I heard there were a few left. Even heard that some of them were trying to rebuild their bastard club, but I can't see Paulo getting mixed up with them. For god's sake, he tried to exterminate their kind."

Hellbilly thought for a moment, then he said, "You're right. Paulo is a lot of things, but you can't deny that he's a mother fucker first and foremost."

"Mother Fuckers Forever Man!" offered Death Mask, solemnly.

"Yeah," answered Hellbilly, sheepishly. "Mother Fuckers Forever Man."

Death Mask returned his attention to the road, but something rotten had invaded his stomach, a dark and slithering thing. For a while, neither man attempted conversion and the car festered with an unsaid worry. The countryside passed by, and eventually they came to the turn off for Brockville.

"Hey partner," Hellbilly said in a perky tone. "I know we're only a couple hours away from Ottawa, but I gotta rock a piss. You cool if I pull off up ahead?"

Death Mask thought about the dark skies they had passed through all morning and the seemingly light sunshine they had come into. It seemed like a good omen against whatever wickedness they were couriering. "I wouldn't mind a bag of chips and a cola."

Hellbilly raised a hand and gave a thumbs-up. "Fuckin' alright! I'm from around here you know. There's a gas station up ahead. It's really more of a truck stop, we can pop in and be back on the highway in no time. Let's be cool though, go do our business, one at a time, make it lickity split."

"Smart plan," said Death Mask as he once again returned his gaze to the window.

Hellbilly took a deep breath and turned off the highway. The pair of Outlaws were so distracted by the thought of a quick pit stop, that they failed to notice the green Harley-Davidson following them.

C H A P T E R   4

The station was small with only a handful of parking spots and a shop that wasn't any bigger than your average convenience store. Despite its cozy nature, the place was buzzing. Travelers jockeyed for position at the gas pumps, and folks darted in and out of the shop with armfuls of snacks and drinks. Hellbilly found a spot towards the back of the lot and backed the Taurus in.

Just as he finished parking, Hellbilly's front pocket vibrated and the biker let out a startled shriek. "What in the alabaster fuck!"

"It's an amber alert," said Death Mask, who already had his phone out and was looking at it. "For that Delaronde kid again. Says they will be releasing new information about the case shortly. Doesn't seem like you need a separate alert for that, but whatever helps, I guess."

Hellbilly shook his head and grimaced "That's a fucked-up situation man. You gotta be pretty low to take a kid like that."

"So, you think he was taken?" Death Mask asked.

Hellbilly scowled a little. It seemed like his new friend was inferring that he didn't completely believe the boy had been abducted. "Don't you? People pray on indigenous kids, man. They think they're all easy pickings 'cause the coppers never take those cases seriously."

"No doubt," said Death Mask. "I don't have any kids, but I couldn't imagine what it would be like to know some creep had his paws all over my child. I'd be going crazy. I got no patience for goofs."

Hellbilly felt a pain in his chest, similar to the wiggling anxiety he experienced earlier, but this time it was deeper. "You mind staying with the car first? I gotta rock a wicked piss, man."

With a wave of his sharp chin, Death Mask gestured for Hellbilly to go. "All good. But don't be hat shopping in there or anything. I don't wanna waste time fucking around here."

Hellbilly undid his seat belt, hopped out of the car, and then stuck his head in between the frame and the door. With a giant grin, and while tapping on the roof, he joked, "No problem, Sarge! Hey you got a big noggin, maybe we're the same size. I can get two for one stetson's in there, you know? They'll be made out of straw, but that's fine for a couple of classy gents like ourselves."

Death Mask smirked, he even had the hint of a twinkle in his eye. Hellbilly returned the look, slapped the roof twice, then slammed his door shut and took off across the parking lot.

Most of the snow had been cleared, but the area was still slushy and covered in patches of ice. Hellbilly had decided to wear riding boots for some reason, and he slipped twice while making his way to the front door. Worse than their grip, the boots provided little protection from the cold, and as Hellbilly stepped onto the paved walkway, he felt an electric tingle of frost run through his feet. He was shaking off the sensation when he saw a green motorcycle pull into the station.

The rider of the Harley was dressed head to toe in black gear and wore a visor that was tinted so dark, Hellbilly couldn't see the man's face. It was a freezing cold day, with drifts of snow cascading across the blacktop, and Hellbilly was amazed that someone had the balls to ride in it. None of the Dead Mariachis were still riding, and they hadn't been for at least a month. Instinctually at first, and then with thoughtful admiration, Hellbilly waved at the rider with two fingers, but the rider did not return the gesture. Hellbilly felt indignant, but then a little silly; he wasn't riding himself and realized that he had no business throwing down his fingers in the traditional rider solute if he wasn't. The Harley-Rider paid Hellbilly no attention and steered the motorcycle into an empty space beside the pumps. Hellbilly brushed off the mixed feeling he had from the encounter and continued on into the store.

The shop was tidy with rows of pristinely faced snacks and fridges filled with single serve drinks. Hellbilly walked past the racks to the back of the shop where a small selection of hats and t-shirts graced the corner nearest to the washrooms. He saw a black cowboy hat with *Mr. Goodtime* written in neon pink on it and briefly thought about buying it for Death Mask as a joke, but decided against it and continued on into the bathroom. The pisser smelled overly clean, more like a dentist's reception area than a rest-stop. Hellbilly recalled how, not so long ago, places like this were all independently owned and operated, and each had its own flare. One stop might be themed, like the Dukes of Hazzard, while another was decorated entirely in neon and swimwear. As a child, Hellbilly's favorite stop was in New Brunswick, and was aggressively themed to honour Jesus Christ and the Virgin Mary. Every time his family stopped there, the lady-owner would give him and his brother free candy and a piece of paper with a bible verse printed on it. Hellbilly never cared for the bible verse, but his mouth watered in anticipation of the candy every time they made the trip out east. Now, the Jesus and Virgin Mary themed stop was gone. It had been replaced years ago by one of the big gas chains and looked similar to the stop Hellbilly found himself in now. Even the bathrooms smelled the same.

After pissing, Hellbilly took a moment to check himself out in the mirror. He combed down his long hair, checked his teeth, and then left the washroom. On his way out of the shop, he grabbed a root beer, a large pepperoni stick, and a pack of cigarettes. He was unwrapping the smokes when he stepped out of the front door. Immediately he felt an odd swirling sensation in his gut. Something was wrong. It took him a moment to piece it all together, but as he scanned the parking lot, the picture took shape. There were extra cars now and they weren't lined up waiting for gas or parking spots. They were covering the exits. A pair of Crown Victorias blocked the east and north exits, and a Ford Expedition covered the west. All of the vehicles were painted black, had long antennas, severely tinted windows, and were idling.

For a moment, Hellbilly thought about running. There was a young dude sitting in a Honda Civic, scrolling on his phone, not twenty feet away. If Hellbilly could pull the kid out of the Civic, he thought he could crash through the back of the Crown Vic on the east exit and be on the highway in thirty seconds. It was a fleeting fantasy though, immediately replaced by the intense sense of duty he felt towards his new partner, who was sitting in the passenger seat of the Taurus. Hellbilly finished unwrapping his smokes, lit one, and then strolled through the parking lot without looking at the blockade.

From the corner of his eye, Hellbilly saw the Harley-Rider. The rider's helmet turned and followed Hellbilly across the parking lot. Knowing that the menacing figure was watching him worsened the uneasy feeling that had been developing inside of Bill since he stepped out of the shop. With calm and measured strides, Hellbilly made his way to the Taurus and opened the driver's side door. Death Mask was as rigid as a corpse when Hellbilly sat down. The small man had his hand deep inside his jacket, presumably on his weapon, and kept his gaze centered straight out the front window.

"They pulled up almost as soon as you went inside," said Death Mask while barely moving his lips.

"Have they done anything besides sit there?"

"Nope," Death Mask replied, calmly.

"Cops?"

Death Mask tilted his head from side to side, as though he were pondering the idea. "I'd say that's the best case scenario right now."

Hellbilly nodded and turned the engine over. "I don't know about you partner, but I'd rather not go to prison for whatever is in this fucking trunk."

Death Mask nodded once and kept his eyes on the black cars standing between them and the open road. "Then we need to get the fuck out of here."

Hellbilly put the car in drive and pressed the gas. The Taurus inched forward, but hadn't moved more than four feet when the door to the Expedition flew open and a man in blue jeans and a dark coat stepped out. The man held a gun in his hand, but kept it by his side. Hellbilly allowed the Taurus to roll forward another few feet until the man from the expedition raised his gun and pointed it directly at the driver's side of the windshield.

"TURN OFF THE ENGINE, AND STEP OUT, SLOWLY!" commanded the man. At the same time, the passenger doors to both Crown Victorias popped open. A middle-aged woman dressed all in black appeared by the east entrance, and a tall man wearing a full parka exited the car by the north one.

A plethora of scenarios raced through Hellbilly's mind. He thought about gunning it towards the expedition, or maybe taking his chances ramming through one of the Crown Vics. He wondered if he should draw his weapon and start firing. It briefly entered his head to do exactly as he had been instructed by the officer and get out of the car with his hands up, but that thought was immediately shirked. Then, a scenario he hadn't considered played out.

The Harley-Rider dismounted and walked towards the Taurus. Hellbilly looked over at Death Mask, who seemed extraordinarily puzzled himself. The Expedition man tilted his head to the side, and then commanded the rider to stop moving, but the rider did not stop. When he was three feet from the Taurus, the rider flicked open his visor and Hellbilly caught sight of the savage eyes of the Red-Golem from the garage. Death Mask saw those eyes too, and another pang of recognition flooded the lizard part of his brain, yet he still could not place where he knew the man from. Then, without warning, Winston produced a sawed-off shotgun from his jacket, spun around on his heels till he faced the Expedition, and fired at the man standing by the passenger door. The Ford caught most of the shot, but a few pellets landed in the officer's leg and he buckled.

With speed that rivaled a world-class sprinter, Winston dashed past the driver's side door and took cover behind the Taurus. The woman from the east side of the lot raised her weapon and Hellbilly heard three low *THUNKS* on his door. Bill ducked under the steering wheel just as his window exploded and a fourth *THUNK* opened a hole in the roof above his head. Glass rained down on him and Bill tried to brush it away, but the shards scraped his scalp and lodged themselves into his palm.

Outside, the man from the Expedition straightened himself out and was about to unload on the Taurus, when five deafening explosions erupted from the passenger seat beside Hellbilly. The volley of thunder, which Death Mask has unleashed, ripped through the front windshield leaving a pentagram of holes and spider-webbing the rest of the glass. The officer flew backwards and collapsed by the Expedition's back tires.

From behind them, by the north entrance, Hellbilly heard the exchange of light popping sounds from two distinctly different guns, and realized that the Red-Golem and the other cop were shooting at one another.

Hellbilly reached into his jacket and pulled out his Baretta just in time to hear a second splattering of bullets collide with the driver's door. Hellbilly sat up, reached over the busted window frame, and blindly fired in the direction of the east-side of the parking lot. Another volley of gunfire pummeled the car, and Hellbilly felt a searing hot pain detonate on the left side of his face. The biker screamed and pressed his hand over his pained eye. His fingers immediately became warm and damp and sticky.

A lull happened, and aside from the screaming gas-station patrons, the world seemed quiet. Hellbilly peeked over the cusp of the driver's side window and looked out. He heard the footsteps too late but saw the female cop racing towards the Taurus with her gun already trained on Hellbilly's face. The biker's balls retracted and his heart bellowed inside of his chest, but just before Hellbilly received his eternal reward, Death Mask rose to his knees and opened fire.

BAM BAM BAM BAM! The female officer and her driver both went down.

Winston zipped across the driver's side of the Taurus and dashed towards his bike. The rider looked over his shoulder and aimed his sawed-off shotgun right at Hellbilly. This time Hellbilly didn't hesitate. He opened the door and rolled out of his seat. Without grace, he plummeted to the hard surface below and cracked his elbow like a stick as he landed. The Red-Golem fired a blast from his shot-gun, and the pellets scattered through the driver's side of the car. With his remaining good hand, Hellbilly fired at the Golem from below the open door. Three shots collided with the center of Winston's chest and sent him stumbling into his Harley.

Hellbilly's victory was short lived though. His face was blasted with fractured cement as two bullets decimated the tiny portion of concrete in front of him and then lodged themselves in the Taurus. The teams from the north entrance had survived their melee with Winston and were now firing at the sedan. Hellbilly couldn't tell if both cops were shooting at him, or if one was shooting at Death Mask, too. All he knew was there were bullets coming in and coming in fast. Using his feet to kick off from the car's frame, Hellbilly spun himself around until he was looking in the direction of the cops. He fired at the driver and missed. The passenger saw Hellbilly's shots and drew a bead on the biker. Suddenly, the tall man's head exploded into a crimson mist. Death Mask had reloaded his weapon and resurfaced just in time to cover Hellbilly beautifully, giving him a chance to line up his shot on the driver once more. Hellbilly fired a round at the man in the parka and this time the bullets landed in the officer's crotch. The driver doubled over and Hellbilly sent another slug into the top of the man's skull. It made a wet and hollow sound as it entered.

There was more gunfire, this time coming from back by the Expedition. The final cop was standing in the open and firing towards the Dead Mariachis. Using the front dash as cover, Death Mask fired towards their attacker. BAM BAM BAM!

"GET BACK IN THE CAR!" Death Mask screamed.

Hellbilly looked up just in time to see his partner propel himself across the front seats of the sedan. With his right hand on the steering wheel, Death Mask reached towards the driver's floor and pressed the gas-pedal.

Hellbilly stumbled into the car just as it began racing forward. Neither biker could see what direction the Taurus was headed, but a moment after they had begun moving they heard a thump and the car rose on one side and then fell back down to the ground. As they crashed their way back onto the road, Hellbilly looked up at the rearview mirror and saw the last cop rolling across the asphalt lifelessly.

"Move man! MOVE!" Hellbilly commanded, and Death Mask moved out of the way quickly.

Hellbilly grabbed the wheel with his good hand, straightened himself into something resembling a driver's position, and slammed his foot on the gas. Like a chugging rhinoceros, the family sedan gunned forward slowly, screaming at Hellbilly for the furious demands he made of her. The Taurus accelerated through an intersection, causing two other cars to swerve out of the way. Hellbilly, Death Mask, and the Ford now found themselves heading north, away from the scene of the crime and away from the highway they belonged on.

CHAPTER 5

The Taurus screeched and bumped up and down along the frigid country highway. Hellbilly's door kept opening, and it refused to latch when he tried to shut it. Death Mask stared out his window, looking back towards the scene of the gunfight. In contrast, Hellbilly scanned the approaching highway frantically, his eyes darting from car, to tree, to sign and back to the road, then repeating this same cycle over again.

"JESUS FUCKING CHRIST!" Hellbilly screamed as he punched the steering wheel with his good hand, which immediately became fire red and throbbed.

"QUIET!" Death Mask shouted. Hellbilly felt a surge of anger, and wished, for just a moment, to shove the little man out the window and send him rolling into the snow-covered ditch.

Caleb closed his eyes and his face took on a serene quality, like a monk in deep meditation. After a time, Death Mask pulled his body back into the car and plopped down on his seat. "No sirens, yet. We have a fighting chance."

"A CHANCE TO DO WHAT EXACTLY?" Hellbilly screamed like a frothing mountain lion.

"Get out of this thing without having our shit pushed in!" There was a chilling pause next, and Death Mask took it as an opportunity to discharge the magazine from his pistol, and count his remaining bullets. "Fuck, I only have four rounds left. We need more ammo, and we're gonna need to ditch this car soon, too."

Hellbilly laughed wildly and stared at his partner. "We can't ditch this fucking car man! Paulo ain't gonna let us walk away from whatever's in the goddamn trunk, just cause we fucked up!"

"We didn't fuck up," Death Mask said sharply. "Someone wants what's in this trunk, or they want what's in this trunk to be found with our sorry asses holding the keys. It was a fucking set-up, man."

Hellbilly thought for a moment. The entire job had seemed odd from the get go, right down to the garage where they met. There were plenty of safe houses and friendly businesses where they could have congregated. The garage wasn't one of them, it wasn't a known spot. It seemed like it had been picked at random by Paulo. Paulo, who seemed so fucking on edge at the meeting, so strung out, so aggressively cheerful. *"Sometimes I dip my hands into something other than cookie jars... on those occasions I have to be discreet,"* Hellbilly heard Paulo echoing in his mind.

Rage filled Hellbilly's veins, it flooded his face and turned his ears maroon. Then, a loathsome thought entered his mind. A thought that was so frustrating in both its simplistic logic and contemptibleness that it caused Hellbilly's heart to race. The Taurus came to an intersection, and without slowing the biker jammed the steering wheel to the right and followed a rough looking road northbound. He knew the road he was turning onto, just as he had known the turn off for Brockville by heart. He was almost in Bastard Township, the miserable place where he grew up, and he could glide through the backwoods of this area without ever opening his eyes. Through gritted teeth, Hellbilly said, "We can ditch the car at my old man's place. He lives up by Otter Lake."

"How far is that?" Death Mask asked.

"Forty-five minutes, less if we giv'er."

"Well," said Death Mask as he pushed the front windshield to the side. The entire thing came off the frame and fell to the road with a thump. "We're in a red car with no windshield, filled with bullet holes. I don't see much point in trying to play it cool right now, do you?"

Hellbilly didn't look over at his partner. He couldn't see any point in being subtle either. All he could think of was the road and the vibrations it sent up the ancient steering wheel which he gripped tightly. With a mosaic of anger, fear, shame, and remorse, Hellbilly pushed the gas pedal to the floor. The sedan vibrated as it picked up speed and dashed down the country roads of Bastard Township towards the McConnell family home and all the hell that came with that.

———————————|———————————

Winston opened his eyes. He looked around and saw the destruction surrounding him. His chest throbbed with a dull searing pain. There were people screaming somewhere in the distance, but as he looked around the pumps and parking lot, he couldn't see anyone. The Scum Fuck sat up, then forced himself to his feet in a pain-filled effort. He glowered at the corpses that littered the parking lot. The cops had failed, miserably, to apprehend Death Mask and Hellbilly. But to be fair, Winston had also underestimated the men.

He knew they would fight back, but he hoped it would be just enough to open up an exit for him through the cops. He didn't expect them to live, nor to blast their way out of the trap that had been set. Now, he had to clean up this mess. Paulo would be angry about how things had gone down, but that didn't matter to Winston. He had his own bosses to answer too, bosses who would be far more furious than the fat juice-head President of the Dead Mariachis could ever be.

Snow started to fall again. Winston found his cell phone and dialed a number he knew by heart. The phone only rang once before it was answered, but no one said anything on the other end.

"It went sideways. I need the boys and the freaks, and I need them now. I'm out by Brockville. They're headed north. I'll keep on 'em, and I'll let you know where they end up."

Without receiving a reply, Winston hung up the phone. He righted his Harley, threw a leg over the seat, and fired up the old hog. As he rode past the Ford Expedition, the final cop — who had been run over while Hellbilly and Death Mask made their escape — reached out in a feeble attempt to solicit Winston's help. The Scum Fuck rode past the dying man and grinned wickedly beneath his helmet. A moment later he was leaving Brockville, heading north along the same road as the Dead Mariachis he tailed.

———————|———————

Except for the farms, trees, and the occasional lake, there was nothing on the road which Death Mask and Hellbilly traveled. The maple trees along the horizon had all shed their leaves and were nothing more than barren gray husks shaking in the merciless chill of winter. The fields glistened with pristine white snow that was clean enough to eat, not at all like the grimy slush that Death Mask and Hellbilly were used to seeing in Toronto. Occasionally, on their frantic travels, the bikers passed a herd of cattle huddled together for warmth, and once a family of horses frolicking. Under different circumstances, the drive might be considered pretty, but not at the moment.

Hellbilly pushed the Taurus to its limit, and the car made sure he knew how upset it was. The tires spun constantly through the frost and snow, but always managed to catch something solid just in time to avoid a catastrophe. They passed a single lone car on their journey and the driver stared at them, bleary eyed, as they drove by. Both men knew, without a doubt, that the operator of that vehicle would eventually report them to the police. After fifteen minutes they came to a fork in the road and Hellbiily continued left. Immediately, the terrain became rougher and the trail more uneven.

"Maybe ten more minutes from here," Hellbilly said, breaking the silence that had befallen them. "It's not far."

"This is a hell of a place to grow up, man," Death Mask said, looking out his window at the expanse surrounding them. They passed a field that was empty except for an abandoned and snow-covered trailer, the kind you might hitch to a tractor to use to haul bales of hay during final days of summer.

Hellbilly glowered, and in a rust-filled voice said, "I didn't grow up here. This is where the good folks live. Our place is deeper into the woods."

They continued northbound. Every time Hellbilly took a turn, the road became more and more decrepit and bleak. Finally, they came to a backroad, surrounded by evergreens and bordering a damp looking marshland. It was at this moment that both of their cellphones went off.

Death Mask pulled out his phone first, and as soon as he looked at the device, his face became sour. A moment later, it hardened into a violent purple as blood rushed into his skin. Suddenly, the short biker threw his phone at the Taurus' dash, and punched it repeatedly. Hellbilly winced at the unexpected violence, and turned his attention to his partner just in time to see Death Mask toss the phone out the window.

"Jesus man! What in the fuck, bud?" Hellbilly exclaimed.

"We're fucked!" Death Mask answered. "Give me your phone."

"What? What's going on man?" Hellbilly felt a swirling sensation invade his stomach again.

"Just give me your phone. Please."

Hellbilly hesitated for a moment, but eventually pulled out his Samsung and handed it to Death Mask. Without a second thought, Caleb threw Hellbilly's cell out the front window. It shattered on the road ahead of them, and a second later, the Taurus ran over the remains.

"That bad, huh?" asked Hellbilly.

Death Mask took a deep breath and then cracked his neck by quickly jerking it to the left. "They updated the amber alert for that Delaronde kid. Two suspects. First male; six foot four, two hundred fifty pounds, long hair, wearing all black. Second male; five foot five, balding, a hundred and forty pounds, wearing all black. Last seen in Brockville Ontario, driving a red, older model Ford Taurus, license plate unknown. Suspects opened fire on OPP missing persons detectives. Consider armed and dangerous. Call nine one one immediately if seen."

"Jesus Christ!" Hellbilly spat. His head felt heavy. There were pieces of a puzzle in front of him, scattered across the vast icy landscape, demanding to be put together, but he couldn't make them fit. Then, the voice of Paulo Renaud once again cut through the noise in the back of his mind. "*I mean it when I say you better not look in that trunk, and you better not let anybody else look in there either*", and all of sudden everything came together. "Is there a kid in the trunk of this fucking car?"

The bikers looked at one another. Horror, shock, rage, and fear were all plastered across their faces. Hellbilly slammed on the brakes and the Taurus skidded twenty feet before coming to a full stop in the middle of the frozen gravel road.

"PAULO YOU PIECE OF FUCKING HUMAN GARBAGE!" Hellbilly yelled. Hellbilly bowed forward and massaged his eyes with his good hand. "I knew this job was fucked."

"We need to look in the trunk," Death Mask said in a calm tone.

Hellbilly moaned and placed his forehead on the steering wheel. "Do you think Paulo is working with the Scum Fucks on some kiddie diddler thing?"

"Hellbilly, we need to look in the trunk." This time Death Mask's voice had more urgency to it.

"Like hell!" Hellbilly smashed the steering wheel and glared at Death Mask. "There is NO WAY that the head of the Nomads is working with our biggest fucking rival club, a club that you and I have BOTH killed members of, on some god damn GOOF child-diddler thing!"

Without emotion, Death Mask repeated, "We need to look."

Hellbilly punched the steering wheel. Then he punched it again, and again, and again. The car shook and the steering wheel bent backward and looked like it was going to snap off, but it held. When he was finally out of steam, Hellbilly stopped hitting the wheel. His hands were flush with pain and his left arm throbbed from knuckle to elbow.

Death Mask turned to his partner and asked if he was alright. Hellbilly nodded and cradled his throbbing hand. Then, speaking plainly, Death Mask said, "We need to look in that trunk, man. If there is a kid in there, we need to know that. It changes our options."

Hellbilly nodded in agreement. "Sure."

"This club is the most important thing in the world to me," said Caleb Driscoll. His eyes were steel. "I've given so much to her. But I know how I'm looked at by some people. By Paulo especially. He thinks I'm gonna make a play for him at some point. You know what's really fucked up about that though?" asked Caleb rhetorically.

"What's that?" asked Hellbilly while staring blankly at the steering wheel in front of him.

"I would never. I don't care about moving up. I'm the Leslieville Sergeant at Arms, that's all I've ever wanted to be since I was a little kid. I'd be happy to spend the next 40 years of my life in that chapter, doing tricks and following trucks around the country. I don't know why Pualo hates me so much, why he'd sell me out to the Scum Fucks, but I'm sorry you got mixed up in this." Death Mask's eyes had reddened. He looked away from his friend in the driver's seat and covered his face.

Hellbilly looked up from the steering wheel and allowed his mind to drift to a darkened bedroom. He remembered the feeling of having his head buried between two long and smooth legs and smelling the intoxicating scent of candied perfume and musk. In front of him, above the warm spot which he devoured with a frenzied avarice, a trail of shooting star tattoos guided his eyes to the curve of an elegant hip. The owner of those exquisite tattoos rose and fell, writhing at the pressure and release of Bill's tongue, her taste and moan bringing him to within a hair of the little death.

"God damn it…" Bill grumbled. "I fucked Paulo's wife."

CHAPTER 6

"You know, you don't have to be here," said the woman, as her face warmed in the tangerine glow of a cigarette.

Hellbilly brushed a lock of long brown hair behind his ear and smirked. "Pretty sure that I do have to be here, ma'am."

"Oh jesus! Don't *ever* call me that again, Billy!" The woman leaned back against the porch banister and propped herself up onto her elbows. Her eyes danced over Hellbilly's chest, briefly met his gaze, and then fell back to her cedar beams at her feet.

"Sorry Olivia, I can't help myself."

She curled her red lips, and looked up from the porch. This time when her eyes met Hellbilly's, they remained. "It's okay, just means your mama raised you right. You still call her that?"

"Yeah, I still call her mama." Hellbilly exhaled a plume of gray smoke through the hairs of his beard and upwards into the night.

Olivia chuckled and took a drag from her own cigarette. "Most guys just have moms, but not Bill McConnell. Nope, Billy's got himself a mama."

The spring air drifted between them. It was ripe with the scent of maple blossom and earth and also carried the flowery sweet smell of Olivia's perfume. She tilted her head to the side and her dark, wavy hair fell off her delicate shoulders. Her locks caught the porch light behind them and looked as though they were on fire. To Hellbilly, it seemed like Olivia had a glowing halo around her.

Bill watched his companion's chest rise and fall beneath the thin fabric of her halter top. A warm rush of heat invaded his cheeks and his stomach fluttered. "Yeah," Hellbilly said, drawing in another breath of tobacco and trying desperately to ignore the thumping in his chest. "What can I say, I'm a hick."

"Don't sell yourself short. You're a smart cookie. Besides, this is Windsor, we're all hicks around here."

Hellbilly laughed, with a little more condescension laced within it than he would have liked. "Darlin', compared to where I grew up, this is high society."

"Just because we aren't from Bastard Township doesn't mean we're from fifth avenue either. Mr. Brockville hillbilly!" When she said '*Bastard Township*' Olivia used an exaggerated mocking tone, which Bill thought was adorable.

"See, that right there shows just how much of a hick you are. Brockville's a big city."

"Didn't look that big, the one and only time I worked there."

Hellbilly shook his head and smirked. "Doesn't matter. I didn't grow up in Brockville. We lived about an hour north actually. The place I'm from doesn't even have a name. It's just a shack in the middle of the woods, off a dirt road, off of a county road. We never even got lost travelers there. If you didn't know it existed, you'd never find the place."

"Well, maybe I'm not a hick, but I'm still a small town girl at heart." Olivia nudged Hellbilly with her shoulder and then shot him a sly grin.

"Paulo's not. He's high fashion and bright lights, Mr. Montreal in the flesh."

Olivia recoiled at the mention of her husband's name, but continued to watch Hellbilly from the sides of her eyes. "He's from Hochelaga-Maisonneuve, that's not exactly Senneville or Madison Avenue."

"Maybe not, but I doubt anyone would mistake him for a grunt these days."

With a hint of a scowl, Olivia pouted. "He earned everything he's got, you know. He's done his bit."

"Shit, I know that. I wasn't saying he didn't earn his spot," Hellbilly said quickly, as the gravity returned to his stomach and punched him in the gut. "He's come a long way and it shows. That's all I meant."

A gust of wind rustled the woman's hair and rolled over her skin turning it to gooseflesh. She crossed her arms in front of her and rubbed them.

"Here." Hellbilly removed his leather vest, the one with his club patches on it, and handed it to Olivia. "Take this."

She turned, presenting her milky-smooth back. Hellbilly allowed himself to look at her. He traced the curve of her neck, from her ear down to her shoulder, and studied the fine hairs that stood up in the crisp night. Then, he draped his cut over her back. The garment covered her entire frame twice over and drooped past her bum, a fact that caused Hellbilly a pang of regret. As she turned back to face him, Olivia blushed and said, "Thanks!" Then she leaned back against the banister and took another drag from her cigarette. A pleasant silence followed; it cut through the chill of the night and had a warming effect.

"Gloria must be a little bit pissed that you're here," Olivia said, finally breaking that silence.

"Ahh, she gets it."

"Still… she does know right?"

Hellbilly nodded and looked away. "She's my wife and I tell her everything. We have a full disclosure kind of deal. Does Paulo know?"

"He knows you're here."

"About the other thing, I mean. About us."

Silence returned, but this time it was an intruder and carried with it only the cold.

Conspicuously, Olivia didn't answer the question about her husband and instead asked Bill, "How's Emmitt doing?"

For a moment, Hellbilly thought about calling her on this attempt to divert the conversation, but he immediately realized that there would be nothing to gain from doing so, and that really, she had given him a clear answer. "He's good. Looks like his mom more and more each day, thank Christ. Would have been a shame if he'd inherited my ugly mug."

"He's in school now, right?"

"Almost, starts in the fall. Glor and I went to Giant Tiger last night and got him a Spiderman backpack, but we ain't giving it to him just yet."

"Wow! Friday night at the Giant Tiger! You and Gloria sure know how to keep the romance alive!"

"I know, it's a little tame, but I like tame sometimes. More and more actually."

Olivia smiled, but her eyes were melancholy. "No, no, it's sweet. I just can't believe you have a kid in school."

"You can't believe I have a kid? You're married to the king of an outlaw motorcycle club. You're the queen old lady, girl! How in the fuck did that happen?"

"What can I say? I give good head," Olivia said as she raised both eyebrows and bit her lower lip.

Hellbilly blushed and Olivia's smile widened.

"God damn! We are getting old, man!" Hellbilly outed his cigarette on his boot heel and stared out into the night.

Olivia turned, squaring her shoulders, and took a step towards Bill, closing the gap between them. Hellbilly felt the warmth of her body and caught her scent as it rose through the air. "Billy, can I ask you something?"

"Sure."

"What the fuck is going on, man?"

The question caught Hellbilly off guard. He shifted in his weight away from his friend, creating a modicum of distance between them. "You know I can't talk about that."

Olivia threw both arms in the air and then flung the rest of her cigarette onto the lawn. "Well Paulo isn't telling me shit, and I got prospects and hang-around following my ass every time I go to the grocery store. And full-patch members setting up shop on my front porch. Did you know Dom was here the other day? For the whole goddamn day. The Sergeant at Arms, sitting on my front porch doing crosswords puzzles and reading a fucking John Grisham novel. I didn't even know that bald gorilla could read!"

Hellbilly's smile returned. "His daughter told me he keeps a stack of Harlequins by the john."

"His daughter?" Olivia scowled. "You banging Misty Di Forno?"

Hellbilly couldn't contain his laughter this time and he guffawed straight from his belly. "GOD NO! First off, I'm straight with Gloria these days, and even if I wasn't, I wouldn't touch Misty. She's got her dad's face."

"Plus, her tits are smaller than Dom's." Olivia shot back, with an impish look on her face.

The pair paused and then erupted in a fit of laughter like a coven of cackling witches. When the final sputtering giggles petered out, Olivia touched Hellbilly on the arm and drew herself close. "Look, I know it has to do with Robby Balls-Out getting killed. He was a founding member, and a fucking Nomad. Those type of guys are supposed to be untouchable. I get that it's serious Bill, I just need to know how serious."

Hellbilly shook his head. "If Paulo ever found out I told you about club business, he'd fill my guts with cement and throw me in the Detroit River."

"Billy, I've known you since you were a hang-around working the door at Kitty's; being sweet and walking me to my car after my sets were done. We go back a long way. Hell, I've known you longer than I've known Paulo, really. And, if I'd been working that first Saturday shift that you worked, instead of Gloria, it'd probably be me and you picking out backpacks at Giant Tiger on a Friday nights." Olivia leaned in and nuzzled herself into Hellbilly's arm. "Please Billy, tell me what's happening. I won't say a word, I promise."

Hellbilly pulled two cigarettes from his pocket, lit them both, and handed one to his good friend. In the distance, an owl screeched and something small screamed as it faded from living to dead.

"You know that the Scum Fucks tried to make a move deeper into Ontario, right?"

Olivia nodded her head inside the crook of Hellbilly's arm.

"Robby getting killed had something to do with that, but I don't know what. That kind of information doesn't make its way down to us foot soldiers. It stays amongst the *inner circles*."

"Jesus. So, the Scum Fucks are coming after us?"

"I guess so. Did you hear about Robby's wife, Vicky?"

"Only that she got roughed up."

Hellbilly took a long drag from his cigarette before continuing. "When they gunned down Robby in his own driveway, they grabbed Vicky, too. They took her with them. I don't know exactly what happened, but they had her for hours, and she was beat up real bad when they found her. She was wandering around some truck stop up by Napanee. I heard she was naked as a jay-bird and bawling her eyes out. Apparently, she wouldn't tell anyone what happened."

"Jesus Christ…" Olivia's face dropped. Even in the dim light of the front porch, Hellbilly could see that she had lost some color. "Why would they come after her? They're trying to hurt Old Ladies?"

"They're savages, Liv. They ain't right." Hellbilly reached out and embraced Olivia. She hugged him back, tight, and buried her face into the barrel of his chest. "We're gonna handle these fuckers though. I can promise you that. But, for now we gotta take precautions."

Olivia nuzzled deeper into Hellbilly's arms, deep enough that he felt the pounding of her heart. "Paulo 's gonna use this as a chance to move up the food chain," she said without looking up. "I overheard him talking to Dom and Cliff about it. He said that half the Nomads want to retire anyways, and if he can jump on this and handle what's going on, it'd bode well for him to get one of the thirteen spots at the Nomad table."

Hellbilly nodded. "Makes sense. They're gonna have to replace Balls-Out anyways, probably a few more before all of this is over. Paulo'd be good for the Nomads. He's got a good head on his shoulders."

"Heavy is the head that wears the crown though," Olivia said absently.

"Is that Shakespeare?"

Olivia turned sharply towards her friend, smirked, and punched him in the arm. "What! Who told a hillbilly like you about Shakespeare?"

"Well, it sure wasn't my wife."

"Really, I'm shocked! I always assumed you married Gloria for her towering intellect."

"I married her cause she can make a mean cheesecake and has an ass like a ripe melon."

Olivia pushed Hellbilly away from her and feigned disgust. "Uhg, I knew it! Underneath that aww-shucks good-old-boy facade, you're just another sexist bitch!"

"You better watch it girl. I'm something of a badass you know."

"YOU watch it! Isn't my husband your boss?"

"Oh yeah, sorry." Hellbilly took another drag from his smoke and chuckled.

In the dim light, Hellbilly saw a look of sorrow glass over Olivia's face. Then, like a whisper, she said; "Goddamn it... I sure wish I'd picked up that first Saturday shift you worked."

Hellbilly searched himself for a reply, but found none. Vaguely, he recognized the nearby sound of pebbles being crushed between cement and rubber, but as the sound grew closer, the biker was so preoccupied that he failed to process the danger it carried with it.

Without warning, a searing heat crashed into Hellbilly's arm and sent him spinning like a top. The crack of the bullet followed a moment later. On his way down, Hellbilly grabbed Olivia and pulled her with him to the floor. Bullets whizzed over their heads, displacing the air in hot gusts, and then collided with the house behind them. Dozens of tiny explosions sent shrapnel made of brick and mortar flying through the air. The road was alight in white hot flashes, and the sound of popcorn cooking in a gasoline drizzle. Hellbilly rolled on top of Olivia, vividly aware that he needed to protect the wife of his president. Two rounds slammed into the meat of his leg. They would have torn through Olivia's small body, ripping through muscle and shattering bone, had Bill not been covering her.

"Vérifie-les! We ain't leaving without making sure they're dead!" Echoed a commanding voice from the driver's seat of a brown Buick.

Hellbilly heard footsteps. One set coming up the front lawn, and the other up the driveway. He spun onto his back, careful to cover as much of Olivia as possible, and with his good arm, pulled out his Baretta. The first man he saw was short, heavy set, and wore a balaclava. The man raced towards the porch, and as he entered the front light, Hellbilly fired four shots in succession. A cone of dark mist jetted from the man's skull and glistened in the porch light. The attacker fell to his knees and slumped over slowly, colliding hard against the concrete landing that existed between the driveway and porch's steps.

Two more bullets ripped across the front lawn. One caught Hellbilly in the side, snapping his ribs like a wishbone, and puncturing the bottom of his right lung. For the rest of his life, Hellbilly would remember the sensation of air rushing into his body in such an unnatural manner; it was a hollow and wet feeling that rattled and stung. With both sides of his body on fire, and fueled by pure adrenaline, Hellbilly unleashed a storm of bullets through the banister.

The hedge at the end of the lawn shook, the windows on the house across the street imploded, and a voice shouted "Tabernac!"

Hellbilly leapt to his feet, nearly collapsed from the unexpected pain, and then scanned the lawn. A second man, also clad in a balaclava, was crumpled in the grass. He moaned and punched the ground over and over again. On the road, by the end of the driveway, a brown Buick idled. A bison of a man occupied the driver's seat, his face obscured by shadow. On the driver's left arm, Hellbilly noticed a tattoo, one that he had seen many times before, of a dog taking a shit that was surrounded by buzzing flies. Hellbilly felt the first waves of shock invading his body and shook as though he'd been standing in a blizzard without any clothing.

The attacker from the lawn stood up and began hobbling towards the Buick. Hellbilly refused to look away from the real danger, lurking in the driver's seat of the getaway car though. In the distance, sirens blared. As the attacker from the lawn reached the Buick, the driver said something low and in French.

The attacker stopped approaching the Buick. His shoulders slumped. The man took a deep breath, and then spun around and raised his weapon. Hellbilly fired first and true. The man slumped against the Buick and collapsed in a pile by the side of the road. Red lights were shining at the top of the street, as if the coming dawn were blinking in and out of existence. Using two fingers, the driver of the Buick saluted Hellbilly, and then pulled away.

Olivia screamed, but to Hellbilly her voice sounded far off and distant. He looked down at her and saw that she was covered in red. "Jesus, girl! You okay?" he asked.

"Billy! You're bleeding everywhere!"

Hellbilly realized that he was covered in blood, his own blood. It painted his legs and shirt, and was soaked through his beard. His eyes began to drift in and out of focus. Absently, he tossed his gun into the front lawn. For a moment, he thought that the pistol was floating away, but he heard it thump down onto the ground and knew then that his mind was playing tricks on him. He heard car doors opening and someone yelling. Hellbilly placed both hands on the top of his head and then dropped to his knees. All of a sudden, he was shoved to the ground and someone pressed down hard on his injured shoulder. As Hellbilly faded into unconsciousness, he felt something cold and metallic ensnare his wrists.

Death Mask's mouth hung open.

"It was years ago, before Paulo was a Nomad, before they were even married. But, they were engaged. Paulo was President of the Windsor Chapter back then, and he was running all over the place for work, and being a cooze-hound every time he was out of Olivia's sight. My old lady was pregnant, and we were having troubles. Liv and I have known each other for years, always been friends. I helped her move some furniture one day while Paulo was out west, and shit just happened. And, it happened a few times after that as well I guess."

Deathmask grinned, and then laughed. It was a maniacal sound that seemed ill-practiced, the kind of hacking screech produced by someone who rarely exercised that part of their vocal chords. Caleb wiped a tear from his eye and said, "We are so fucked, man."

A tickling sensation hit the back of Hellbilly's throat and then, like a sneeze, he burst into laughter, too. The brothers filled the air with chortles and snorts, neither man had laughed like that in years, not so genuinely, not so unrestrained. In the field across from them, a pair of freezing cows chewed cud and watched the rabid scene unfold; a pair of bloodied bikers laughing like madmen while sitting in a relic of a car that had no windows left and was riddled with bullet holes. Eventually, their laughing subsided. Hellbilly looked over at his friend, who he thought looked peaked and maybe even a little scared. They locked eyes, and nodded gently to one another. Together they stepped out of the car and walked to the trunk. Hellbilly was thankful to find that there were no bullet holes on the back of the car. He took a deep breath, put the key into the lock, and opened the hatch.

The boy inside didn't look like he was eleven years old. He was small, so very small. He had sharp features which were made even more severe by the gauntness of his malnourished face. His black hair and porcelain white skin stood in stark contrast to each other. His eyes were closed, and in the corner of his lips was a dried up white substance that was probably residual foam from some sort of seizure that he'd had. He was dressed in a gray sweatshirt that was easily three sizes too large for him, and faded jeans that were tight and probably meant for an eight-year-old girl. He had no shoes. The only good thing in the entire scene was the gentle rise and fall of the boy's chest, which meant that for better or worse, Oscar Delaronde was alive.

Hellbilly's heart grew colder. The sight before him was a sin. No child should ever look so horribly pale and thin and broken.

"We're ten minutes from your dad's place, right?" said Death Mask.

Hellbilly nodded. "Yeah."

"We can make it there and figure out our next play, but we need to get off the roads asap. Are you okay with us bringing this heap of shit into your old man's life?"

Hellbilly scrunched his face tightly. "Why not? That bastard ain't done nothing but throw piles of shit into mine."

Death Mask took off his jacket and placed it over the sleeping child. Hellbilly did the same. Both men stood in the cold, dressed in only their long sleeve t-shirt, emblazoned with Dead Mariachi insignia and numbers. They closed the trunk, returned to their seats, and carefully drove away.

Outside, the daylight began to weaken and the first hints of peach and fuchsia dusted the afternoon sky.

P A R T   2 :   S T O P ;   T H A T   W A Y   M A D N E S S
L I E S !

C H A P T E R   7

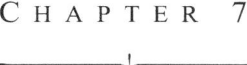

Renee Delaronde sat beneath a tall white pine tree in the center of a
meadow and watched the northern horizon ahead of her. It was
nighttime, but the indigo skies held no stars, and somehow Renee
knew that they had been plucked from the canopy and hidden away
by something vile. The winds that caressed her body deepened with
every passing moment, chilling her, causing her skin to pebble and her
breath to cloud. Renee placed a hand on her chest, and realized that
instead of her usual clothing, she wore a deerskin dress adorned with
porcupine quills. She pulled the dress tightly around her body, but it
did little to shelter her from the cold. She stepped forward and the
frozen blades of grass threaded between her toes left little cuts in her
webbing. There was something warm beneath her feet. Renee could
feel it fighting against the frost.

Snow began to fall from the cloudless sky. It was gentle at first,
like sugar frosting blown through a fan, but soon the ground was
covered in white and the field was a blizzard of slashing ice and harsh
gusts of wind. Renee tried to breathe, but the air she took in burned

with the stench of sulfur and it made her cough. Her lung erupted with excruciating pain and she doubled over. At her feet, Renee found two pieces of firewood lying beside each other. She picked up the pieces and studied them. She knew the pieces of wood were meant to be together, but for the life of her she couldn't figure out what else they were for.

"You need to make a fire," echoed a voice inside Renee's skull.

"I CAN'T!" She cried out, "I've lost my fire!" A rush of sorrow filled her womb and pulled Renee down to her knees. She wept. Tears froze onto the mother's cheeks and snow covered her like a blanket.

Something began to warm her knees and her belly. Renee looked down and saw that the ground was glowing. The glow reached out from the base of the pine tree like hundreds of long fingers and reached all the way to the horizon. The firewood in Renee's hands pulsed in time with the glow. She tucked the two pieces under her nose and took in their woodsy smell. The sweetness of the logs blocked out the stench of the air.

Then the rumbling began.

It came from the horizon like an earthquake in the sky. Flashes of red, which crackled and seared the air, came next. Then, from over the crest, a magnificent bird appeared. The creature had a brilliant scapular of blue and gold feathers and a righteous orange lion's mane. Its eyes sizzled with the red lightning that had illuminated the sky and every time it flapped its wings the heavens roared with thunder. Instead of talons, the raptor had two human hands that were bright red, and it clutched a black ship with glowing sails. The ship cut through the storm like a fire-orange sword that had come straight from the blacksmith's forge and melted away the blizzard. Renne looked closer and realized that standing on the bow of the ship, holding a flame in his hands, was her son Oscar.

The monstrous bird and the great black ship radiated warmth and protection, and the flame in Oscar's hand grew brighter. Renee's feet tingled with warmth. She looked back down at the ground and saw that the roots of the pine tree had melted a trail for her. Renee leapt to her feet and started running. The grass tried to catch her and the snow attempted to flood the trail, but was beaten back by the heat of the pine tree's roots. As she raced towards her son, Renee held the pieces of firewood above her head, and they began to sizzle and spark.

The great bird saw Renee approach and cried out, but when it did, something horrific returned its call. The sound was so deafening that it forced Renee to cover her ears and made her stumble in stride.

Behind the bird a vulgar stampede of black goblins followed. They clamored over one another, biting and gnashing, and clawing as they ran. The horde reached into the air and tried to swat the bird and the ship down to the ground. The thunderbird flapped its booming wings and tried desperately to move away from the fiends.

Renee heard barking. She looked east and saw a pack of ravenous black dogs with piss-brown collars flanking the protectors who carried her son. The dogs had eyes that burned orange like cholera-laced coal and their coats dripped with blood. In the front of the pack was a hound whose face was made of zippers. He howled with a mouth of shattered teeth.

Suddenly, the skies tore open and became the flapping wings of an enormous black bird.

"CAW!" The cry shook the entire meadow.

The black abomination flapped its wings and glared at Renee. It had a treacherous beak filled with human teeth and molted feathers that festered with lice and leeches. With another thunderous "CAW," the filthy crow swooped down and charged towards the thunderbird, the boat, and the boy.

Renee stopped in her tracks. Her guts turned into ice. The crow reached the trio, spread its terrible wings and brought a frost hurricane to the field.

The thunderbird veered towards the west and began flying away from the meadow. Renee reached out for her son. Oscar saw his mother, reached out towards her, and screamed, "ISTÁ!"

Renee woke up on her couch in the same burgundy hoodie and blue jeans she had been wearing for three days. Her head swam as if she had been drinking heavily the night before, even though she hadn't had anything more than half a glass of water throughout the previous day. She rolled onto her back and looked around the living room in a groggy sort of way. The thought of cleaning the place hadn't occurred to her since Oscar went missing, and now piles of empty chip bags and soda cans were scattered around, and there was a strange orange stain on the carpet which Renee couldn't remember the origins of. Her scan of the room brought her to a puffy old chair beside the couch, and she saw that it was covered in dirty clothing. The sight of the messy chair bothered her. That chair was where Oscar sat like a pretzel and watched cartoons or hockey. It had no business being so dirty. Afterall, she thought, what if he came home and saw it looking that way.

Renee sprung up from the couch, suddenly filled with the need to clear off the chair, and clean the entire house. She stumbled over to the recliner, grabbed the clothes, and bunched them into a smelly pile. Then she carried the pile down the hallway, into the furnace room, and threw them into the washing machine. As she came back into the living room, Renee realized how hot it was inside the house.

When she returned from the press conference the night before, Renee was chilled to her bones. Part of her worried that if she fell asleep, Oscar would walk through the front door and she would miss that beautiful moment when he first came home. So it had become her routine to stay awake for as long as possible, until her body was exhausted and could no longer handle being conscious, and then pass out wherever she found herself. She was so tired last night that she was shivering when she came into the living room. She cranked the thermostat all the way up, made herself a sandwich, and brought it to the couch. She couldn't remember the last time she had eaten anything, but as Renee stared at the sandwich, the thought of putting the damn thing in her mouth made her feel sick. Eventually, sometime just before dawn, she fell asleep and drifted into a cold meadow filled with terrible monsters.

But there was something strange about the meadow she found herself in. It was familiar, like a beloved painting she walked past everyday, but it didn't belong to her. It was someone else's meadow, someone else's dream, and it had been violated.

Renee looked out her living room window and across a field of snow. She placed her arm on the sill, and then her forehead against the cool glass. She took a deep breath and steadied herself. The hot living room air was stale and it had the faint stench of burning matches. On the other side of the field, Renee saw the horizon darken and heard the cry of her son,

"ISTÁ!"

CHAPTER 8

The Taurus slowed. They came to a narrow lane bordered on one side by a frozen wetland, and on the other by a thick forest filled with evergreens and sparse maple trees. Hellbilly turned the car onto the lane and followed the path down the marshy shoreline until a dwelling came into view. The house only had one story, was a little shy of the length of a semi-truck trailer, and only a little wider than a single room might be. The red vinyl siding was cracked at one of the top corners, revealing the original tar-paper which the shack had been constructed out of. Scattered throughout the front lawn were snow-covered truck parts; a bumper near the front door, a pile of exhausts and mufflers off to the side, and a lonely truck-bed by the swamp. Completing the scene was a garage, which was nearly as big as the house, and an ancient looking Dodge Ram 1500 that appeared to be rotting in place. Hellbilly stopped the Taurus twenty feet behind the Dodge and scowled. After a long absence, William McConnell was finally home, and he didn't care for it one bit.

"So, this is casa de la Hellbilly is it?" Death Mask asked.

Bill didn't answer at first, he just silently stared in the direction of the shack. Then, quietly, he said, "My brother and I slept together in the living room on a pullout couch. Every single person in this goddamn town knew that we did."

Death Mask looked down and fidgeted with the ring on his index finger. "Folks always do like to make sure you remember your place, don't they?"

Hellbilly nodded. "That they do."

"Just your dad inside?"

"Should be." Hellbilly touched his wounded eye and winced from the pain. "My mama died in '15. Breast cancer."

"Sorry to hear that."

Hellbilly shrugged and as he did, as if on cue, a pan light over the front door came on and an old man stepped outside. Long white hair and a belly-length beard framed the man's incredulously ugly face. He sported an expression that was equal parts confused and hostile. The man was unkempt in all manner of the word; his shirt was stained, his jeans were threadbare, and the flannel vest he wore was falling apart at the seams. Everything on him sagged, from his lips, to his ears, to the gut that hung past his groin. In the man's left hand, he carried a sixteen-gauge pump-action shotgun, but didn't seem to be able to do much more than drag the cannon beside himself.

Death Mask's first impression was that the man looked like a David Allen Coe impersonator, to whom the years had been savagely unkind. "I assume that's your pops?" He asked.

"In the flesh," Hellbilly answered.

"He looks like a character."

"He's a piece of shit," Hellbilly growled. "As soon as we figure out what we're gonna do, we need to leave. And be cool about what you say in front of him, he's half a rat."

Bill opened his door and stepped out slowly with both hands raised above his head. With the adrenaline of the gunfight gone and the pain of his injuries setting in, Hellbilly lacked the fluid grace he had possessed only an hour earlier, and it took him more effort to stand than he had expected.

"It's just me Pop!"

Pete McConnell frowned as viciously as if he'd just found a maggot in his soup. "What the fuck you want? I ain't got any money fer ya!"

"I was in the area and came to say hi," Hellbilly answered, defiantly.

"Bullshit!" screamed the elder McConnell, with spit flying from his mouth. "Your car looks like a fucking Panzer after D-Day! What kind of shit-storm are you in now, boy?"

Hellbilly walked towards his father with his hands still raised above his head. The snow crunched beneath his feet, and when he breathed out, a plume of vapor appeared. The passenger door opened and Bill looked back just as Death Mask stepped out of the car.

"That one of you Mariachi buddies?" Pete raised the shotgun with one hand and used it to point at Death Mask. "I don't let Dead Mariachi shit go on inside my home."

Hellbilly reached the front door, stopped directly in front of his father, and lowered his hands. Pete's eyes were glassed over and the same sour scent of alcohol seeped through his pores that Bill remembered from his childhood. "Nice to see you too, pops."

"I mean it about the Mariachi shit," Pete said with a frown.

Pushing past his father, Bill replied simply, "I know pops."

The shack was deceptively warm, but that warmth was marred by the stench of body odor, stale smoke, and mildew. The walls of the kitchen and living room, which were really just the same small room, were lined with fake plastic wood paneling that had darkened with age into a deep yellowish-brown, like stale piss. On the far wall, opposite the front door, hung a confederate flag with a laughing Hank William Junior in the middle. The flag was held in place by thumb tacks and flanked on both sides by stuffed deer heads. Below it was the yellow and green chesterfield that Hellbilly and Patrick had slept on throughout their childhood. When Bill saw that piece of furniture he winched. Opposite the kitchen was a hallway that led to the bathroom and the only bedroom in the house. On either side of the hallway's entrance were two shrines; one with two celtic crosses and the portrait of a woman who shared the same nose and eyes as Hellbilly with the name "Ruth" underneath, and the other with a framed blue denim vest adorned with a three piece rocker that read "Leadbellys," "MC,"and "Bastard Town" in blue writing on a gray background and had the picture of fat drunken cartoon hillbilly in the middle.

The psychedelic twang of Gordon Lightfoot's *Wreck of the Edmund Fitzgerald* buzzed out of a radio that sat on a round table covered in porno magazines, newspapers, plates, cutlery, and a large ashtray piled high with cigarette butts and ash. Pete followed his son into the shack, flung his shotgun down on the table, groaned as he sat down on a hardwood chair, and then lit a half-smoked cigarette which had been hibernating in the ash-pile. "Your face is all fucked up, too. In case you hadn't noticed."

Hellbilly scanned the room. It was a little grimier now that his mother was gone, but for the most part it looked the same as it had before she died, same as when Bill left at sixteen, and just as it did when he was a child and used to cry himself to sleep.

"So, who is the little fella with ya?" Pete asked, as Death Mask entered the room.

In a curt tone, Hellbilly replied, "He's a brother of mine."

Pete blew out his first puff of smoke into a massive blue cloud. "Don't be stupid, you only got one brother."

Death Mask gestured towards the framed rocker in the corner, and in a chipper tone he asked, "You were a Leadbelly?"

"Yeah, I was." Pete barked. "What the fuck do you know about the Bellies?"

"We patched most of you over, back in the day," Death Mask answered, then he turned to Hellbily and added, "Freaky-Frank, from Kingston, he was a Belly."

Hellbilly nodded to indicate that he was aware of this.

"Frank Hoffstetter's a faggot!" screamed Pete, as he slammed a hand down on the table. His eyes were furious.

Hellbilly stepped towards his father and instinctually pointed with his tender arm, an action that reminded him of how much pain he was in. "Frank's been a Dead Mariachi for twenty years longer than he was a Leadbelly. He's a good guy and loyal. Shit, the man was Vice-President of the Kingston Chapter for ten goddamn years. You'd be wise to watch your fucking mouth when you talk about him."

"He suck your dick so you'd say that, or did he let you suck his?" Pete hissed. "Maybe the Mariachi's don't give a shit about having a fancy foot in their club, but that bitch packed fudge when he was in

Milhaven and was one vote away from getting the boot from the Bellies when you fellas waltzed in and gobbled up every good, god-fearing, and honest Motorcycle Club in the area. Anyone who joins that wannabe riding club of yours has a touch of lavender to 'em! Every single one!"

Death Mask was shocked to hear someone so blatantly disrespect a member of the Dead Mariachis, let alone the club as a whole. In any other situation, throwing around a wild accusation about the sexual exploits of a former vice-president, then damning the entire Dead Mariachi nation, after having received an explicit warning from a Double Mariachi, would have meant a visit to the nearest intensive care unit or morgue.

"You're one to talk," Hellbilly shot back, red faced and eyes bulging, "considering the company you keep!"

Pete frowned. "Just what the hell is that supposed to mean?"

"I saw Roy Hatch's truck outside. You keepin' it for him while he does another bit? What he do this time, fuck a little girl?"

Pete stood and pointed at his son. His left hand stayed on the table, close to the shotgun. "Look at you passing judgment! That man has been nothing but kind to you your whole life, but you're gonna cast a stone aren't ya? And for what? Some slut threw herself at him and he gave in! Big deal, he's a man ain't he?"

"Well, the last girl he raped was thirteen and his niece's daughter, so I'm not sure your argument holds a lot of water pops. As far as I'm concerned, real men don't prey on children." Hellbilly immediately shot back.

"You got a lot of balls to come into MY HOUSE talkin' shit!" Pete screamed. "Just where you get this fucking attitude from I'll never know. If your mother could see you now."

"Watch it…" Hellbilly said in a flat tone that simmered with violence.

"You've hated me for years boy! Like I'm some jack-off! You ever had an empty belly growing up? Go to school without any shoes, or a jacket? So, I kept you and your brother in line when your mama couldn't, for that you hate me?" Pete stood up quickly and kicked over a nearby chair, sending it flying into the living room couch. "I'd die fer either one of you boys, but do I get any thanks? I did things to protect you that you'll never know, never understand, and I worked my ass off every goddamn day oh my life so that you could sit around and get fat!"

Hellbilly threw his hands into the air. "I'm so sorry that your lazy ass had to work for a living so that I didn't starve from neglect. Maybe if you hadn't drunk half of every dollar you ever made, we could have had more than this shithole for the four of us! You ever think of that, you old bastard!"

"Oh, I'm a bastard? And lazy?" Pete stomped on the floor.

Hellbilly pointed at his father. "You're a piece of shit as a man – and a father."

Pete stopped. His fury subsided faster than it had grown, and an evil smirk opened his face wide. "Speaking of pieces of shit fathers, how is little Emmitt doing these days? Not so little anymore, I bet."

Hellbilly froze in place, overwhelmed by emotion and adrenaline. The already long and wild day had squeezed every bit of sanity he had and compressed it into a keg of gunpowder. The mention of his son's name, and the righteously evil smirk on his father's face, threatened to ignite that powder keg right here and now. Pete knew damn well that Bill hadn't seen his son in years, and he knew how hard it had been on him to go through prison without seeing his boy. The word *"KILL"* flashed through Hellbilly's brain in red neon, but he couldn't make his body move and he ended up standing still and silently gawking at the obscene cruelty of his own father.

"Yeah. that's what I thought, tough guy," said Pete with a satisfied grin.

Before Hellbilly could tear his father apart and cause a brand-new crisis to plague the already cancerous day, Death Mask stepped in between the family members. In one proficient motion, which had an almost artistic flair to it, Death Mask scooped up the kicked over chair, spun the thing gracefully in his hand, then slammed it onto the floor and sat down at the table with Pete. From his pocket, Caleb produced a soft pack of American cigarettes. He took out three, lit one, and handed the other two to Pete.

Pete stared at the offering in wild disbelief. His hand drifted closer to the shotgun. Hellbilly watched, confused, and increasingly alarmed.

"Bill here never did mention your Christian name, Mr. McConnell. Mine's Caleb, Caleb Driscoll."

Pete looked down at the tiny man with a frown. "It's Peter, used to be Stinky, but now it's just Pete."

Caleb smiled. "To get a name like Stinky, that means you either smelled like Calvin Kline back in the day, or hot-sweaty-ass. I don't see you as the type to let the ladies suffer while they tickled your taint, so I'm guessing it's the former, am I right?"

Pete let go a single chuckle, took the cigarettes he had been offered, and sat back down. "It was just Brute, but I lathered myself up in that shit when I was a kid."

"Bet you got that pussy because of it though, didn't you?" Death Mask said wickedly.

The old man guffawed, outed his beat-up smoke and with his tarnished brass zippo, lit one of the fine smelling cigarettes Death Mask had given him. Pete took a long draw from the fresh and luxurious American dart and then clapped the lighter shut on the table. "You know what part of Ireland your people come from Caleb Driscoll?"

"Limerick," Death Mask answered as he pulled a drag from his own cigarette. "On my mom's side. Her parents were born there."

"Not named after your daddy then?"

Caleb checked out his cuticles, but didn't pay them any attention. "Ahhh, no. I never did get to meet him."

Pete grunted and then used the two fingers he held the Marlborough in to gesture to Hellbilly and himself. "We come from up north, in Derry. My father killed some limey police officer and had to hightail it over here with my mother, who was pregnant at the time. Course Bill's only half white."

Death Mask nodded uncomfortably and looked over his shoulder at Hellbilly.

"My mom was Ojibwe," Bill said, confirming the needless disclosure of his racial identity.

"I used to live with a girl that was Bear Clan. She made a mean frybread." Caleb offered in solidarity.

Hellbilly folded his arms in front of himself and looked at his feet. "I don't know what clan I am. My mom was part of the sixties scoop, she was raised around here by a couple mean-ass Catholics. All I know about her people is that they were from up around Thunder Bay."

Caleb nodded, then leaned back in towards the old man whom he shared the table with, and looked Pete directly in the eyes. "Mr. McConnell, Bill and I got ourselves into a bit of a jam. You were part of the life, you know how it goes. We need a place to get ourselves collected. We'll do it quick and then we'll be on our way. Might need to shave and throw some crappy paint on the car we came in. Unless you know someone selling a ride for cheap?"

"You outta give us Roy Hatch's piece of shit truck and let us be on our way," Hellbilly said venomously.

Pete glared at his son. "That truck's the only damn thing Roy has left, and I said I'd look after it for him. You ain't taking it on some joyride, boy."

Death Mask rapped his knuckles on the table, drawing Pete's attention back to him. "If you did think that Mr. Hatch would part with that truck, it would be greatly appreciated, and we would make it worth his while. In any case, we're only gonna be here an hour or two, and then we'll be out of your hair. Like I said, we just need a minute to breathe and to figure out our next step."

Pete looked over at his son. Bill was still staring at his feet, trying desperately to avoid eye contact, and languishing in the shame of needing his partner to take over diplomacy with such totality. "You better not get me into a jackpot here, son. I'm too god damn old for any monkey business."

Caleb smiled and crossed his heart in a similar way to how Paulo Renaud had earlier. "Criss cross applesauce. 'Sides, anyone asks, just tell them we gave you no choice. We ain't looking for you to lie on our behalf, sir."

Pete scowled. "Fine, but tell your partner to keep his trap shut while he's in my house."

Caleb raised a hand in Hellbilly's direction, requesting silence. Then he reached into his pocket and produced a billfold, stacked fat with cash. He counted out nearly half the stack, $1,500.00, and handed it to Pete. "That's for your trouble, and I'd say the club owes you a favor on top of it, too."

Pete's eyes went lecherously wide. "See boy, now that's fucking classy. I hope you're spending lots of time with this fine fucker right here. Maybe he'll convince you to make some child support payments even."

Hellbilly took three long strides towards the table, but before he could reach his father, Death Mask shot up and intercepted him by placing two hands on his chest and gently pushing back. Caleb looked his partner in the eyes and gained Hellbilly's attention. "We need to go check on the cargo inside the trunk and have a little palaver. Come on, let's get ramblin' partner."

Hellbilly sneered, but acquiesced to Death Mask's request. He turned and stormed out the front door, pushing it open with enough force that it bounced off the side of the shack and slammed back into the doorframe.

Before leaving, Death Mask turned to Pete McConnell and added, "If you think Mr. Hatch would part with that truck, I'd be happy to toss you the other half of my billfold."

Pete grunted. "Maybe. Let me think it over."

Death Mask nodded a thank you in Pete's direction, then followed Hellbilly back into the cold.

C H A P T E R   9

Outside, the eastern cobalt sky glistened with the first stars of twilight, while the western horizon buckled beneath the crushing fuchsia and plum weight of dusk. Hellbilly hobbled across the front yard, through frost crisp air. Plumes of vapor escaped his mouth. When he was half-way to the car, a hand grabbed him by the shoulder. Hellbilly turned and found that Death Mask had caught up with him.

"I want to be respectful of how I ask this…" the small man said, trailing off intentionally and inviting Hellbilly to finish the question.

"You wanna know if we can trust my pops?" Hellbilly frowned.

"You two seem like you have some shit to work on, and that alert went out to every cell phone in the province."

Hellbilly chuckled and stared at the thin row of trees that separated his father's yard from the swamp. "That old bastard don't have no cellphone. Shit, there's only a fifty-fifty chance he even has a landline these days. And thank Christ, but it's only 5:30, so he hasn't seen the news yet."

Death Mask took little comfort from this answer, and his face reflected that dread. "Let's say he did know?"

"Well, we left his ass alone, so if he knows, and he thinks there's a reward or something, then he's already called the cops. I'd be worried he'd try and call one of the clubs too, but there ain't a Mariachi left in the world that would listen to anything he has to say, and he damn sure don't know any Scum Fucks."

The evening darkened, and an unsettling quiet fell. Death Mask looked around the yard, scanning it for interlopers, but saw nothing except the trees. "I don't think that boy in the trunk was ever meant to make it to Ottawa, and I don't think we were either." Both men paused for a moment and stared at the ground. "As hard as it may be to believe, we need to assume that we were set up by Paulo. So, we need to think about our options, because we can't head just back to Toronto. I know it stings, but we have to assume pretty much everyone who is four-thirteen could be tainted. "

Hellbilly hated what his partner was saying, but he knew it was right. "We're gonna need some help man. I'll get the keys to that truck, even if I have to hog-tie that old bastard and take em, but then what?"

Death Mask looked over his shoulder, checking that the shack's door was closed one last time. "I don't know. Paulo has a lot of reach."

In the distance the deep caw of a crow echoed.

"Fuck!" said Hellbilly, not as a disagreement, but rather as an affirmation. His mind raced through a rolodex of people, friends, family, and acquaintances, but no one felt safe. He had a cousin in Smith Falls who was straight laced, but if his old man did call the cops, that would be the first place he'd suggest they look. His brother would be no help. Pat had been living in Kingston for years now, and slamming fentanyl into his veins the entire time. Hellbilly's little brother took every chance he got to make himself feel like a big shot, and if his badass outlaw biker of an older brother suddenly showed up on his doorstep begging for help the entire junkie community would know about it. Eventually, someone would tell the Kingston Chapter of the Dead Mariachis, and they'd come looking for them.

"How do you feel about Fast-Eddy?" Death Mask asked.

Hellbilly squinted. "Did you not just say we couldn't trust anyone who was four-thirteen? Shit man, I love Eddy, but that mother fucker is a tried and true Double Mariachi. If Paulo has already gotten to him, he'd have no choice but to turn us in."

Stoically, Death Mask said, "He'll come if I call."

"No fucking way!" Hellbilly gasped. "You willing to put your life on that? That if you call Fast-Eddy, the next call he makes won't be to the goddamn Paulbearer?"

"Yes," Death Mask said, as he raised both of his hands in a calming gesture. "If it was anyone else, I'd say you were right. But Eddy and I have been through some serious shit man. We've done things together, things nobody else knows about, not even Paulo. Shit, Eddy comes to Christmas dinner with my mom, and my uncle works on his bike. He's family."

Hellbilly shook his head. "That's what everyone says until they're sitting in the defendant's box, or standing in a grave they were made to dig for themself."

"If I call him, he'll come. He'll hear me out, and he'll help if he can. He won't sell me out either. If he can't help, he'll tell me straight up and we'll figure out another plan."

Hellbilly took a step towards his partner. "You need to be one hundred percent sure about that, compadre. Are you?"

Death Mask took a deep breath and contemplated. Then, with resolve, he affirmed. "I am. He'll come."

Hellbilly looked back towards the swamp and let his mind wonder. He saw a large black bird perched on the branches of a dormant maple tree. It seemed like the creature was staring at the bikers and watching their conversation unfold. "Okay then. When we get back inside, I'll ask my old man about the phone, so you can call Eddy."

"Good." Death Mask said. The word escaped him as a puff of breath with a release of tension.

With the conversation over, the men continued their journey to the ogre of a vehicle they had arrived in and opened the trunk. Oscar was awake, but barely. His tiny frame shivered so desperately that it caused the two coats on top of him to rub together, creating a crinkling aluminum foil sound. Using his thin hands, the boy covered his face. Dark eyes blasted through the slits between his fingers. When the child blinked, his eyelids moved one and then the other. The bikers noticed now that the child had bruising beneath both eyes and that his lips were swollen and purple.

He didn't realize it, but Hellbilly had bunched his hands into fists and was bouncing them into his hip aggressively. The sight of the bruises on the child had pulled Bill deep into a tunnel filled with anger and brutality. He yearned to drive his hands through whoever was responsible for the sin he was witnessing. A bright rush of pain caressed his lower lip, and Hellbilly realized he was biting himself. The sensation pulled him out of his dark tunnel and back into the moment. Then, like a father gently waking a sleeping child, Hellbilly reached into the trunk and placed a comforting hand on the boy's shoulder.

"Hi there."

The boy's eyes went wide, but he struggled to keep them open.

"You're safe little man. I don't know who did this to ya kid, but you're safe with us. I promise."

Sheepishly, the boy removed his hands from his face, but kept his faltering eyes on Hellbilly. "Is it nighttime?" the boy asked in a whisper.

"Not quite yet, but pretty soon," Death Mask answered. Hellbilly looked at his partner, and saw that his face was stricken with worry and anger.

The boy recoiled again, bringing his hands under his armpits and his knees to his chest. From the fetal position, he let out an anguished whimper. The sound of the child tore into Hellbilly's chest and left a gaping wound in a spot the biker had long believed untouched. He placed his hands into the warm cocoon of the coats, wiggled them underneath Oscar's humble frame, and lifted. The child's body was sharp and boney, devoid of muscle. He felt like a bag of feathers. Hellbilly had never seen someone so underfed and mistreated in real life. Only photographs of the Holocaust or the Residential Schools held such grim images.

Bill turned with the boy in his arms. "Let's take him inside and get some food into him. My old man's not good for a lot, but he'll have waffles or some shit."

The twilight stars sparkled and the fuchsia of the western sky disappeared, leaving only traces of plum behind.

Halfway back to the shack, Death Mask stopped. He grabbed

Hellbilly's arm and silenced them both. "Listen!" he said, in a tone that was serious and only just above a whisper.

It took a moment, but in the distance Hellbilly heard the gentle hum of an engine. "That's a V-twin." He said as a sinking feeling crept into his stomach.

Death Mask squeezed Hellbilly's arm tighter, "There's more than one of them, a truck or something, too." Caleb looked at his partner intensely. "I don't think coppers are riding motorcycles in the dead of winter. We need to get inside, right now."

Hellbilly started running first, but it was Death Mask who won the race to the front door. Caleb propped open the door with one foot and drew his pistol all in the same motion. With his free hand, Death Mask ushered his partner and the boy inside and like a battering ram, Hellbilly trudged into the shack headfirst.

Pete watched his son fly into his living room with an armload of child and immediately spat beer all over the floor. "Jesus Christ, Billy! Where the fuck did that kid come from?"

Hellbilly ignored his father and brought Oscar over to the chesterfield. He lay the child down and was careful to keep both jackets on him. Then, with his enormous hand, Hellbilly pushed back the boy's hair and looked deeply into his eyes. "Don't worry kid, it's gonna be just fine."

"Are you out of your fucking mind?" Pete screeched. "How old is that boy? Ten? Goooooooooooood DAMNIT William! What in the hell is going on?"

Hellbilly glared at his father. "Shut the fuck up old man!"

"HELLBILLY!" Death Mask scolded. Then, switching temperatures, he turned to the elder McConnell and spoke softly. "Pete, don't mind him, but listen to me. I know I said we were going to get out of here as soon as possible, and we will, but we might be in more of a jackpot then I thought. Do you have any more guns in here?"

Pete's jaw dropped wide open, he placed both his hands on his temples, and shook his head from side to side. "Oh no! No, no, no, no! What happened to two fucking minutes ago, and '*we just need a moment to breath*?'" The last part Pete said in a mocking tone like he was a child poking fun at his teacher.

Death Mask leaned over Pete McConnell and seemed to become twice the size he had been a moment earlier. "You saw the car we came in, right?"

Pete nodded with a scowl.

"Well, the people that did that might be on their way, and if they do show up here, Mr. McConnell, they're not gonna give a shit if you helped us or not. They are just gonna kill you. Kill you, kill me, kill your son, and kill that boy over there."

Peter's expression grew serious.

"So, Stinky Pete, last of the Leadbellys," Death Mask said as he leaned forward, "I'm gonna ask you again, do you have any more guns around here?"

Pete exhaled a big breath and then stood, forcing Death Mask back a step. "I got some hardware in the basement, but it ain't much."

"Good," Death Mask said plainly. "Thank you for that. Do you have a phone that I could use?"

"You gonna call the cops?" Pete asked.

"No," answered Death Mask, "and you ought not to either, Pete. Pretty sure calling the cops would only get us killed faster."

Pete picked up his shotgun and cradled it in his arms like a newborn. He scurried over to a nearby door which was nestled beside the kitchen area and flung it open. Behind the door was a staircase leading downwards and into darkness. "Guns are in the basement, I'll bring what I can. Phone's sittin' right beside Hellbilly, under that stack of papers." Pete motioned to a side table by the boy's head.

Death Mask smiled and thanked Pete, who in turn grunted and headed down into the basement.

Hellbilly brushed the papers off the side table, revealing a beige telephone with a short chord. Death Mask walked over, grabbed the phone, and dialed a number that he knew by heart.

As the phone rang, the boy's eyes opened wide. He pulled his legs to his chest, and in a frigid voice said, "It's nighttime."

"That's okay," said Hellbilly. "Doesn't matter what time it is. We're gonna figure out a way to get you home."

Oscar began rocking back and forth softly. His eyes became grim and distant. "It's too late. They're almost here."

Hellbilly placed a gentle hand on Oscar's shoulder. "Who's coming, kiddo?"

With a blackness that chilled both Hellbilly and Death Mask, the boy answered, "The dead."

Eddy was standing over a 1957 Studebaker when his cell phone rang. His fingers were covered in a mixture of gummy brown engine lubricant and thick grainy black grease, so he stepped away from the car and wiped his hands. He looked down at the vibrating cell phone on the table, but didn't recognize the number. That wasn't unusual though, Dead Mariachis often called one another from prepaid burner phones or landlines with no name assigned to them, so that the government couldn't track their calls. Five rings later, Eddy pushed back his slick blonde hair, and answered the phone.

"Hey."

"It's Caleb."

"Cay-hey-hey-HEY-leb! How the hell are you doing, man?"

"Look, um, I don't know what you've heard so far, but I'm in a bit of a bind."

Eddy heard a wavering in his friend's usually steady voice, and it gave him a sinking feeling. "What's going on brother?"

"I need a favor, a big favor. I'm into something deep here, and Paulo Renaud might be involved."

"That's heavy man."

"Eddy, you and I go way back, we've been through it man…"

"Yeah… we sure have."

"So, if you can't help, I'd understand. You have your own shit to deal with, and what I need might put you in conflict with our club, with Paulo especially."

"You're killing me brother, just out with it."

Caleb took a deep and purposeful breath. "Did you hear about what happened in Brockville yet?"

"Judy said something to me about a shootout with some cops. It's got something to do with that missing kid too, I think."

Eddy waited for his friend to continue, but Caleb remained silent. Coming from the other end of the phone, Eddy heard nervous and heavy breathing, the sound made him feel sick.

"What the hell is going on Caleb?"

"I don't want to say much more over the phone man, but you know me, you know I wouldn't hurt a kid. And, you know I wouldn't go picking a fight if I didn't have too, especially not one I was gonna lose. I need your help man, but like I said, it's a big ask. If I'm right, Paulo's gone turncoat, and he might be in bed with whatever remains of the Scum Fucks. If you help us here, and if we can't turn it back on Paulo's pink handed greasy-ass, you might end up in the dirt right beside us. So, if you have to say no that's okay. I'd understand that."

Eddy shook his head and felt his bowels gurgle. His stomach suddenly felt rotten and ready to purge itself. Death Mask was right, this was a big ask and a heavy accusation being made, but Eddy did know Caleb. They had been through the trenches together, and if his friend needed help, then by-god he was going to help him. "My uncle has a place near Sharbot Lake. Remember, you came up when you were dating that Allison chick, and we all went water skiing."

"Yeah, I remember. Nice little cottage."

"I can meet you there in a few hours."

Caleb let out a measured and controlled sigh. "You're amazing. I'm gonna owe you for the rest of my life."

"Fuck that, I already owe you, man. Okay, so what do you need me to bring?"

The line went quiet for a moment and in the background Eddy heard his friend speaking to someone.

"A couple days' worth of food, and some water. A change of clothes would be nice too, shit without DM stuff all over it. My partner is a big fella, like your brother Al. You know him. He told me about the time you got your dick snagged on a hooker's tooth."

Eddy smiled on the other end of the phone. He knew right away that Caleb was talking about Hellbilly, and it made him feel better to know they were together. Bill would keep Caleb safe, and Caleb would keep Bill level headed. They were a good match.

"Kids clothes, too." Caleb continued. "For like, a small eleven-year-old, I guess. I think we have a car, but we may need a replacement, so if you have anything you are working on that could go missing from the shop it might be helpful. Any cash you can spare, and guns Eddy. I think we'll need some guns."

"Okay," Eddy said without emotion.

"After you hang up with me, you gotta go radio silent man. Ditch your phone, ditch Judy's phone. Tell her to get out of town and make it look like you went together."

"Her mom's been sick for a while, the guys all know about it. Wouldn't be too much of a stretch to say we headed up to Collingwood to see her on short notice."

"Okay, that's great. Sorry to hear about Judy's mom, though."

"Don't worry about that right now."

"I have another favor to ask." Death Mask thought about leaving well enough alone, but something in the back of his brain had been nagging at him, clawing to break free ever since he saw the dog-shitting tattoo on the Red-Golem in Paulo's garage. His entire world was about to get flipped upside down and he knew it had something to do with what he had done to the leader of the Scum Fucks almost a decade ago. "Can you swing by mom's place? Don't tell her anything about what's going on. Just say that I'm working on an older foreign bike or something, and that there's an article about replacing parts in one of my magazines. There's a stack of 'em in my closet, grab one, any one, but while you're in the closet, tucked in the back, there's an old suit bag with a leather vest inside. Bring it to me, please."

Feeling very dry all of a sudden, Eddy licked his lips. "Sure man. It's gonna take me a few hours to get everything and get my ass up there. Can you hold out till around midnight?"

Caleb thought about it, but realized there was no other option besides saying yes. "Whatever you need. I'll make it work."

"Okay," said Eddy. "I'll see you then."

"Eddy, thank you."

Eddy nodded to himself and hung up the phone. He looked around the clutter of his garage and felt his knees begin to weaken.

CHAPTER 10

Caleb placed the phone back on the receiver, carefully, and then stared at the back of the room. He felt oozy, like something horrible was seeping out of his pours. The warmth of the cabin, which originally felt inviting, suddenly seemed stagnant and oppressive. An intense urge to race into the cold and dunk his head in the nearest snow bank pounded against his brain.

"What did Eddy say?" Hellbilly asked. His hand was still resting tenderly on the boy's shoulder.

"He can meet us at his uncle's place by Sharbot Lake."

"Jesus!" Hellbilly snorted. "That's great! Bit of a drive, but we can make it. Especially if we have Roy's truck."

Just then, Pete appeared at the top of the stairs. The elder McConnell had several boxes of ammunition in his arms as well as a small caliber hunting rifle. In his waistband were two pistols and a hunting knife. Pete tossed the ammunition and rifle onto the countertop. He pulled out the knife and one of the pistols, then tossed them onto the table as well. The other gun he kept in his waistband. "I'm keeping my Glock and my shotty, but you two can duke it out over the peacemaker and the rabbit gun."

Hellbilly walked over to the table and picked up a box of 9mm shells. "My baretta takes nines."

"You can have one damn box! But, I'm keeping the rest for my Glock!" Pete snapped.

"Looks like there are some forty-fives here, too. Should be fine for your ACP," Hellbilly said, signaling to Death Mask with his chin.

Pete wheezed and swayed a little from one side to the other. Finally, he slammed his sixteen gauge into the floor and used it like a cane to steady himself. "Those are for the Peacemaker your grandaddy owned."

"I don't think he's gonna be using it pops," Hellbilly replied. The biker looked at the collection of guns and ammunition his father had piled onto the table. It wasn't much. He picked up the .22 and examined it. The gun looked like a Winchester, but was nothing of the sort. It had been made in Denmark by a company that didn't exist any longer, and Hellbilly remembered using the firearm as a child to hunt whistle-pigs. "I'll keep the .22. Death Mask, you should take the Peacemaker since you're using that ammo anyways."

Death Mask approached the table, gathered the long barrel revolver in his hand and examined it. He cracked open the cylinder and tossed in six shells. "Looks nice enough, big fella, but if it's needed, I doubt I'm gonna get a chance to reload it. It was your grandad's, you oughta keep it." Then, without giving Hellbilly the chance to argue, Death Mask shoved the gun into his hands, picked up the small caliber rifle, and began loading shells into it.

Hellbilly felt the weight of the revolver in his hands. It wasn't a true Peacemaker, not the black-powder kind, this was a replica built in the mid-1960s. It looked like something out of a spaghetti western but fired modern shells and was more accurate than its ancestors. A surge of power invaded Hellbilly's remaining good hand. This gun felt right, it felt strong, and it made Hellbilly feel safe. The biker tucked the weapon into his belt and allowed the sensation of it to inspire him. For the next few minutes, the gang loaded and checked their weapons. Finally, after ensuring that his Baretta was in working order, Hellbilly placed the knife and sheath on his belt, along with the peacemaker. It was then that the putter of a V-Twin engine began to slowly rumble down the driveway.

Pete's face became severe. He hobbled to the front widow and pushed back the curtain. "I don't suppose you boys are gonna be happy to hear that there's some Scum Fuck in my front yard taking a gander at yer ride."

Hellbilly and Death Mask were startled, but not surprised to hear this news. They raced to the window on the other side of the door and looked out. Sure enough, the Harley from the gas station was circling the Taurus, only now the rider wore a brown leather vest that had a cotton patch of a cartoon dog taking a shit in the middle of it. The words "Scum Fucks," "MC," "Nomads," circling the dog in brown letters on a pale green background. Both Hellbilly and Death Mask had heard rumors that the Scum Fucks were still around, but it had been a nearly ten-years since either of them had seen anyone bold enough to wear their rockers. On his second pass of the Taurus, the Scum Fuck stopped his bike and dismounted.

"You boys gonna tell me about who this son of a bitch is?" Pete asked.

Hellbilly ignored his father and cocked back the hammer on his Baretta. "We should ice him while he's looking at the Ford, I'll do it."

With his heart pounding, Hellbilly took two steps towards the front door, but was stopped when a Death Mask grabbed his forearm in a vice grip. "Are you out of your fucking mind? He's not alone out there. We have no idea how many there actually are."

"There's a bunch of 'em!" said Stinky Pete, while still looking out the window.

The glimmer of half a dozen motorcycles shone through the front window. The bikes bopped along the ice-covered driveway. Their headlights bounced up and down, illuminating the frost in the air and creating a dazzling display that looked like a landing UFO. The sound of the machines was deafening; filled with thunderous pops and growls. When they rounded the bend, the first thing Hellbilly noticed was how dirty all of them were. The convoy was covered in mud and ice and salt from the roads. The bikes were all rusted and frayed. The riders wore leather pants, full face masks, and their cuts were disheveled. Everyone, except for the original rider, had a side-rocker displaying the chapter name, "Montreal."

Following closely behind the convoy was a dark Chevy Tahoe, which pulled up behind the Taurus and blocked it in. Two men stepped out of the mountainous sport utility vehicle, and Hellbilly was not surprised to see that they were his former chapter brothers Domonic

Di Forno and Clifford Tibbs. Unlike the Scum Fucks though, neither Dead Mariachi wore their cuts. For a strange moment, Hellbilly was comforted in knowing that he wouldn't be killed by someone wearing a Dead Mariachi rocker.

The light from the motorcycles flooding the front windows and prevented the occupants of the McConnell home from witnessing the final plum shades of the day disappeared over the horizon, leaving only the blackness of night behind.

Hellbilly peeked out the window, and caught sight of the Scum Fucks who had circled the Taurus. The man reached up, undid his chinstrap, and carefully removed his helmet. Steam escaped, and when the rider's grotesque face finally emerged it danced with hot mist.

"It's that red-headed freak from the garage." Hellbilly said with a hiss. "I don't get it, I iced his ass back at the gas-station."

"Maybe he had a vest on," Death Mask said calmly.

Hellbilly spat on the floor. "I'm gonna fucking kill Paulo!"

"Let's worry about getting out of this thing first," said Death Mask.

Another terrible mechanical sound screamed down the driveway, and like an ocean liner crashing through an iceberg, a busted up yellow school bus roared into view. The mammoth vehicle smashed into a set of trees, just past the curve in the driveway, and came to a halt. Cliff and Dom stepped backwards and placed the SUV between themselves and the bus. The Dead Mariachis pulled out their sidearms and coward at the sight of the aged vehicle, but the Scum Fucks never took their eyes off the cabin.

The bus was a rusted heap of chipped paint. Its wheels sagged so badly that the rubber had cracks running the circumference of the tires. The windows were gummed up, but behind their translucent brown grime, hands slapped and smacked against the glass. Slowly, the front door slid open, revealing a deep blackness. A horrible screech radiated from inside and beneath it, a thumping and grinding sound echoed. Then, the things emerged.

They were people, but they weren't right. Their eyes were barren and their skin was pale. They moved unnaturally, in a way that was contorted and twisted. One of them fell and then continued on all fours, like a centipede. As they escaped the bus, the creatures battled one another, biting and clawing each other and trampling over any of their cohorts that had the misfortune of falling to the ground. Once free of their confines, the ghouls raced towards the woods. They let out hooting noises and yipped until they finally vanished into the depth of the forest. The last thing to exit the bus was a particularly large and beastly looking creature, with four terrible slashes on its face and the top of its skull exposed. The thing caught sight of Dom and Cliff, and began making its way towards them. Unlike its counterparts, this beast was so large that it had no choice but to amble towards its prey like the killer in a slasher movie, slow and methodical, and violently calm. Dom raised his gun, but Cliff seemed so scared that he was unable to do anything. The Red-Golem stepped in between the beast and the Dead Mariachis and pointed into the forest. The creature stopped its approach, snarled, and then retreated into the woods to join the rest of its kin. Trees and shrubs cracked and shook, and the sound of gnashing of hungry teeth rose into the night.

"It's alright. I'll go with them," said the boy. Oscar had crept up soundlessly and was now standing behind Hellbilly and Death Mask. The noise of his quiet voice cut through the horrifying clamor outside and caused both bikers to gasp.

Oscar was wearing only his sweater, the coats he had been given were left on the couch. Hellbilly reached out, took the boy by the slender shoulder, and pulled his boney frame in close. "You're not going anywhere with those creeps. You're staying right here with us and we're gonna keep you safe."

The boy looked directly at Hellbilly, his eyes were cold and black. "If you don't struggle when they eat you, it'll hurt less."

Hellbilly's eyes went wide, Death Mask shook his head and attempted to rid his mind of the horrible thing he had just heard, and from the other side of the room Stinky Pete yelled, "WHAT IN THE ALABASTER FUCK DID THAT BOY JUST SAY?"

"Don't pay that any mind pops. We got more important shit to worry about," Hellbilly commanded.

"You got any windows looking out back?" asked Death Mask.

Still in shock from the statement Oscar had just made, Pete gestured with his shotgun towards the hallway. "In the bedroom."

Death Mask grabbed the twenty-two and dashed towards the hallway. He slipped through the dueling shrines and was lost to the other side of the shack.

Hellbilly listened to the ragged footsteps outside, and to his horror the sound drew closer. Sweat dripped down his forehead like a trickling stream and collected in a pin's head on the tip of his nose. He wiped away the salty moisture and raised his Baretta to the window.

Winston saw Hellbilly through the glass and winked. Then, the Red-Golem raised his hands, and the forest fell silent. "Hello in there! And, make no mistake, I know you are all in there. I saw that you tossed your cell phones a ways back. I found 'em on the road. That was smart for the cops, but it's not how we were tracking you."

Two more Scum Fuck arrived and rode down the lane, nearly toppling as they passed the bus.

Winston smiled. "My guys just cut the phone lines to the whole road, so now you're in there all alone and you ain't calling anybody for help."

Hellbilly's vision narrowed, and his heart slammed against his chest.

"Look guys," Winston continued, "the truth is we're gonna do what needs to be done here, but we all just wanna get home. Between us and the freaks, you ain't gonna make it through the next hour, let alone the night. So, if you come out nice and easy like, I'll kill you quick. But if I have to send in the hounds, I promise it'll be painful for ya."

Hellbilly's tongue filled with venomous thistles. "If you try to come in here, I'm gonna shove my Beretta so far down your mouth, you're gonna shit gunpowder! What you ought to do is go home, lather that ugly ass face of yours up with vaseline, then shove it up Paulo Renaud's prolapsed ass!"

The things in the forest giggled when they heard Hellbilly yell. The sound was profane.

"Ho ho ho ho! I like that spirit," said Winston. "I *really* do! But no, you fucking hick, I think not. You see, the freaks," Winston used his middle finger to wave a circle around the yard, "the freaks just want to feast, and they are gonna. There is NOOOOTHING I can do to stop them. But, the question is; do I let them eat you while you're still alive, or as you lay unconscious and dying? So, do us all a favour, you fucking hillbilly, get your little buddy and come out of that god damn shack."

From the darkened woods there came another communal laugh, this one even filthier than the first. Hellbilly looked down at Oscar and squeezed the child's shoulder, trying to show him that he wouldn't even think of handing the boy over.

"That's a lot of big talk coming from some chicken-fucker riding a geezer-bike!" Pete, for some inexplicable reason, decided to yell.

Winston chuckled and shoved his hands into his pockets. "Is that your old man in there with ya, Hellbilly? Dom here said you was from this area. C'est bon! Old man, I think I would have liked you under different circumstances!"

Hellbilly shot a dagger stare at his father, but Pete didn't see it. His fear-stricken face was immovable from the window. Pete was glued to the events happening outside.

"Let the boy go, Bill!" said a new voice, one that was far more reserved in tone. It belonged to Dom. "You and Caleb ain't gettin' out of this. You both went against Paulo, in your own ways, so that checks been cashed. You can make it easy on yourselves, though. I know you don't have much ammo left after that little pop-off at the gas station. Come on outta there and I'll make it quick for ya. One Mother Fucker to another."

Dom's use of the ingratiating term "Mother Fucker" riled something inside Hellbilly. He gripped his Baretta tighter and leaned into the window. Hellbilly's mind saw a loose string in something Dom had just said, and pulled at it; the fools outside thought they were low on ammo, maybe even out. Granted, they didn't have much, but they were more flush than the bozos outside thought. Hellbilly felt a surge of adrenaline chug through his neck, and it made him smile with hope.

"Dom!" Hellbilly called out. "If for some reason you live long enough to see Paulo again, you make sure to tell him I'm gonna find him and I am gonna cut his fucking head off!"

"You're goddamn right we are!" Death Mask shouted in agreement from the bedroom.

"Okay then.," Winston said, and clapped his hands together. "Sounds like negotiations are breaking down. I guess we're doing this thing. Don't say I didn't warn ya." Winston placed his index finger and thumb into his mouth and blew out a high-pitched whistle. Right away the ghouls descended.

The first gunshots came from the bedroom, where Death Mask was. The tiny biker fired in two short bursts, and every time he did, something outside screamed. Hellbilly found himself distracted by the sound of gunfire and didn't see the woman in the woods at first. She came out of the trees like an attacking wolf and ran towards the front door in an all-out sprint. When Hellbilly finally noticed her, she was already past the Taurus and halfway to the front door. She was dressed in a thin white blouse, pencil skirt, and flats. Her hair flew behind her like a storm. She ran wildly. Every third or fourth step she took was a misfire, and she stumbled constantly, but somehow maintained her stride. It seemed like she didn't know how to use her legs correctly, like they didn't truly belong to her. As she entered the space where the pan light shone, her face came into view. She was pale like an apple core, with sunken eyes that were milky and hostile, and bulging with rage. She had no lips, only long savage teeth that snapped frantically at the air. She was both alive and rotting at the same time, a feral husk ripping through the night in a frenzy, aroused by the prospect of carnage. Worst of all, though, Hellbilly recognized her.

"Olivia…"

A child-like fear paralyzed Bill. He realized that Olivia meant to cause him harm. She was no longer the woman he had shared cigarettes with, whose body once gave him the most intense pleasure he had ever experienced. Now she was a demon that wanted to kill him. Hellbilly knew he needed to act, but the image of Olivia's backlit face on that chilly spring evening wouldn't allow him to pull the trigger of his gun. Then, when she was not three paces from the window, her head exploded into a brown-rust mist.

"God dammit boy!" screamed Pete. "You gonna shoot or keep your dick in your hand?" Hellbilly's father fired another round out the window and a man in a corduroy vest twirled like a ballerina.

Hellbilly snapped out of his daze and buried the thought that his friend had just been killed in front of him. He looked around the yard and saw an entire horde of grizzly abominations descending upon his childhood home. A teenager in a denim jacket appeared by the Taurus. The boy snapped with a putrid mouth and slashed with blackened fingernails as he ran towards the house. Hellbilly lined up on the boy's chest and fired two shots directly into his heart, but the boy kept moving forward. Hellbilly fired again, three times now. The boy fell to the ground, but right away stood up and continued on. Panic and terror crawled up Hellbilly's chest and invaded the sides of his head like a pair of rotting fingers dancing along his flesh. He fired again and this time caught the boy just above the eye. The teen fell into a heap and rolled two paces before coming to a dead stop.

Pete fired his shotgun, sending a punk-rock chick flying backwards. The punk-rock girl shook off the assault and leapt back to her feet. Pete fired again, this time hitting a business man by Roy Hatch's truck. The business man's shin exploded. He fell to the ground but immediately started dragging himself towards the cabin. Pete lined up on the businessman and pulled the trigger, but nothing happened. The elder McConnell switched to his Glock and continued to fire out the window, hitting almost nothing and emptying his pistol in just a few seconds. The window in front of Pete imploded. Three sets of hands protruded through the frame and slashed at the warm air inside. Pete staggered backwards and tripped. He fell completely on his ass and sprawled out like a shell-racked turtle. He stared up at the window, shocked by the feral humans invading his home. Then, to his horror, a grizzly looking man in a decaying flannel shirt pulled himself through the window frame and fell onto the floor. Pete raised his Glock again and fired.

CLICK. Nothing.

As the ghoul reached for Pete, Hellbilly looked on. William was flooded with emotions; he saw himself as a child cowering before a red-faced and towering patriarch who screamed at and berated him. He remembered the shame and guilt that came when his father found his collection of porno-magazines in the woods and announced it to the entire family. He recalled sitting in a prison cell reading about the painful way his mother had died, but receiving no words of comfort in the letters his father had written. If it had been only these memories that invaded Hellbilly at that moment he would have let the ghoul continue its attack, but those weren't the only things he thought of. There were happy times as well; like when Bill was seven and Pete let him take a gulp of beer while the Leadbellys played cards in the garage. Or the time Pete took just Bill to go fishing and the two spent the whole day sitting peacefully together by the riverbank, and the beautiful way his parents danced liked teenagers whenever Buffy Sainte-Marie came on the radio.

Hellbilly drew a bead on the dead thing's head and pulled the trigger. Blood splattered against the basement door, flew into the kitchen and coated Pete's face.

"I think you gotta shoot them in the head!" Hellbilly yelled. Pete looked at his son in stunned relief, and for the first time in many years the pair shared a smile.

The McConnell reunion was short-lived, though. Something crashed into the front door, causing it to buckle, but not break. Soon after, a melting human leapt through the front window. It was a woman of severe decay. Her arms had no flesh on them, the sandstone of her kneecaps was exposed and her hair looked like seaweed. The rotting woman turned her head slowly and looked at Hellbilly. She opened her maw, which was filled with sharp brown teeth, and howled. The thing crawled towards Bill and rattled off a wet sounding chuckle as she did. Hellbilly aimed his Baretta at the mushy face of the woman and fired. Her head jerked backwards and a jet of brown sludge coated the shrine that belonged to Ruth McConnell.

Six gunshots came from the bedroom, and Death Mask screamed, "FUCK! FUCK! FUCK!" He raced into the living room, fell onto the floor, immediately rolled onto his back and fired upwards at a heavy-set man who followed closely behind. A single bullet caught the man in the eye and he fell with a SPLAT onto the floor just in front of where Death Mask was.

"Thanks for the tip!" Death Mask yelled from his back. "But, there's more coming!"

Several wild looking people appeared in the hallway and the other front window imploded with bodies as a cascade of freaks poured into the living room.

Pete stumbled to his feet, threw his Glock at the incoming horde, and yelled; "Get in the goddamn basement!"

Time slowed then.

Hellbilly looked down at Oscar, who seemed resigned to a grim fate, grabbed the boy by the wrist and pulled him towards the basement door. Pete stepped out of the kitchen, iron skillet in hand, and began waving the frying pan in front of him. As he reached the door, Bill heard two loud DONG sounds and knew that his father had connected with something's head. Hellbilly was first to the door. He grabbed the knob, pulled the door open, and as soon as he did, he felt Death Mask collide with him. Together, Death Mask, Oscar, and Hellbilly rolled down the stairs into the basement. Hellbilly jerked his body to the side and used himself to shield Oscar from the worst of the tumble, but his bad elbow hit the stairs and sent hot flames rippling through his torso. When they finally came to a stop at the bottom of the steps, Hellbilly felt an ache running through his entire body.

A wretched scream drifted down the steps. Hellbilly looked up and saw his father. Pete was on his knees, crawling towards the door, covered by a mountain of fiends. The front door exploded and fell to the ground, crushing one of the ghouls as it did. A new horde of apple-core faced beasts entered the house. Hellbilly raced up the stairs and reached for his father. Pete shuffled forward, trying to get to the door. A woman with fire-red hair grabbed the old man by the shoulder. She reared back, thrust her teeth into Pete's cheek, and ripped his flesh away like the crispy skin of a baked turkey. Blood spurted from the wound, and Pete's eye rolled backwards. Hellbilly screamed, "NO!," and tried taking three steps at once, failed, and fell directly onto his chin. Pete's eyes returned from the sunken place where they had been and he looked into the desperate face of his son. From the front pocket of his vest, he grabbed a set of keys and threw them into the basement. Just after that, a man in a trench coat grabbed his arm and bit into his wrist. Hellbilly heard a crunching sound as the man shattered Pete's bones. Another ghoul jumped onto Pete's back and immediately sunk its mouth into his neck. A scarlet fountain shot out of the puncture and slammed into Hellbilly's face. Mustering what little strength he had left, Pete shuffled forward one last time, and with his free hand he grabbed the basement door. Then, Peter McConnell, last of the Leadbellys, looked into his son's eyes, yelled "GET!" and slammed the door shut.

Hellbilly stayed on the stairs, lost in the moment. From behind the door, he heard a wet slurping sound filled with snapping and sucking, and behind that gruesome noise was the whimper of his father. He could tell that Pete was in agony.

The stairs shook. Death Mask raced past. The short biker grabbed an extension cord from off the wall, slid it underneath the door, and then tied it tightly to the railing. Death Mask used the other side of the chord and looped it around the handle. For now, the door was secure.

CHAPTER 11

The basement was a dust-filled crypt. Unfinished cinder blocks, zebra'd with rusty-brown streaks, lined the walls. The floor sloped to one side and was uneven, as though the concrete had been poured directly onto unflattened earth. Mummified spiders hung from exposed beams, swaying in the cool breeze of the tomb. It smelled dank, like wet moss, and was dark except for the soft glow that came from the wood stove that heated the rest of the house. Death Mask descended the stairs carefully and helped Hellbilly to his feet. The now oldest living McConnell was still in a daze, but through muscle memory he reached up and pulled on a slender chain, which turned on a single hanging light bulb that cast shadow-devils into places where the light couldn't reach. Directly at the bottom of the stairs was an empty gun safe, which was really just a refurbished highschool locker. Beside it were boxes of magazines, Christmas decorations, clothing, and motorcycle parts. Shelves, tools, and workbenches filled the rest of the space, leaving only a narrow path through the wreckage. As the light and shadows constricted the labyrinth, Hellbilly felt his heart pump harder and faster, and he couldn't shake the looming feeling that he was going to die down there.

The door at the top of the stairs THUMPED, and Hellbilly knew that it wasn't going to be long before the ghouls broke through.

"You got any ammo left?" Death Mask asked, in a tone that was direct, but soft.

"A couple of rounds in my Beretta, that Peacemaker, and my knife" Hellbily replied absently, and another THUMP cracked through the silence of the cellar.

Death Mask looked around and saw the keys that Pete had thrown into the basement. He scooped them up and held them closely to his chest. "Hellbilly! Please tell me there is a way out of this basement. If we can get to that old truck, then we can get the fuck out of here, man."

Bill heard his partner, but Death Mask seemed far away, and his voice was covered in static. Oscar walked over to Hellbilly and looked at him. The boy tilted his gaunt face to the side and studied his protector. A look of sorrow was plastered on his face. "You should kill yourself now, before they come through the door. You can't stop them."

Something inside of Hellbilly's head went fuzzy. He rushed towards the boy, grabbed the child by the shoulders and shook him. "What the fuck are those things, kid? They ate my dad. THEY ATE MY DAD!"

There was a sudden pressure under Hellbilly's armpits, which hurt, he was lifted to his feet and tossed gently away from the boy.

"Relax!" said Death Mask, as he placed himself between the child and his friend. "I'm sure the little man here is just as confused as we are. Who knows what these fuckers have done to him."

"Them?" The boy looked to the top of the stairs just as another loud THUMP erupted. "They don't do anything to me, I belong to the Monster. But, I stay with them, in the darkness. I've seen what they are."

Death Mask wondered what the boy meant about belonging to "the Monster," He took a deep breath and stared at the child. "What do you mean?"

"Those things are dead." Oscar continued, seeming to assume Death Mask was asking about the ghouls. "They don't think, can't talk, they just mumble a little bit. I saw one of them get torn in two once, but it could still move, could still hunt. It still ate like the rest of them later that night."

"Ate?" Hellbilly asked.

The boy stared at the ground. "People. They always eat people. People that nobody misses. Just like me."

Hellbilly shivered, but dropped to a knee and looked Oscar in the eyes. "No, not like you, buddy. You're missed, kid. Your mom, she's been on the news for weeks telling anyone who will listen all about you. About how she's gonna find you and bring you home."

"That's right," said Death Mask, "She's on the news every damn day. The whole country is worried sick about you little man."

"My mom?" Oscar asked in a soft voice. The boy's face changed, his eyes lightened and his lips spread out. Hellbilly placed a hand on Oscar's shoulder. The child looked both concerned and thoughtful. He was a small mouse, with the first embers of hope burning in his chest.

"Me and Death Mask here, we're gonna get you back to your mama. See, we're brothers, sort of." Bill looked up at Caleb and the pair shared a moment. "And for the time being, you can be our little brother, okay? So, I promise you little brother, we're gonna get you back to your family, to the place you belong, back home."

"Home?" Oscar's voice drifted and he looked up at the door just in time to hear another THUMP.

Caleb wanted to ask again about the Monster, but knew that they were running short on time. He had to search the basement for things that could help get them out of this mess; weapons, tools, a forgotten window, anything. Caleb began moving boxes aside and searching. It was only a matter of time before the door at the top of the stairs gave way and the ghouls descended.

There was another THUMP, and it caused Hellbilly to look up and realize that he was kneeling beside his father's workbench. The space was greasy and cluttered with tools and beer cans. Bill was about to look back at Oscar when he noticed a beautifully ornate wood picture frame near him on the bench. Inside the frame was a curly haired little boy, with stained clothing and a devious smile on his face. Hellbilly stood, walked over to the bench, and picked up the frame. It was the same picture that Bill had hanging from the rearview mirror of his truck. He looked from the picture of Emmitt, to the pale boy in the oversized sweater, and back to his son. Tears swelled at the bottom of Hellbilly's eyes and then poured down his cheeks.

"What's the deal with this storm drain?" Death Mask called from the other side of the room.

Hellbilly looked at his partner, who was standing where the floor sloped and pointing at a metal grate at the bottom of the wall that was the size of a microwave. "Used to be a well, but the county-men said there was e-coli in the water. The basement floods, so my dad kept it as a drain. It leads out to the swamp. Kind of gross actually, makes the house stink like shit in the summertime."

As serious as he had ever been in his life, Death Mask looked his partner in the eyes and asked, "If we got this grate out of the way, would there be anything stopping us from reaching the swamp?"

Lightning crashed inside of Hellbilly's brain. There was another grate on the other side of the tunnel, but he knew his father used to take it on and off to clear out leaves and debris. He raced to his partner and started kicking and punching the grate. Death Mask joined in, and with a well-placed kick to the side, dislodged the slated piece of metal from the wall. A few tugs later, and the entire plate was free. The tunnel that appeared was slick with sludge and ripe with the awful stench of fermented decay.

Hellbilly looked at the slender opening and doubted that he could fit though. "You two go first, and if I can, I'll follow you. Otherwise, I'll hold them off."

Another THUMP echoed through the cellar, followed by the crinkling sound of wood breaking. The door was about to give way.

Oscar stared at Hellbilly, a crease appeared on the child's forehead. Hellbilly took the hand of his newly acquired ward and brought the child over to the opening. "You can get out of this thing, kid. You just follow Death Mask here. He'll keep you safe."

Caleb lightly punched the kid on the shoulder and smiled. "I'll go first, okay? I'll make sure it's safe. Then, you follow me, and Hellbilly is gonna be our tail-gunner."

Hellbilly squeezed the boy's shoulder. "We're all gonna be fine, kid. You just keep moving forward and don't look back, no matter what you hear."

The boy smiled awkwardly, but it was there. The gesture made Hellbilly's heart warm. Turning from the child, he said to his partner, "There's another grate on the other side. It might take some elbow grease, but it'll come off."

Death Mask nodded. Then, the small man climbed into the hole and disappeared.

"You're coming right?" asked a tiny voice. Hellbilly looked down at the child. The boy was shivering, and his eyes were desperate and deeply brown.

"Of course," Hellbilly answered, forcing himself to smile.

"Promise?" Oscar asked.

Bill pinched Oscar's chin and said, "Yeah kid. I promise."

The boy nodded. Another THUMP and CRACK rang out, and as Oscar dropped to his knees and followed Death Mask into the hole, a panel flew away from the door and fluttered down the stairs. A legion of rotting arms penetrated the new hole, probing blindly for anything that could be maimed. One of the creatures found the extension cord and ripped it away.

Hellbilly reached down and wrapped his hands around the handle of the Peacemaker. His stomach turned and his testicles retreated. Blood pumped so loudly through his body that it was deafening and it blocked out the mad sound of fingernails scraping against wood as the fiends tore apart the door at the top of the stairs. As soon as Bill had seen the tunnel's entrance, he knew that his road had ended. He couldn't squeeze through the small hole, couldn't drag himself into the darkness and the sludge. He was going to die in his father's basement, a sacrifice to a child who he had only known for a few minutes. One of the ghouls fell through the door. Hellbilly saw its snarling face, its savage teeth, and its heat-seeking eyes.

Then he felt the frame in his other hand. Bill ran his thumb over an ornate rose that had likely been carved by his father and thought about the boy in the picture, and about how he had failed so completely as a father.

William stood behind a thick gray metal door. He waited as the guard entered a smaller room off to the side, confirmed something on a clipboard, and then returned. A moment later, the red light on the ceiling turned green, and the door opened into a larger beige room. Hellbilly was led through the door and seated in one of the stalls. A woman with wavy blonde hair sat on the other side of a plexiglass window. Her arms were crossed in front of her and she tapped her fingers along the inside of her bicep nervously. Hellbilly smiled at his wife, but realized that his son was nowhere to be seen, even though it was visiting day. He picked up the two-way phone attached to the divider, and Gloria did the same.

"Hey babe," Hellbilly said, taking a deep breath, "Been a minute since you came to see me."

Gloria stared at him, her eyebrows furrowed. "Did you know what they were up to?"

"Who?"

"Don't play stupid with me. Did you KNOW what they were going to do?"

Hellbilly had heard rumours about the raid on the Scum Fucks' clubhouse. He wasn't a shot caller by any stretch of the imagination, but he had gained some clout for defending the wife of Paulo Renaud, and was being kept up to date on what was happening outside of Collen's Bay Correctional Facility. He watched Gloria's anticipating eyes and desperately wanted to answer her honestly, but also knew full well that their conversation was being recorded and certainly listened to.

"Gloria, I have no idea what you're talking about. Where's Emmitt?"

Gloria's lips thinned. "Nova Scotia, with my mom. Once I get out there we're going to stay for a little while. Then, I dunno, figure out what to do next."

"Why are you going there, Glory? If you stay in Windsor, I can get the guys to keep an eye on you."

Gloria shifted in her seat uneasily. "I don't need you to have the guys in Windsor look after me, Bill. Emmitt doesn't either."

"This thing with the Scum Fucks isn't over, they might still be looking to hurt us. We know they like going after Old Ladies and families..."

"So what?" Gloria's face was suddenly bright red. "Me and Emmitt are in danger now? What the hell did you get yourself into, Bill?"

Hellbilly felt shame and doubt crunch him into a ball. He looked down at his shackled hands and thought that they looked old and withered, as though they belonged to an elderly man of eighty rather than a young man barely through his mid-twenties.

Gloria took a deep breath and continued. "I need to go home, for a while at least. I need to figure out how to have a peaceful life. I deserve one. Emmitt does too."

"I want that also, Glory."

Gloria shook her head. "No Bill, you don't really want that. You think you want that, but it ain't you."

"Is this about the club? You knew I was involved when we met."

"GOD DAMMIT BILL!" Gloria yelled. The guard by the door glared at her and took a single step forward to show that he wouldn't tolerate that behaviour. Gloria waved him off and shot him a placating look which said she would behave. She dusted herself off and then returned to the conversation with her husband. "This is *not* about the Dead Mariachis. There are plenty of guys in the club who ride around, drink a few beers, but still make it home in time for dinner and don't end up in jail for killing a man."

"It was self-defense," Hellbilly said into his hands.

"I guess that's why you only caught seven years for shooting off that illegal gun you had. Your lawyer told me that the crown wanted to give you life originally, Bill. How would that have played out between you, me, and Emmitt? He'd have had his own family by the time you got out."

"Don't take him, Gloria." Hellbilly looked up with red watery eyes. "Don't take my boy, please. I'm a good father."

"You are a good father Bill, but this is about the choices you make, choices that keep hurting this family."

"Every choice I have made is to protect this family."

"Is that why she was wearing your cut?"

An uneasy silence filled the space between husband and wife. Bill shook his head, and then, playing dumb, asked, "What are you talking about?"

"The night when everything went down, I went to Paulo's house first. I didn't know you were already at the hospital. When I got there, Olivia was standing beside a cop, giving him a statement, and she was wearing your fucking cut, Bill."

"It was cold that night, Gloria. I let her wear it, so she could keep warm. That's all."

"Your cut, Bill? It was cold out, so you let her wear your goddamn cut?"

"She's the president's wife. What was I gonna do?"

"You mean besides telling Paulo you couldn't guard her in the first place? That your wife would be pissed off about you two spending time together? Even if she were cold Bill, you were at HER house, how about you tell her to go inside and get her OWN fucking coat!" Gloria's eyes raged, then suddenly calmed as an ocean of understanding washed over them. "Paulo has no idea about you two, does he?"

"There's nothing for him to know about, Gloria."

"No, how about the fact that you fucked his wife?"

"They weren't married when it happened. Not quite."

"But, we were." Gloria rapped her fingers along her arm again, then looked away. In a distant voice she continued. "I'm taking Emmitt home with me, and when you get out, I don't want you to follow us. Don't come to Nova Scotia, Bill. Go ride Harleys and drink, mess around with your Dead Mariachi friends, and get in shootouts with dudes who like the same shit you do but wear different coloured vests. You'll be happier, we'll be happier."

"I'm his father…"

"Maybe, when he's older, he'll look you up. I won't stand in the way if that happens, but until then, just leave us alone, Bill." Then, swiftly and without looking back, Gloria stood, hung up the phone, and walked away.

Hellbilly watched his wife cross the room and wait for a moment as the outer door opened for her. He followed her through the windows as she raced down the hall, holding her face while her shoulders bounced up and down in sobbing heaves. After she was gone, he sat motionless in his seat, with eyes that stung from the hot sensation of tears.

Finally, the guard gently tugged on his sleeve. "Come on big guy," said the guard. "Hold it together until we get you back to your cell. I'll let you put a sheet up over the bars, and we won't bother you for the rest of the day. I'll even bring your supper to you, if you want it."

Shaking, Hellbilly stood. The guard led him through the first gray door and down the hallway, back towards the general population. As they moved, Hellbilly's body felt distant, like he was nothing more than a walking corpse.

It had been warm on the day the picture was taken. They brought a cake with them to the park and played outside for hours; throwing frisbees, roughhousing, and kicking a soccer ball around. Near the end of the day, while Bill was giving his son a piggy-back ride, he leapt over a puddle and Emmitt threw-up all over his head. Bill wished he'd understood how important that day was while he was having it. He wished he'd soaked up the broad smile of his son and the sound of Gloria's laughter. He thought about the ways his life had turned out, and knew right then that more than anything in the world he wanted to see his son again, and that he was going to keep the promise he had just made to Oscar Delaronde.

Hellbilly smashed the picture against the wall. He ripped the photograph out of the frame, folded it, and stuck it in his back pocket.

He looked at the freak who was through the door and saw the thing pointing at him. Something about the freak's look, the way it smirked and seemed to call its shot like some cocky teenager playing billiards, enraged Hellbilly. He wasn't going to die here. If he had to fracture every rib in his body, Hellbilly was going to squeeze through that tiny hole, open the grate on the other side, and make a break for it. Hellbilly let go of the Peacemaker, grabbed the Beretta, and raised it. Then, he fired the final two 9mm bullets into the freak's grinning face. The creature collapsed in the doorway and a cackle of filthy laughter erupted from the other side. Hellbilly dropped the gun, then threw himself onto his stomach, sucked in his gut, and squeezed into the muck-filled entrance of the tunnel.

CHAPTER 12

The tunnel was pitch black and slick with gristled rot. Hellbilly pulled himself through the catacomb by digging into the walls with his fingernails, wiggling his chest from side to side, and pushing forward with his back feet. As he moved, his face raked through tar-like black grime. Decay and congealed mold entered his nose with every disorganized thrust. When he drew in air, Hellbilly's lungs filled with a sweetly rancid scent that was so terrible it short-circuited his olfactory. His lungs constricted too, and it felt like he brought in less oxygen with every breath he took. He tried to take another deep breath, but the sludge in his nostrils prevented it. Bill pushed his nose into the air while trying to blow out and expel the slime, but his head hit the ceiling and forced his face back into the muck. Cold, greasy, putrid ooze smeared across Hellbilly's face and lodged itself inside his bleeding eye wound. Startled, he pulled himself forward, attempted to flee from the spot where the slime had met his blood, but he miscalculated how high up his mouth was and ended up dragging his teeth though the sludge. The concoction that invaded his mouth tasted salty, coppery, and spoiled, like bad meat covered in pus and maggots. Hellbilly wretched and spilled bile directly in front of himself.

Behind him, the basement had turned into a frenzy of snapping and scratching. The creatures tumbled down the stairs and threw boxes from one side of the room to the other. Hellbilly realized that they were searching, which meant they were perplexed by the disappearance of the bikers and the child. If that was true, then only the cocky looking bastard on the stairs had seen them entering the tunnel. The other beasts had no idea what happened to their prey in the few minutes since they'd seen them enter the basement.

Hellbilly dragged himself through the pungent mire and over the pool of vomit he had made for himself. Oscar slipped, and there was a splat sound as his head touched the grime. Then, without warning, Death Mask screamed, "Ah fuck!" and fell into something liquid. The boy stopped moving and Hellbilly bumped into the child's feet.

With an echoey voice, Death Mask called out, "Hold on kid. Give me a moment," and sloshed through some kind of vile bath. "Okay. Take my hands," he said. Hellbilly felt the boy's feet glide away from him and heard them softly dip into the waters ahead.

"You got any light up there?" Hellbilly asked, as he continued to labor forward.

"My lighter's gone and I have no flashlight or anything," Death Mask replied, sounding as out of breath as Hellbilly felt.

When Bill reached the precipice of the tunnel, the texture of the walls changed from smooth stone to cut out rock. He grabbed onto the lip of the exit with both hands, and pulled himself forward. Hellbilly tried to bring his head upward, but he hit the top of whatever chamber they were in, and the biker was forced back down. The sudden change in weight distribution made Hellbilly shift forward and caused his body to betray him. Bill avalanched into a pool of vile water and became completely submerged.

Warm festering liquid touched every part of Hellbilly and entered his body through his eyes, ears, and open wounds. Hellbilly flailed upwards and his hands ran through a blanket of scum. His feet touched the bottom of the chamber and sank into a floor of sludge. He tried to walk forward, but found no traction. In his panic, Hellbilly gasped for air and a rush of putrid water filled his mouth and lungs. Hellbilly's eye popped open, a reflex to the trauma he was enduring, just in time for him to collide face first with something long and round. He skidded along the floor, hoping to find something to hold on to, and finally found a strong arm. Death Mask lifted Hellbilly to his feet and Bill was able to steady himself finally.

Hellbilly realized that he was waist deep in a cesspool of fermenting water that had been left to rot when the chamber was sealed up. Probably the backflow from the swamp had kept the chamber ripe with bacteria, and could even have brought with it various shit-logs from the wildlife nearby. The rank liquid dripped down Bill's long hair and saturated his clothing.

Bill hacked and ejected septic water from his lungs. He ran his tongue over his teeth, collected the tunnel-muck that had coated them black, and spat it into the cesspool. With his hands shaking from fear, his cheeks glowing red with embarrassment, and his skin tingling with rage, Hellbilly scanned the darkness. Along the wall, where they had entered the chamber, was a pinpoint of light, and behind it were the vague sounds of chaos.

Death Mask squeezed Hellbilly's arm. "You okay brother?"

"Fuck no," Hellbilly answered, still spitting out the muck from his teeth.

"But good enough to help me find that grate?"

Hellbilly nodded, then remembered he was in pure darkness, and answered, "Yeah, man."

Although the three amigos could stand in the chamber, neither adult was able to be upright. Hellbilly crouched, and prodded the wall with his good hand. Finally, he found another short tunnel, this one leading upwards. He reached inside the tunnel and found something that felt like a steering wheel. He tried to turn it, but the plate wouldn't budge. Oscar coughed in the darkness and a terrifying "woot" came from back in the basement. Hellbilly felt around the grate and found a small lock along one side. He pulled out his buck knife and jammed the blade into the keyhole. At first, the cylinder refused to yield, but Hellbilly torqued the thing with as much force as he had left to give, and the lock clicked open just as the blade snapped.

"Let me go up first, I'll look around," Hellbilly offered. Death Mask agreed and then adjusted the boy in his arms. Quickly, Hellbilly reached up, found the edge of the tunnel, and pulled himself out of the sarcophagus. He rolled out of the opening and collapsed on the snow-covered ground. Above him, the night sky was filled with stars and racing dark clouds. Pedals of snow fell softly onto Hellbilly's nose, gracing him with their sweet chill. The liquid that drenched the biker's clothing steamed in the moonlight and drifted away into some unseeable void. For just a moment, Hellbilly thought about staying right where he was until the freezing winds slowly took him away into nothingness, but then he remembered the look in the boy's eyes when he'd promised to follow him into the tunnel. Hellbilly rolled onto his chest and pushed up with both hands. The snow burned his palms and fingertips, and his muscles grinded like a rusty gate as he rose to his feet. His bad elbow sizzled with blue flames, and his forearm screamed.

When he was finally erect, Hellbilly looked around the yard. He had come up no more than twenty feet from the back of the house, and only a leap away from the edge of the swamp. If it was springtime, the marshy waters would have been right up to where they had come out, perhaps they would have even drowned down in the chamber. Bill heard calamity inside the house; glass breaking, drywall being ripped apart, and those things slurping and feasting on his father. His chest tightened and his belly became a deep well of blackness. Because the house blocked them, Hellbilly couldn't see the Scum Fucks, nor the bus, but he knew they were directly in front of where he was. He could see Dom and Cliff though, smoking and leaning against their SUV. Neither of them seemed aware of Hellbilly's presence. Beside the Nomads, was Pete's small garage where he'd kept tools, camping gear, odds and ends, and of course his motorcycle.

Suddenly, two small hands appeared from inside the drainpipe. Hellbilly bent down, grabbed Oscar, and pulled him up and out of the tunnel. The boy hugged Hellbilly as he came out and began shivering as soon as he touched the air. Hellbilly put the boy on the ground and rubbed his shoulders. Then, the biker lifted a finger to his mouth, asking for the boy to remain silent, and pointed towards the Nomads by the SUV. Oscar's face became very serious and he nodded.

Death Mask was already half out of the chamber when Hellbilly reached him. He grabbed the smaller man and hoisted him the rest of the way out. The pair of bikers stumbled backwards, but caught themselves before they fell. They looked at each other and then at the boy. Their clothing was already becoming ridged, and tiny icicles had formed in their noses, but the stench of the tunnel and the old well remained. It was nearly unbearable.

Silently, Hellbilly and Death Mask closed the grate again, sealing the sarcophagus. As they did, Hellbilly thought he heard the sound of the dead emanating from within the bowls of the chamber, and wondered if the creatures had found their way into the tunnel leading to it. With the grate closed, the comrades scanned the property, searching for a way to execute the next phase of their plan.

"I still have the keys to that truck," Death Mask said as he patted his pocket.

"Give 'em here?" asked Hellbilly, his teeth chattering. "They'll probably have the shed key on 'em too."

Death Mask reached into his pocket and threw them at Hellbilly, who caught them in mid-air. Hellbilly looked at the key set which was bound by a metal Las Vegas keychain and his heart sank. Instead of the Ford key he was expecting, there was just a narrow motorcycle key that belonged to a 1980s Harley-Davidson Wide Glide.

"Holy fuck!" Hellbily whispered violently. "These ain't the keys to the truck, man. They're for my dad's chopper."

Death Mask felt his own heart sink. He shook his head in disbelief. "Maybe we can get Dom and Cliff's SUV?"

Hellbilly knew that was unlikely and offered up the only realistic solution he could think of. "At the very least, I'll say this; the old man's bike will run. Might run like shit, but it'll fucking run, you can believe that."

Death Mask scowled. "You wanna take a fucking motorcycle out of here?"

Hellbilly's face went wonky. "Maybe. Might get us the fuck out of here if we have no other choice."

The prospect of riding an aging chopper out of a zombie infested backwoods shack in the dead of winter tickled something just right inside of Death Mask. Despite the cold, despite his fear, despite the pain in his body, Caleb couldn't help but smile. "Alright partner. Let's giddy-the-fuck-up then!"

Hellbilly felt a tingle of excitement. He remembered wheezing down the crumbling limestone quarry road on that skeleton of a sportster which he'd stolen from Pete's shop. He looked down at Oscar, whose eyes glistened with hope and fear and bewilderment, and saw the boy shivering inside of his ice crusted sweater. Hellbilly knew he was going to get the boy out of this horror-show no matter what, but first things first, he needed to get him something warm to wear.

Hellbilly looked at the shed, beamed a wide-open smile, and whispered. "Mother Fuckers Forever Man!"

CHAPTER 13

The distance from the well to the garage was only about sixty feet, but to travel as the crow flies would have been suicide. From where they had come out, Death Mask could see the Nomads, Dom and Cliff, watching the carnage unfold inside of the house. Even though they were covered by the house and not in view, Caleb also knew that the entire Montreal Chapter of the Scum Fucks, and their red-headed leader, were also watching the frenzy.

Hellbilly tapped his partner on the shoulder and then led everyone towards the woods and away from the cabin. The tree line was thick, and it provided immediate cover, but the brush was so dense that it was hard to travel though, and the moonlight became lost in shadow and barely touched the ground. The winter air froze the rank droplets of cesspool water onto all of their skin. It tore at their lungs and chilled their bones making it hard to travel. Still, the trio were able to move through the trees and bramble quietly, rarely stepping on branches nor hardly ever allowing the snow to crunch beneath their feet. Twice, Hellbilly stumbled on the uneven ground, and once the boy fell right to his hands. Each time one of them fell, they simply righted themselves and continued on as if nothing had happened.

Hellbilly stared straight ahead and without focus, as though he'd been hit in the temple and had not yet recovered. Death Mask's cheeks and nose burned because they were so cold, his hands were numb and his feet ached. The boy was the worst off of all three of them though; the child's skin was bluish gray, his hands quaked, and his eyes were distant. A strange chattering sound bounced off the trees, like a cicada emerging in the dead of winter, but Death Mask quickly realized the sound was coming from Oscar's teeth as they clanged together. He pulled the boy close and tried to warm him. Oscar snuggled into Death Mask's arm. Oscar let go of a breath he had been holding in, but no mist came from the boy's mouth because his little body had acclimatized to the cold. As they rounded the side of the cabin, with Oscar still tucked in his arm, Death Mask blew out a white cloud of frozen mist. The plume drifted out of the forest and into the front yard where it caught the porch light.

Dom's face hardened. The Nomad looked towards the woods, and squinted. Death Mask stopped in his tracks and grabbed Hellbilly by the elbow. Bill turned, saw that his partner was staring into the yard, and looked towards the front of his childhood home.

A row of Scum Fucks lined the front yard. They rested casually against their idling bikes, like they had stopped for coffee during a ride, and watched the carnage unfolding inside. The flippantness of the way they stood enraged Death Mask, and caused him to ball his hands into fists and breath heavily. He wondered how much the lackadaisical bikers knew about the freaks in the cabin. Were they pawns finding out for the first time that their club was involved in a truly horrific evil, or were they willing participants in this unholiness? In either case, none of them seemed to be taking the madness as seriously as they should be. Standing in front of the Scum Fucks was their red-headed leader. He bounced on his feet with nervous anticipation, like a boxer waiting for a fight to commence. He seemed fully invested in the frenzy, enthralled by the horrors, and excited by the violence. The porch light waned and then grew, illuminating the Golem's face, and in that shimmer Death Mask saw wild and predatory eyes filled with bloodied yearning and a mouth coloured burgundy from scar tissue.

Dom appeared to complete his scan of the tree line and his attention returned to the house. Cliff and he leaned against the Tahoe, but they did not seem as comfortable with the savagery as the Scum Fucks did. Death Mask felt certain that the Nomads were only now realizing just how diabolical their alliance with the rival club really was.

Death Mask felt a tug on his sleeve and looked down. Oscar had gathered the attention of both Dead Mariachis, and in a serious voice he said, "They can't smell us. They have no idea we are here. We need to keep moving."

The Dead Mariachis looked at one another, affirmed that they each felt safe to continue on, then kept trudging through the woods as silently as possible. A moment later, the group rounded the garage and the structure slid in between them and the rival bikers, concealing their escape from the eyes of their pursuers. The garage was an unpainted pine box with patchwork shingles on the roof and chipped white paint on the window frames. Between where the three amigos stood in the forest and the garage, was a minefield of scattered vehicle parts, hubcaps, and sterling wheels mostly. The group had to tiptoe through them carefully. When they arrived at the back wall of the garage, Hellbilly pointed up at the window. "Unless he's changed in his golden years, the old man never locks that window," Hellbilly said, as he simultaneously scanned the yard for cannibals.

Death Mask reached up and ran his hand along the bottom of the frame. White flakes fell onto his nose and he blew them away. Finally, he found a gap big enough to slip his fingers into. He lifted the window till it was all the way open, grabbed onto the inside of the frame, and hoisted himself into the garage. Caleb fell hard, but made little sound as he did. He rolled on the freezing concrete floor and felt a new aching in his shoulder. As he stood, the air inside the garage warmed and provided him with the wonderfully sweet smell of engine grease and metal. The place was dark, with just enough glow to allow Death Mask to see around. There was a workbench along one wall, covered in tools, rags, bolts, and small parts, and at the end of the bench was a set of shelves. On the bottom shelf were two large red jerry-cans of gasoline. On the next bench, there were boxes filled with camping gear – including a small stove and tent. The door on the far wall had slim windows along the top, but Death Mask was too short to see out of them. Beside the door was a rack of coats, snow pants, and some old boots. Finally, sitting directly in the middle of the garage, lit up in the moonlight like a statue in a museum, was the Wide Glide. Its gas tank was painted midnight blue, and it had blood-orange flames. The bike had a king and queen seat, saddlebags, and a classically thin front tire attached to forks that were extended ever so slightly, giving the bike an extension that made it look gothic. Though obviously well ridden, the shovelhead appeared to be in fantastic condition. On a balmy summer evening, Death Mask had no doubt that the bike would fire up immediately, but 1980s Harley's were notoriously faulty, and he had his reservation that the Wide Glide would start in the dead of winter.

"He comes out here every day and fires her up," said a raspy voice by the window. The shock of hearing someone speak sent a current of fear up Caleb's spine, and caused him to clutch his chest and whirl around. His hand was already on his knife before he realized that the voice belonged to his partner. Bill had Oscar by the armpits and was shoving the child through the window. "He likes to hear her purr, though I don't think he's ridden her much since mama died."

Death Mask reached up and took the child in his arms. He lowered the boy to the floor, and started rubbing his shoulders. Oscar looked pale and cold. Caleb couldn't help but feel pity at the sight of the boy.

"There oughta be some sleeping bags on that shelf over there, and some clothes by the door," Hellbilly said, as he doubled over and fell through the window.

The shelf with the camping gear had two sleeping bags on it, both of which were surprisingly high quality and thick. Death Mask retrieved the bags and brought them back to where Oscar stood. "Take your clothes off, they're soaked and freezing, and won't do you any good anyhow. Wrap yourself in this. They'll keep you warm," he ordered the boy.

Oscar stripped himself of his oversized shirt and tiny pants, he even kicked off the ridiculous white shoes he'd been wearing, and then shoved his bare self into one of the sleeping bags.

"Get the other one," Hellbilly said, and Death Mask did. With a great bear hug, Hellbilly lifted the boy and shoved him into the second sleeping bag. The bags were meant for a grown man, and the boy sank into them until only the top of his head was visible. Death Mask looked at the child, hidden within the great blankets and smiled. Oscar looked up at the biker and attempted to return the grin, but the gesture came out as more of a grimace than anything.

Hellbilly walked over to the workbench and found a brown leather bag, similar to something a bowling ball would be carried in. He unzipped the bag, reached in, and pulled out a shimmering skullcap helmet in the same midnight blue as the Wide Glide, with the word "Leadbellys" running along the centre in sparkling silver paint. Then, Bill walked over to Oscar and placed the helmet on the boy's head.

"That's better than nothing! And if we take a tumble, you're about the only one of us who deserves to have their noggin stay in one piece," Hellbilly exclaimed, as he lifted the sleeping bags, with the boy tucked gently inside, and placed the heap onto the front seat of the Wide Glide.

Death Mask gathered the coats, pants, and overalls from the rack beside the door, and tossed some over to his partner. He also found a brown toque, a red and black checkered trapper hat, and a single pair of mittens. The bikers turned away from each other and dressed themselves in the grease-stained garments. Hellbilly looked just fine in his father's wool lined denim coat, chainsaw pants and work boots, but Death Mask looked comical. He wore coveralls that came down past his feet, snow pants that shielded his entire chest, and a blue and black flannel coat that made him look a hundred pounds heavier than he was. He didn't bother to change his shoes for the rubber boots available. Death Mask wore a size eight, and the boots were size thirteen at least, but he removed his socks and stuffed his boots with old greasy rags from the workbench.

"You look like a tiny Michelin man in that get-up," Hellbilly smirked. He tossed the trapper hat on top of his head and threw the mittens to Death Mask.

Caleb gestured the mittens back towards Hellbilly, but he waved them off and pulled out a pair of snow-mobile gloves from underneath the workbench. "So, your plan is for all three of us to ride that chopper out of here?" Death Mask asked as he placed the mittens on his hands.

Hellbilly shrugged and threw a leg over the bike. He pulled himself into the riding position, and placed Oscar on his lap. "Unless you got a better plan?"

Death Mask placed both hands on his hips. He studied the rickety old bike and shook his head. "You know, you're only gonna have one chance to start that thing, right? Maybe two, but that'll be it. Those creatures are gonna hear us as soon as we open the door, and they'll come running."

Hellbily caressed the choke on the side of the engine, pulled it out, and thumbed the start button. "She'll start. She always starts."

Death Mask watched his partner as he succumbed to some childhood fantasy about the motorcycle he was sitting on, but his attention drifted to the gas cans on the shelf. He looked at a pile of rags on the workbench, and then at a camping stove sitting beside a tent. With a smirk, he asked Hellbily if he'd ever made a Molotov cocktail. With vigor, Hellbily replied, "Why yes, yes I have…"

C H A P T E R   1 4

———————|———————

Winston licked the tattered remains of his lips, and stared pensively at the fray inside the cabin, which appeared to be winding down. The attention of the freaks, once scattered and unfocused, was now concentrated on eating scraps of flesh they had acquired during the dismemberment of Pete McConnell, or on other hedonistic delights. An adolescent male crouched on top of the breakfast table and slurped blood from a clump of scalped silver hair. Beside the chesterfield, two thin females took turns biting a mound of stomach fat and giggling as the gristle dripped down their cheeks. One of the bigger males was feasting on the old man's left arm, and used it periodically to bat away the smaller ghouls who were trying to take it from him. A deer's head had been pulled down by a fat man in a business suit who was missing half his face. The businessman gnawed on the deer's taxidermied cheek while five of the creatures humped each other on the kitchen counter beside him.

As far as Winston could tell, there was no sign of the black-balled Dead Mariachis, nor of the boy they were protecting. A sinking feeling grew in the Scum Fucks' stomach when suddenly a female with matted blonde hair strolled into the kitchen. Winston had seen the messy-looking ghoul enter the basement earlier, just after the bikers and the boy had. As the disheveled thing crossed into the living room, with a lazy sort of stroll, Winston studied her face and saw no signs of blood or flesh. His stomach liquified as he realized that something was wrong.

"FUCK!" Winston shouted in a way that seemed to be more of an exhale than a vocalization. He turned to the man on his left, who had a green mohawk on top of his helmet. The leader of the Scum Fucks motioned for the man to come closer, and when he was within ear shot, Winston grabbed him by the back of the neck and squeezed tightly. "The freaks fucked up! Get inside that shack, and start searching the woods. If those fools are missing again, I am gonna shit an absolute brick!"

With a toss, Winston released the mohawked Scum Fuck, who sprawled out momentarily, but caught his footing enough to stay upright. The mohawked biker motioned for his men to follow him towards the cabin and, begrudgingly, the other Scum Fucks pushed themselves away from their rides and shambled towards the house. As they approached the front door, half of the group, including the mohawked lieutenant, veered off to search the woods.

With his subordinates gone, Winston turned his attention to Dom and Cliff. The Dead Mariachis rested against their black SUV with their arms crossed in front of them. They looked anxious and nonplussed by the happenings. Winston's chest tightened at the sight of the men sitting so casually against their vehicle, and he stormed towards them with his fists clenched. When he was only a few inches from Dom, Winston stopped, looked the gorilla-sized man in the eyes, and through gritted teeth shouted; "Either of you feel like joining in on the search? At this point I'd say that you, and that lazy prick Paulo, will be about as fucked as I am if those idiots get away!"

Although heavyset and slow moving, Dominic Di Forno was a man who had proved himself as an outlaw dozens of times over, and he didn't take kindly to someone from a rival club addressing him in such an aggressive tone. The Nomad Sergeant-at-Arms pushed himself off the SUV and squared up with the small ginger man from the rival club. Now, eye to eye with Winston, and barrel chested, Dominic's face took on a murderous facade. "Ain't nobody as fucked as you are, you shredded-cheese-faced bastard. Now take a step back from me, and remember whose bottom rocker has the name of this territory on it."

Winston smoldered. He was about to lose his mind and do something brash and stupid when the doors to the pine-box garage flew open. Through the dim evening light, Winston saw a tiny-little man in a puffy blue coat waltz out of the building. The man's face was lit up by the marigold flames that danced on the spouts of the two red jerry-cans he held. Winston realized right away that he was looking at Death Mask, who had somehow made his way into the garage, changed clothing, and acquired a pair of make-shift bombs. He watched the Dead Mariachi take two steps forward, and in one fluid motion draw back his right arm and fling one of the jerry-cans towards the SUV, while screaming "Fuck you, you GOD DAMN BASTARDS!" The can flew low and snagged on the side of the SUV's hood. It erupted into a flaming ball which doused Dom and Cliff in liquid fire, and carried on until it collided with the row of Scum Fuck bikes, setting all but Winston's ablaze.

Just before the jerry-can collided with the SUV, Winston had the wherewithal to propel himself backwards. He landed on his ass and immediately rolled away from the fire. As the Scum Fucks' bikes were igniting, Winston reached into his coat and tried to draw his gun, but was interrupted when the second jerry-can was let loose. The red container arched high over Winston's head, and cartwheeled into the front door of the cabin where it spread out like a spiderweb of flames across the front of the house. A terrible chorus of screams echoed from within. One of the Scum Fucks tried to open the door, but the backdraft fueled the blaze. Flames reached into the cabin tickling the curtains and carpet, and finding many other wanting things inside. Within moments the entire home was on fire.

Back at the SUV, Dom and Cliff rolled on the ground and tried in vain to put out the fires on their bodies. It was too late though; the gasoline had drenched them and every time they extinguished one fire a new flame ignited somewhere else. The sky split in two with the cries of their anguish.

Winston fumbled for his weapon, but couldn't get his fingers to work properly. Finally, he curled his hand around the grip of his pistol, but before he could draw, a blinding whiteness exploded in his eyes. The light was coming from a single source inside the garage. It was not fire, but it was fire-bright; as though the sun had come to earth and was hiding inside the small pine structure this entire time. Winston raised his weapon and aimed it as best he could towards the source of his pain. He fired twice, but hit nothing. A volley of bullets returned his gunfire and sounded like they belonged to an archaic weapon from some old western movie. One of the bullets grazed Winston's hand and another tore off a streak from his scalp. He dropped his gun, and instinctively grabbed at the spot on his face that suddenly burned with pain.

From the belly of the pine box garage came a scraping and sputtering sound that was immediately followed by a growling "tum-tum-tum." Winston stood, but nearly toppled over as he did, and watched the light begin to creep forward. In his peripherals, Winston saw a blue streak cross the front yard, and realized that Death Mask was making a break for his Ultra-Limited. The ginger Scum Fuck stumble-ran towards his bike, but there was a ringing in his right ear that pulled him to the side and downward.

Winston heard the "tum-tum-tum" sound approaching. He tried to search for the light, but his vision was unfocused, and he only saw a great expanse of white off to his side. What he could see, if only in a fuzz, was Death Mask sitting on top of *his* Harley-Davidson. The Dead Mariachi's hand moved up and down, and a low muttering roar joined the "tum-tum-tum" sound. Both bikes were alive and running.

Affronted that someone else was on his bike, and revving it, Winston raised his gun and aimed it directly at Death Mask. The barrel drifted from Death Mask's right shoulder over to his left. Winston fired, and again hit nothing. He tried to center the barrel, but just as the iron sights lined up with Death Mask's head, something crashed into the Scum Fuck's side. Winston flew across the yard, towards the fiery cabin, and collided with the frosty ground. He rolled over and over until he finally came to a stop by the porch. Dull throbbing pain invaded the right side of his chest, radiating from underneath his floating ribs and up through his spine and shoulders. He struggled to take a breath and couldn't draw in any air on his first attempt.

As he lay on the ground, Winston looked up and saw that the white lights of the motorcycles had turned red and were quickly getting smaller. The bikes turned around the bend in the laneway, passed the bus, and disappeared. Only the muttering roar of Winston's Ultra-Limited and the "tum-tum-tum" of the other motorcycle remained, and those sounds quickly dimmed as though someone was turning down the volume on a radio.

Dominic Di Forno and Clifford Tibbs eventually fell silent as well. The smell of cooked skin drifted through the air, and the enticing scent eased the pain Winston had felt since the chopper collided with him. The Scum Fuck rose to his feet and stumbled towards the SUV. When he reached the vehicle, he saw the pile of what was left of the Dead Mariachis. Steam rose from Clifford's body and the gentle pops and sizzles of his charring flesh drifted into the air. Clifford "Tank" Tibbs had no life left inside of him, he lay on the frozen ground as a burnt heap. Dominic, on the other hand, squirmed and writhed, and whimpered softly. His face was darkened and crinkled, and looked like a sheet of brittle nori paper. His once blue eyes were bubbling and creamy white, as though they were made of spoiled milk.

Winston fell to his knees and stroked what was left of the Dead Mariachi's hair. He looked into Dom's dying eyes and smiled.

"Winston…" Dom muttered, "Is that you man?"

"Shhh..." Winston offered softly.

"Winston…you gotta help me."

A legion of flaming ghouls escaped the cabin. They poured out of the front door and through the windows and then raced towards the marsh beside the house. The pack hooted and whooped with pain, then crashed through the trees and brush until they finally found the wetlands. Winston heard a loud "CRACK" as the ice on the swamp broke, followed by a deep gulping splash as the ghouls sank into the waters.

With the back of his hand, the Scum Fuck continued to stroke Dom's forehead. A clump of burned flesh stuck to his knuckles and tore away. The blood-murky eggshell bone underneath met the cold air and turned to pink jelly. "Oh, my dear. I'm afraid it is far too late for that." said Winston, as his lips parted, revealing two beautifully elongated canine teeth. Then, with predatory quickness, Winston slammed his mouth into Dom's throat. As his lips made contact with the Mariachi's neck, Winston bit down. His sharp teeth snagged onto a gummy feeling tube, then pierced the cylinder and tore it wide open. Blood rushed into Winston's mouth. He drank deeply, with heavy and satisfying gulps. The taste of salted copper ignited his body in an orgasmic euphoria, blinding Winston to the fists and scratches that

Dominic used against him. It was too late for any fight to be successful though, the vampire had attached himself to his prey and was feasting. A moment later the struggle ended and Dom's flesh became cold.

The pain in Winston's side dimmed to a dull ache and the fragrances of the night became robust and decadent. Even the swamp had a beautifully earthy scent that reminded Winston of freshly cut summer hay. The biker sat back on his knees, looked up at the night sky, and for a moment allowed himself to be lost in an ocean of purple and blue tones with dazzling white stars. Since his transformation, Winston felt the life and energy of the night in a way that he simply had not before. There was an unboundness that existed in the dark, that called to a deep part of his soul and forced him to be naked before the world. The cold air rippled over his skin and chilled the warm blood that dripped from his mouth and pooled on his cut. He relished the sensation as deeply as if he were holding a beautiful woman after a long night of lovemaking.

Lost in his moment of catharsis, Winston barely noticed that he was no longer alone. The three remaining Scum Fucks stood beside him. While still looking up at the splendor of the sky, Winston asked, "Where are the others?"

The mohawked Scum Fuck said nothing, nor did the other two Scum Fucks beside him. That was enough of an answer for Winston. The scar-faced biker scanned the front yard. He saw the mound of twisted motorcycles that had once belonged to his men and knew they would never run again. He listened to the shallow splashes and hoots from the swamp, and realized that it would take an hour, at least, to round up the ghouls. Without saying a word, Winston stood, walked over to the bus, climbed on board, and plopped himself into the driver's seat. The other Scum Fucks followed closely behind their leader and entered the bus in an orderly and single file fashion. Winston leaned against the dashboard and exhaled. His lungs burned and he was wheezing, but his body teemed with fresh blood and was already better now than he had been moments earlier. With a shaking hand, Winston reached over, grabbed a black handle, and closed the front door of the bus. Then, he pressed the start button, put the dilapidated vehicle in reverse, and backed out of the driveway, leaving the dead alone in the cold marshlands of the McConnell estate.

CHAPTER 15

———————

Colleen Driscoll's door was already unlocked when Eddy arrived. He rapped lightly on the entrance to her apartment but received no reply. The uneasy feeling in his stomach, which had been there since he spoke with Caleb, gathered like an approaching storm. For the last two hours, Eddy had been busy packing food and clothing into a dilapidated Dodge Caravan that had been abandoned at his shop, and driving his wife to North York so she could stay the night at her sister's house. After dropping Judy off, Eddy turned his phone back on, just to see what he was missing, and saw that he had two calls from his chapter president and one from Paulo Renaud himself. He hoped the officers were calling just to let him know that Death Mask and Hellbilly had been given a green-light, meaning anyone could kill them without repercussions and that all 4-13 were duty bound to report their whereabouts, but Eddy's friendship with both men was well known and he feared that his absence was already being seen as suspicious. As he turned the door handle, Eddy realized that he was never going to be able to justify his disappearance to the other Dead Mariachis, and as he stepped into Colleen's darkened apartment, he knew that he was a part of whatever was happening with Caleb and Bill, and that he was in it for the long haul.

Only a thin blade of burgundy-blue light illuminated the space. It cut through an opening in the curtain and showed the side of a plant and the corner of a leather barcalounger. Reflexively, Eddy reached into the candy dish beside the entrance, took out a single gumdrop, and popped it in his mouth. It was lime.

"Ms. D! It's Eddy. Caleb asked me to pick up a magazine for him from his room." There was no reply, and the air inside the apartment felt oppressively still. "Ms. D, you here?"

Suddenly, the door slammed shut and Eddy felt a presence behind him, like someone had materialized out of nothing. Two arms ensnared the Dead Mariachi from behind and squeezed. Air was forced out of Eddy's lungs, and when he tried to breathe, he found that he had no room left for fresh oxygen. Eddy kicked off the wall, but the man holding him was immovable, and his arms only squeezed tighter. A splash of white light erupted in Eddy's head, and then dissipated like a receding fog. When the mist was finally gone, Eddy realized that he had been thrown down onto the ground, hard. His attacker grabbed one of Eddy's hands and lifted it into the air while twisting it backwards. At the same time as his arm was being assaulted, a foot pressed down on Eddy's neck, shoving him into the unyielding parkay floor.

Eddy looked up. Standing above him was a strange looking man, who was mostly shielded from sight by the opaqueness of the room. The man was tall and broad in the shoulder, with ornate tattoos running along his arms. And, by god, was he strong. The feature that stuck out most to Eddy though, was the shape of the man's face; he looked like a jigsaw puzzle that someone had decided to ball up and tape back together rather than solve. In all of his life, Eddy had never seen a person whose very existence blasphemed against nature so boldly.

The barcalounger squeaked as someone moved forward and disturbed the leather. Eddy looked towards the blade of light by the window and saw two delicate feet appear. They were small and porcelain white, with neatly groomed French-tip nails.

"I was so excited when I smelled you coming down the hall," said a flowery and feminine voice. "I admit, I was hoping for the little man, but you're sort of a bonus, aren't you? The one that got away."

The foot on Eddy's throat pressed harder, shoving him further into the hardwood. The Mariachi tried to claw at the back of his attacker's calf, but it did nothing to stop the press.

The woman stood and a curtain of white silk fell, covering her ankles and dancing along the tops of her feet. She walked towards

Eddy, and when she was close, the streetlight cut through her robe, revealing every curve and valley on her body. She reached Eddy and lowered herself by going up on the balls of her feet like a wolf, and spreading her legs wide open. Eddy saw a luxurious garden of black hair and the valley that split it in two, and despite his terrible predicament, felt a rush of blood go into his loins. A cascade of black curls dropped into sight, and then the grinning face of the woman appeared. She looked the Dead Mariachi directly in the eyes, and although it had been ten years since their last meeting, Eddy recognized her immediately.

Morrigan Church leaned forward and stoked the side of Eddy's face. He struggled to catch his breath, and in doing so took in the scent of sweet hibiscus and rose, and something putrid underneath them. The scent made him feel dizzy but also calm.

"Where is Caleb Driscoll?"

"I have no idea," said Eddy, through the choking that was being inflicted upon him.

Viciously, Morrigan grabbed Eddy by the cheeks with one hand. She leaned in close until their faces were almost touching. "You listen to me, blonde-boy, and you listen good. Caleb Driscoll is no longer where he is supposed to be, and I want to know where he's going. So, you are gonna tell me darling, or I am going to make a suit out of your lovely skin."

The man standing over Eddy emitted a low and broken chuckle, and when the Dead Mariachi looked up, he saw raging dark eyes, a jagged mouth filled with broken teeth, and a face that looked like a shattered mirror. Despite the living Halloween mask before him, Fast-Eddy knew he was looking at Daniel Church.

What happened next, Eddy could never rightly say. A cloud of pleasure fogged his brain, and he heard himself speaking, but knew that he wasn't saying anything. He heard Daniel chuckling once again and then, suddenly, there was only darkness and pain.

PART 3: MY MASK IS A DEATH MASK

CHAPTER 16

———·———

Renee stared at the large blue and white tiles at her feet, took a deep breath and raised her head. The faces she saw alternated between sympathy and pity, and the sight of them all made her heart stagger. Her cousin, the chief of police, was there, as was her uncle the councilor. Everyone in the room was familiar, they were her friends, her family, and her community. They had stood beside her ever since Oscar went missing, comforted her when the darkest clouds of her life gathered, but it was still hard for her to speak the words that she had come to say. Renee worried that all of the good people in the meeting hall would think she had gone crazy, that after she said her piece, they would turn to each other and whisper with sneers on their lips. She almost returned her gaze to the floor, but before she could, her eyes met the gaze of an elderly woman sitting across from her. Jean looked at Renee with intense eyes that were filled with love and empathy and a desire to understand. The sight of the woman caused Renee to tremble, not from fear, but from the beautiful hope that comes from knowing you are valued.

Shaking, Renee began.

"I know how strange this is going to sound, but I am absolutely sure that Oscar is still alive, and I think he is trying to come home."

The room was silent. Renee fidgeted with the sleeve of her hoodie and stared at the Mohawk Warrior Society flag secured to the wall in front of her. Finally, Jean the Elder smiled and said, "Please Renee, continue."

"I had a dream. It was unlike any dream I have ever had before. Usually, when I dream, it's like I am watching a movie, but this felt real, like I was actually in the place I was seeing. There was snow around me and I could feel the frost. I could hear the winds and I could smell the air. I was beneath a white pine tree and I held two pieces of firewood that were meant to be together."

"The white pine of the Haudenosaunee, the Tree of Peace. And Thayendanegea, the man whose name we honour here, means two pieces of wood bound together for strength," said the Elder.

"Yes," Renee nodded. "I heard a voice tell me to light the wood on fire, but Oscar is my flame and so I had nothing to light them with. Then I saw him, coming over the horizon, standing on a black ship that was being carried by a strange looking thunderbird. He was trying to come home, but he was being chased by goblins and dogs, and a rotting crow. Before he could reach me, the devils made him turn away, and he headed west from where they were. But, ever since I woke up, it's like I can feel him. Like he's a warm beacon cutting through the cold."

"Where is he now?" asked the Elder.

"Moving..." Renee answered.

C H A P T E R   1 7

The bikers took turns ferrying Oscar through an obsidian field of white streaks, but the real cold had come in and the air now bit at everything it touched. Caleb's jacket was littered with patches of frozen grease that were plied against his skin like a sweater of popsicles. Hellbilly's beard and eyebrows were blanketed in ice and his skin was speckled with the white dots of early frostbite. When Death Mask saw his comrade's face, he worried that if those dots got any colder they would blacken into dead flesh. Greased by a day of snow, salt-melt from the plows, and snow again, the roads had become slick and treacherous. The bikes wobbled and skidded everywhere, and traveling in a straight line was impossible. To move forward, the bikers pulled back on their throttles gently and then followed whatever path through the snow they were given. The brakes were useless, every time Caleb tried them, the back tire of his Harley threatened to pull away from him. Hellbilly tumbled a few times, and Death Mask did once as well. Thankfully, they were never going fast enough for the crashes to cause damage, but the falls were always jarring.

Whenever they could, they checked on Oscar, and for the most part, the boy was doing better than either of the Dead Mariachis were. His cocoon of sleeping bags was warm enough that puffs of steam escaped whenever they opened the top, and his helmet seemed to cushion him from harm. Oscar had taken to giving them a thumbs up whenever he was asked about how he was doing, but he never smiled, and hadn't said anything since they'd taken to the road. Still, he seemed as content as he possibly could be given the circumstances.

Outside the small town of Westport, Hellbilly caught the thin front wheel of the Wide Glide inside a schism of ice and the bike thumped down hard into a snowbank. Luckily, Oscar was curled up behind Death Mask in the well-padded passenger seat of the Ultra-Limited, so it was only Hellbilly who endured the tumble. As the bikers pulled the chopper out of the snowbank, a rumbling sound, like a beat-up school bus racing down a barren road, drifted through the air. Both outlaws stopped what they were doing, and Hellbilly's hand neared the Peacemaker in his jacket. They searched the horizon, but the snow and darkness were thick enough that all they could see was a void. After a moment, the sound faded, leaving the men to finish their chore in the cold peace of the night. They said nothing of the sound to one another, but the incident marred the rest of their time, instilling a feeling of dread and stoking the need for them to continue on.

Bill took his turn with Oscar after the Westport crash. He said he concentrated better with the kid on his bike, and that did appear to be true, for it was the last time Bill fell. The outlaws continued on at a modest pace, despite their desperation to reach the cottage, and in the meandering quiet, Caleb's mind wandered. The sound of Pete McConnell being devoured reverberated in his ears, and the sight of Oscar curled up in their trunk was tattooed in the corner of his eyes. Worst of all, though, was the image of the grotesque rotting things that terrorized them in the cabin. Caleb had seen death before, many times, and the moments of carnage which paralyzed other men rarely bothered him these days. He was meant for the fray. But there was something different about the people who attacked them. There was a wickedly unnatural quality to the fiends that made Caleb doubt he was seeing true.

After his time in Afghanistan, Caleb had visions – flashbacks really, of the horrors he had witnessed as a young man. Sometimes it would be a sound that would set him off, like a jackhammer at a construction site or a couple of kids playing with firecrackers. One time, when he was at a carnival, he caught the whiff of burnt pork and it caused him to empty the contents of his stomach in the middle of the midway and shake violently. In those moments Caleb was taken into another reality, a false one, where the eyes of a burned husband and wife stared at him accusingly, and he felt like his mind was about to shatter. Thinking about the dead people who attacked Pete's house brought Caleb to the front step of that alternate reality, and it made him doubt that he was right with the world around him. Yet, Bill had seen those same things, and the boy had too, which meant that the snarling beasts were real. As horrific as it was, knowing that he was not alone in this nightmare grounded Caleb.

Everything that had happened so far that day revolved around Oscar, the Scum Fucks, and the Dead Mariachis. The three things were intertwined in some kind of macabre web, which Caleb tried to untangle but couldn't. At some point, his muscles took over and Death Mask stopped thinking about the road. His mind slipped into a meditative state and he was pulled back to the night when the Dead Mariachis launched their final offensive against their rivals and conducted a massacre at the Toronto clubhouse of the Scum Fucks Motorcycle Club.

———————

"That's him I guess," said Fast-Eddy from his perch on top of a milk crate. "He doesn't look so tough. Unimpressive really."

Bruno the Rose walked over to the same basement window Eddy was looking through and peeked out. "That's Daniel Church alright. Don't get cocky though kid, that son-of-a-bitch has killed more Dead Mariachis than Highway 401."

Eddy dropped his eyes to the floor. "No doubt. Didn't mean nothin' by it, Rosey."

"All good," Bruno whispered as he hopped down from the milk crate.

There were seven members in the Dead Mariachi raiding party, which occupied a small storage room inside the basement of the Scum Fucks' clubhouse. Caleb was the only Prospect. Bruno had been asked by Paulo to lead the forward offensive, and since his apprentice's "college years" were spent fighting through the opium fields of Afghanistan, Bruno had elected to bring Caleb along with him. The raiding party had penetrated the compound by way of a service tunnel, which Paulo found in the original 1940s schematics of the building, from back when it began its life as a warehouse. The tunnel started at a drain water grate on the south end of Toronto's Port Lands and slinked its way under various factories and shipyards until it reached the clubhouse. The squad spent the entire afternoon wading through suspicious waters and dodging questionable looking drips until finally they came to a boarded-up door. Carefully, they removed the rotting pieces of lumber, and to their jubilation found only drywall separating them from the storage room on the other side.

"Okay," said the Rose. "Danny-Boy is here, that means we got about fifteen minutes before they drive a dump truck into the front of this building and start dog-piling these cunts. We're gonna head out into the basement now and stage ourselves at the bottom of the stairs. When all hell breaks loose, I'm gonna count to thirty, just long enough for people to regain their senses and start panicking. Then we're gonna head up them steps and fuck up everyone's day from the inside. Any questions?" Everyone shook their heads or said nothing at all. "Good. Balaclavas down boys. Balaclavas down."

Bruno reached up and pulled down his black ski-mask. Everyone else in the room, including Caleb, did the same. They had been told not to wear anything that could link them to the club, and everyone ended up looking like a uniformed hit squad from a bad comic book movie; in dark hoodies, dark pants, black work boots, and black gloves. They wore no jewelry and their tattoos were hidden. Each man had been issued a "cleaned" gun that would be hard to trace and given a bottle of bleach to be used in the event that their own blood exited their body, in hopes that it would kill their DNA.

The storage room door creaked open and the band of soldiers crept into the basement. Against the wall by the stairs were stacks of beer kegs, old motorcycle parts littered a series of shelves, and a small home gym occupied one corner. Above them, the floor creaked and bopped, and the sound of white-power punk rock drifted down the staircase. Caleb saw Bruno's dark eyes scrunch with anger when he heard the hate-music coming from upstairs. The troop gathered around the bottom of the staircase and Caleb placed himself at the back of the pack, near the beer kegs. Standing in front of him was a grunt from Thunder Bay who swayed back and forth in a jittery and anxious manner. The clumsy man rocked backwards too far, forcing Caleb to shift over, and the Prospect collided with one of the stacks of kegs.

The pile crashed to the floor with a symphony of hollow bangs. Caleb caught one keg on its second bounce, so did Eddy, but the third keg rolled away with a clamor.

Everyone in the raiding party drew their guns, pointed them towards the top of the stairs, and held. For what seemed like an eternity, everyone was silent. Sweat dripped down Caleb's nose, collecting inside the acrylic fibers of his face-covering. His chest tightened and his knees felt gummy, yet as Caleb stared down the barrel of his .45 he saw that the iron sights of his gun stayed in place. His hands were steady.

The music upstairs continued and eventually the Dead Mariachis realized that no one was coming to investigate the noise they had made. Bruno turned to Caleb and gave him a friendly but firm backhand to the shoulder. "You're dumb ass is gonna get us all killed. You wanna live long enough to get your patch? Be fucking *silent* from here on in."

Caleb nodded and turned his head away in disgrace. That's when he noticed what the kegs had been hiding, a door. It was thin and rough, obviously homemade, and instead of a doorknob it had a little rope which released a latch on the other side. Just above the rope was an expensive looking combination padlock, the kind they put on shipping containers.

"I don't remember seeing that door in the blue prints, do you?" Caleb said to Bruno.

The senior Dead Mariachi shook his head. "God damnit! And it's locked, too."

"I can get it open," said Eddy. He rushed over to the door, produced a lock-picking set from his back pocket, and started working on the padlock. After only a few moments, the blonde headed Mariachi had the padlock released. A musty stink yawned as the door opened, and a cold draft filled the basement. On the other side of the door was a narrow passageway, which seemed darker than it ought to be.

"We've gotta check that out," said the Rose. "Who knows what the fuck is in there. Could be a getaway tunnel or a goddamn armory."

"I'll go," Caleb offered. "I was recon for the Army."

"Take Eddy, too." Bruno commanded. "When you two hear shit popping off, get your asses back here though."

The pair of young Mariachis nodded and then ventured into the abyss with Caleb leading the way.

The hallway was poorly constructed. The path regularly shifted from being claustrophobically too thin to uncomfortably wide, it turned more often than it should have, and the angles where the walls met were never at ninety degrees. Caleb felt like they were always climbing, even after they had risen past what should have been the height of the basement, and the trail simply did not follow the floor plan as the Prospect understood it from the blueprints he had seen during their briefing. When they came to a stretch covered by peeling wallpaper, Caleb noticed holes in the wall which created dust-ridden light trails through the hallway. Both men found a crack in the wall and looked out.

The room they saw was big. It had slime-green walls with dark brown trim all around, and on the far side was a mural of the Scum Fucks' dog-shitting rocker. The short muzzled black dog in the painting was more lifelike than on the club's embroidered patches. The beast had dozens of flies buzzing around the maggot infested shit-log that oozed out of its stretched rectum, and the canine's facial expression was one of gleeful agony, as if it shamefully enjoyed defecating in front of a crowd of onlookers. In front of the mural, a Scum Fuck kneeled as if giving a prayer. The member concluded his sacrament by screaming "FUCK YOU DOG," flipping off the wall, and then kissing the shitting anus of the airbrushed canine.

"Savages," Caleb whispered to himself.

The crowd was lousy with spiky dyed hair, facial piercings, home-made tattoos, and vests of both brown leather and acid-wash denim. The bottom rockers of the Scum Fucks' cuts only displayed three territories: Quebec, New Brunswick, and Ontario. The sight of the Ontario rockers made Caleb's cheeks go flush with anger. In the corner of the room, on a stage propped up by bales of hay, a stripper with a c-section scar rubbed ice on her nipples, then tossed the cubes into a nearby beer stein belonging to an older-looking member. Along the wall beside the bar, in a shadowy area with the words "CUMDUMP CORNER" spray painted overtop, two skeleton-thin women in hooker boots gave blowjobs to a pair of extremely drunk Scum Fucks with matching skinned heads.

The music shifted from white power punk rock to dirt-bag country, and a beer bottle flew across the room. It came crashing down in the face of a heavy-set woman sitting near the bar. She collapsed in her seat, but was immediately picked up by a few of the nearby old-ladies. Beside the woman stood a gargantuan man with a bald head and a devil's goatee. The man wore tight black jeans, shit-kicker boots, and had only his open brown leather cut on top. An elegant black crow was tattooed across his chest, celtic knots and Irish Ogham intertwined around his shoulders and neck in an intricate pattern. Twisted black apple trees lined his forearms, making it look like dark flames were coming out of his wrists. Those tree tattoos were freckled with red apples, and Caleb had heard a rumour that each one represented a person the man had murdered. To Caleb, the man looked vicious and deadly, and he wondered if Eddy, having now seen him more closely, still thought that Daniel "Danny-Boy" Church looked "unimpressive."

Church laughed at the sight of the injured woman, then used his heavily tattooed arm to signal the green mohawked bartender to come over. Church said something to the man, and he scurried around the bar, helped collect the woman, and then took her into a backroom away from the noise. Beside Daniel stood a red-headed Scum Fuck with his back turned to Caleb. The red-headed man whispered something into Daniel's ear, and then both of them walked towards the back of the club.

"We should follow them," Caleb whispered to Eddy.

But Eddy shook his head. "We should go back and tell Bruno what's up."

Caleb understood Eddy's view, but didn't agree with it. "He'd want us to stay on Church."

Eddy seemed to ponder the idea and looked like he was about to refute Caleb's position when a shiver ran through the man. Instead of arguing, he simply nodded and said, "Okay, for now."

The pair continued down the corridor. They turned around the big room and after a brief travel, found themselves in a narrow passage with more holes in the wall. Caleb began to suspect that the holes had been put there intentionally. This time, the Dead Mariachis looked out into a conference room with a large maple-wood table in the middle. Sitting at the table were Scum Fuck officers with President and Vice-President flashes, and leaning against the walls were the Sgt.-at-Arms and Secretaries. Just as Caleb's eyes were adjusting to the room, Daniel Church entered and a hush fell over the crowd.

Danny-Boy looked around the room, asserting his dominance over the people inside as much as surveying it. Most of the Scum Fucks looked down at their feet or at the table in front of them, and this act of submission made Church smile wickedly. The biker-king walked over to the head of the table, and with a sudden jolt, turned his head upwards and to the left. A loud crack disrupted the quiet of the room and sent a ripple of tension down Caleb's spine. Church's red-headed compatriot pulled Danny-Boy's chair out for him and then tucked it back in as the Scum Fuck President sat down. Then, the red-headed man took his own seat on the right-hand side of Daniel Church.

Danny-Boy pulled out an expensive looking Cohiba from the front pocket of his cut, struck a match, and lit the cigar. The aroma of exotic tobacco flooded the room and seeped through the holes Caleb and Eddy were looking through. When he finally spoke, Daniel's voice was velvet smooth and as commanding as the crack of a whip.

"First, let me thank you all for coming. I know that for some of you, this gathering is an imposition, taking you away from your businesses and families. I appreciate that you're here." The room seemed to inhale collectively, and Caleb felt the tension rising. "My understanding is that there are some concerns about our relationship with the Catalanos family, and with the actions we took earlier this summer in Windsor and in Kingston."

"More than concerned, mon frère," said an ugly man sitting at the foot of the table. The man ran his fingers over a Hitler-eque mustache which topped a set of gnarly looking teeth with a severe overbite. The man's flash said "President," and his side rocker read "Hochelaga-Maisonneuve." "I am very upset with you, and the decisions you 'ave made over the last few months."

Daniel moved forward in his chair into a predatory position and looked into the eyes of the man sitting directly across from him at the foot of the table. "Yes, Fabien, you've said as much."

"This spring," Fabien continued, "you told everyone in this room that you had come to an agreement with the Catalonos and that we were going to be their exclusive partners in both Ontario and Quebec. Based on that, we all agreed that we would be able to acquire the firepower needed to move into this territory, IN FULL, and that certain steps were needed in order to solidify our position in the area. The problem is, Danny-Boy, now it seems there may be no such arrangement. And, if that's true, then you 'ave opened up old wounds and dragged us back into a war with the Dead Mariachis over nothing. Hell, we've been at peace with that club since 2002."

Daniel rocked his Cohiba from side to side by fluttering his fingers, a conscious gesture he often made when considering his words. "Nico Catalonos himself, has assured me that his organization is ready to do business with us, and to support our takeover of this province philosophically and financially. I have no reason to doubt his sincerity."

"Nico Catalonos doesn't give a shit about *our* territory disputes. He only gives a shit about making money. Besides, he is the youngest of the Catalonos brothers and the biggest fuck-up of the three! He is a capo in name only," Fabien said as he grimaced and shook his head.

"He's still a goddamn Capo." Daniel growled.

"Daniel, we 'ave made some very big moves based on the deal you claim to 'ave with that organization."

"Very big moves!" roared a voice from halfway down the table, belonging to a gargoyle looking man with the entire upper left side of his face concealed by a poorly executed blackout tattoo.

Fabien nodded in agreement with the gargoyle and a smirk appeared on his face. "And yet one of our brothers from Toronto-North, a full patched member mind you, not some junkie informant, saw Marco Catalonos sitting down with Paulo Renaud in that guinea pizza place in Vaughn, not two days ago. Hence the reason we 'ave asked for this little palaver here."

"I invited *you* here," Daniel scowled. "And, in good faith, because I also want answers about what's going on."

Fabien chuckled and the hairs on his mustache vibrated. "I'm sure you want answers, but you also 'ave some explaining to do."

"FOR FUCK'S SAKE DANNY-BOY!" screamed the Gargoyle, who was now standing at his seat and glaring at Daniel. "I HAD ROBBIE BALLS-OUT KILLED ON YOUR SAY SO! Do you have ANY IDEA how much heat that's brought to the Bellville Chapter? I've got Dead Mariachis circling my block day and night. THEY FOLLOWED MY SON TO HIS SCHOOL! You need to tell us what the fuck is going on? Do we have a deal with the Catolonos or not? Cause we're the ones who are out there right now risking our lives over a BULLSHIT story YOU told us!"

Caleb surveyed the room. There was no warmth left in the faces of the men sitting there. Daniel Church was losing the support of his fellow officers.

Fabien raised his right hand in a calming gesture and the gargoyle returned to his seat. "He's right Danny. If we are, as you said, now the exclusive partner of the Catalanos, then what the fuck is the head of that family doing having a sit down with the President of the Windsor Dead Mariachis? The Paulbearer is the biggest player in that entire damn club."

Daniel was silent for a moment, and the look on his face changed from predatory to apprehensive. "I don't know Fabien. I want answers, too. Do you think my skin doesn't boil thinking about this? I promise you, my francophone brother, that I want to know what Marco Catalonos and Paulo Renaud were talking about. And, I promise you this, I'm going to find out."

A thin looking skinhead with a swastika tattoo underneath his left eye shook his head. "You said the Catalonos were a sure thing, that the deal was done."

"I don't control the Catalonos," Daniel snapped. "I'll take responsibility for my part in trusting Nico, but when we decided to make moves, it was because we *all* thought this thing was a lock. You had the same information I did."

"Bullshit!" said an elderly man with gray dreadlocks at the far end of the table. And with that, dissent in the room erupted into murmurs and glares.

"We need a vote!" screamed the Gargoyle.

"Seconded!" agreed the skinhead.

Daniel stood, pushing his chair back, and slamming his fist into the table. "ARE YOU KIDDING ME BOYS? We just re-ignited a WAR with the Dead Mariachis and you want to vote me away from the head of this table? Are you out of your minds? What's the matter with you all? You scared? Here I thought you were ROCK HARD, but you caught a whiff of rank pussy and now you want out? Chicken-shit! The lot of ya!"

Fabien rose to his feet and stepped to the side of the table. "You aren't fit to lead green and brown anymore, Danny-Boy."

A smile spread across Daniel's face, and a menacing look appeared that was framed by creased skin and wolfen eyes. "Green and brown? Huh! Green and brown you say…" Daniel moved to the same side of the table as Fabien. "The last time I checked, our colours were SNOT and SHIT! And you, you goddamn FROG! Don't even know what club you belong to, but you think you have the BALLS to step into my seat?"

The crowd rustled. The men along the walls stood straighter, creating a clear pathway between the Presidents of the Toronto-South and Hochelaga-Maisonneuve chapters.

Fabien smirked. "You're a fool Danny-Boy. As easily deceived by that wop Nico Catalonos, as you are by that hag of a mother you keep locked away in here!"

Like a bull elk, enraged in the heat of mating season, Daniel charged. His counterpart did also. Together they raced head first at one another and collided in the center of the room. Daniel threw a heavy-handed punch that caught Fabien in the temple, sending the man to the floor. Caleb was shocked by the speed and power of Daniel's punch. It made his guts tighten to see such intensity.

As Fabien fell, he grabbed a hold of Daniel's collar and used his body weight to pull the Toronto President into an uppercut. Compared to Daniel's, Fabien's punch was paltry, and the pair stumbled into the wall, sending the lower Scum Fuck officers sprawling.

Next, Fabien reached for Daniel's throat, but Danny-Boy caught him by the back of the head and pulled him down and into his rising knee. A red mist spewed out of Fabien's mouth, covering Daniel's face and chest. Howls of delight erupted from the crowd as the officers cheered the violent circus happening before them.

Fabien stumbled backwards and Daniel stalked forward in pursuit. Danny-Boy grabbed his rival by the back of the head, used two fingers to dig inside his mouth, then placed a foot on the maple-wood table and kicked away. As he did, Fabien's cheek split open, and a cascade of jellyfish pink droplets splattered the floor.

The Hochelaga president screamed in a shrill and high-pitched tone that belonged a half mile under the streets of Paris in the skeleton laced catacombs, and a sickening quiet moved through the other officers. In that vacuum, Daniel soaked up the sound of Fabien's screams, and allowed them to fill him with a delicious satisfaction.

Daniel tossed Fabien to the ground, and with blood dripping over his face, scanned the room once again. No one met his gaze, not the Dreadlocked Scum Fuck, nor the Skinhead, not even the Gargoyle. The only man who didn't look away when Daniel's eyes passed over them was the red-headed goon next to him, who excitedly grinned from ear to ear. With the room quiet once more, Daniel walked back to the head of the table, picked up his cigar, and took three deep puffs. He exhaled between each toke, and the clouds he emitted grew in tandem with the brightness of the orange glow at the end of his Cohiba.

"So," said Danny-Boy, "Now that that's out of the way. Let me be clear about something. I don't know what Marco Catalonos and that fat fuck Paulo Renaud were doing together, nor what their bitch asses were talking about, but I *am* gonna find out. And, when I do, I promise you all, we are going to put an end to the bullshit games being played here. Because my brothers, it ain't me pulling on your strings. It ain't me lying and cheating you out of an honest day's pay. I was told, by Nico Catalonos, that we had a deal, and just like you all, in my mind, a deal is a mother fucking deal. So, we're gonna get what's ours. Now, anyone else got anything they'd like to discuss with me?"

Before anyone could answer, there was a knock on the conference room door. The red-headed goon glided over and opened the door, revealing a frail old woman dressed in a sheer white nightgown. She was a tiny thing with narrow shoulders, thin hips, and a curved spine. Her translucent flesh and sunken eyes gave her a wraith-like appearance, and as she tip-toed through the room, her knees knocked together. The only thing about the woman that had any substance to it at all was her hair, which, despite being magnificently white, was still lush and curly.

"Daniel, there are people here making an awful racket. Can you please come and tell them to be quiet?" Morrigan said, in a voice that sounded like it belonged to a skittish forest creature.

Daniel stood tall and straightened out his cut. He produced a cloth from his pants pocket and wiped away the first layer of blood that Fabien had left on his face. "Gentlemen, if that's all the business we have to discuss tonight, then I am truly sorry for your long travels. But please, you are my guests, enjoy my hospitality while you are here. If you need anything, my Road-Captain will see to you. He's behind the bar, or nearby it. Now, if you don't mind, I'm gonna take my mother back to her room."

The table nodded in quiet unison.

As he reached his mother and took the old woman's arm, Daniel looked over his shoulder at his right-hand man and said, "Winston, would you be so kind as to join us?"

The red-headed goon stood and quickly took over holding the door. When Daniel and his matriarch had left the room, Winston looked back with a final visceral smirk, and then closed the door behind them all.

There was no debate this time, Caleb and Eddy followed the tunnel again. Whenever they came across a hole in the wall, they stopped and took a peek. Behind the first peephole was the room where the broken faced woman was resting. The next peephole showed the inside of a closet. And the third looked into a bathroom where a drunk couple fucked against the sink like a pair of sloppy hippos. Finally, as the hallway threatened to fall into a valley of black,

Caleb and Eddy came across a square of light and realized they were looking at a door, the first door they had seen since entering the crawlspace. Caleb peeked between the crack beside the frame and saw an office with green carpet and deep brown walls.

A moment later, Daniel, Morrigan, and the red-headed goon entered the room through the main entrance, which was directly across from where Caleb was spying. The red-headed goon closed the door, and Morrigan immediately leapt into her son's arms. She squealed like a joyous baby pig while Daniel spun her around in a great bear hug. When he lowered her to the ground, Morrigan came up on her tiptoes and kissed her son on the lips.

The old woman's physique had changed since leaving the boardroom. No longer did she appear withered and frail, but instead robust and comely. Her back was straight, her shoulders were squared, and her hips were wide and inviting. Morrigan's complexion had returned to a healthy cream tone that was youthful, and her lips were a deep rose color. Even her magnificent white hair seemed to have darkened.

"Oh, my beautiful boy! How radiant you are tonight."

"Thank you," Daniel said as his cheeks flushed.

"Those *things* back there, you know that they all wish they could be you, my love! They wish they could be your toenail, or the flecks of dead skin falling off your arm. They wish they could feel what *you* feel, see the way *you* see, and do the things that *you* do!" Morrigan's hand reached up and grazed the hairs on Daniel's chest. "They are nothing but shriveled worms, desperately pining to be the snake they see slinking through the tall grass."

Caleb felt a surge of power ooze through his head, like he was standing on the outskirts of a wave running through a lonely bay. His mind went fuzzy, and Caleb felt sick. When he composed himself enough to look over at his partner, Caleb saw that Eddy's eyes were closed and that his hand was planted firmly on his gut.

"It's not over," Daniel said. "They'll break off into groups now, and figure out who supports Fabien and who supports me. And, if it's no longer Fabien they want to throw their chit in with, then they'll rally behind someone else. My time at the head of the table is coming to an end." Daniel looked down at his feet and then, like he was giving confession, said, "I sometimes wonder how my father would have handled these kinds of things."

With lightning quick reflexes, Morrigan grabbed her son by the face. "You always worry about that man, but you have two fathers, don't forget that! One for your body and one for your soul. You just walked into a room full of murdering bastards and pissed all over them. That was your *other* father speaking through you just now, your divine father. No need to worry about the pathetic little biker that once was."

"She's right about the other officers," said the goon-faced Winston from across the room. "I've been keeping tabs on everyone, Danny. Fabien had his little clique there, but this was his moment to make a move, and let's be honest, that was a pretty feeble coup. I think you can stop worrying about a mutiny. At least for now."

Somberly, Daniel replied, "Maybe…"

The biker-king left his mother's embrace and crossed the room. He moved to the hidden door and placed his forearm on the frame, a gesture which startled Caleb with its intimacy. The enemies were only a few inches away from one another now, separated only by a door.

"There is something strange about this night, isn't there?" Daniel said.

Morrigan crossed the room and hugged her son from behind. "Yes, there is."

"Did you read your tea leaves today?"

Morrigan nodded. "And the ashes of a dead bird. It may be tonight that we finish the ritual."

The air around Caleb chilled, and a foulness invaded that could be felt, but not seen nor smelled. Daniel stared at the door, and Caleb almost believed that the man was looking right at him.

"I'm not ready for that."

Morrigan scowled. "It doesn't matter if you're ready. I've lit the fires and warmed the pit. So, if the time is right, then whether it's a bird or a ship that comes to greet you, we will do what must be done."

With that, Morrigan walked over to the other side of the room to a dresser, and opened the bottom drawer. She pulled out a bulbous flask, and brought it to her son. "Drink this, and then we'll wait downstairs for whatever is coming."

"I can keep watch up here," Winston said with a nod.

Morrigan laced her arms through her son once again and pulled him into her. "Then that's settled, isn't it?"

Daniel looked at the flask, studying its matted exterior and the intricate network of runes that surrounded it. He took a final study of his mother, then opened the container and drank its contents in a single long gulp.

"Good boy," Morrigan smiled.

The ground shook then, and the walls vibrated. Dust fell from the ceiling, covering the Dead Mariachis. Caleb raised his .45 and aimed it at the door while Eddy reached into his jacket and pulled out a long and perforated cylinder grenade.

"What the hell was that?" Daniel shouted.

Winston opened the door to the office and stuck his head out into the clubhouse. Gunfire echoed through the hallway, and from the main room screams could be heard.

"IT'S AN ATTACK!" Winston shouted back.

"It *is* the day, and *now* is the time," Morrigan grinned. She grabbed Winston by the arm and commanded his attention to her. "Help us down into the chamber, then come back and guard the entrance. You understand your place tonight don't you Winnie? You know what you might have to sacrifice for Daniel?"

Slowly, but without a shred of trepidation, Winston nodded. He left Morrigan's clutches, walked over to the hidden door, and opened the passageway. As the red-headed goon approached, Eddy pulled the pin on the grenade, and when the door peeled open, revealing the now confused Winston, the Dead Mariachi kicked the Scum Fuck in the balls and shoved the grenade into his face. The Goon fell backwards and the door closed under its own weight. Caleb and Eddy dropped to the floor just as the hallway erupted in blue light and a BANG deafened them.

From the office came a haunting cry. Caleb jumped to his feet and threw open the door. The red-headed goon was rolling on the ground, clutching his face and screaming horrifically. Smoke drifted up from the man's mouth and cheeks as the skin on the lower part of his face bubbled. The stink of Winston's sizzling flesh brought Caleb back to that farmhouse in Afghanistan and fogged his brain. As he stepped into the office, Caleb saw a huddled mass of humans on the other side of the room, and for a moment, the Prospect thought that two charred faces were looking at him with accusatory eyes.

Caleb stopped dead in his tracks and whispered, "I didn't throw the grenade this time."

The huddled mass moved. A lightning quick hand appeared, holding a revolver, and Caleb snapped back to reality in time to see the first muzzle flash from the gun. The Prospect rolled out of the way and raised his forty-five. Danny-Boy fired again, but this time Caleb returned the call of bullets, and caught Daniel in the leg. The biker-king barely acknowledged the injury. Instead, he fired his last round, and Caleb felt a white-hot searing pain in his side.

Gunsmoke clouded the room. Caleb gathered his bearings, but just as he began to understand, the fog around him the now empty revolver barreled into his nose. The pistol hit him like a ten-ton stone and pulverized all of the bone and cartilage in the centre of his face. Caleb's body seized for a moment, blinded by blue-electric pain, and as he tensed, his Colt pistol fell to the floor.

Now it was Eddy who burst into the room. He had a small Uzi and sprayed the place with bullets. Winston took two slugs to the butt and Daniel took one more to the arm, but otherwise, Eddy's attack was fruitless. Danny-Boy leapt to his feet, crossed the room like a cheetah, and slammed into Eddy like a rhinoceros. The pair sprawled backwards into the hallway and the Scum Fuck king unleashed a hell-storm of fists into the face of the Dead Mariachi.

Caleb hobbled to his feet, but as soon as he found footing, someone pounced onto his back. The Prospect reached up, grabbed a handful of thick curly hair, and yanked down hard, but the owner of the hair refused to yield. Morrigan and Caleb twirled around the room like an out of control top, colliding with desks and dressers, and finally slamming hard into a wall.

In the crawlspace, Daniel had coloured Eddy's face violet and charcoal. The Scum Fuck stopped his assault, and looked up at his mother who was pinned between Caleb and the wall. Danny-Boy grabbed Eddy by the hair and slapped the door with his free hand. "MOTHER!" he screamed impatiently. Morrigan bit into Caleb's collarbone, and the pain was incredible enough to force the Prospect to let go of her hair. Daniel dragged Eddy into the darkness while the lady in white crossed the room.

Before she entered the hallway, Morrigan looked back at Caleb with a greedy smirk and asked, "Are you coming, dear?"

Caleb looked over at the other door, the one that led into the clubhouse where a firefight was taking place.

"By the time you get help, we'll have skinned your friend alive," Morrigan giggled. "Follow me instead and come find out who you really are."

And then she was gone.

Caleb considered running into the clubhouse and trying to get help. He hoped that if he could find one of the invading Dead Mariachis that he could get some backup for his plunge into the abyss, but in his heart, he knew that effort would be futile. He was on the wrong side of the battle. And even if he could fight his way through the battalion of Scum Fucks and reach the front line, he was almost certain to be shot by his own troops. Only Bruno and the other raiders might have the wherewithal to realize how deeply Caleb had made it into the compound. The others would assume he was just another nazi-punk-biker, and shoot. There was no time to risk it. If he wanted to save Eddy, Caleb had to follow Daniel Church and his vicious mother. So, the young man, the veteran, the wanna-be outlaw, scraped his .45 caliber handgun from the floor, kicked the red-headed goon once for good measure, and followed the Church family into the darkness.

Just inside that dim hallway, Caleb found a long and decrepit staircase that led downwards. The steps were loose at the stays and angled so steeply that it felt more like climbing down a ladder than anything else. Every time the Prospect touched a new rung, it cried out and rattled. Then, without warning, Caleb reached the landing and his foot sank. The floor was dirt and the chamber he found himself in reeked of must and sick almonds. Only a dim glow, which came from the other side, illuminated the room. The walls were coarse and earthy, plied with rotting wood boards and rusted old spikes that belonged in a pioneer village. Using one of the rough and crumbling walls, Caleb guided himself towards the light, and on the other side of the chamber he found an opening that was just big enough for him to squat down and duck-walk through.

The gravity of the situation befell Caleb; he was alone in a dark room, with the deadly leader of his rival motorcycle club, and an aged but violent woman. He had no backup and nobody knew where he was. For all he knew, the hole lead into a tunnel, and if he turned back now, Daniel Church would drag Eddy to god knows where and murder him. There was no other choice, so Caleb swallowed a dry piece of air, raised his gun, and rolled through the opening.

On the other side of the hole was a chamber, this one much larger than the room Caleb had just been in. The walls were stone here, and they had scratch marks all over them, as if by some impossible means a person had carved out this place with their bare hands. It was cold inside, despite the oil drum fire in the center of the room, which was the source of the light. A round metal bowl, like a witch's cauldron, hung over the fire, suspended by a metal hook. And beside the cauldron were two blankets with intricate needlework on them.

Morrigan stood completely naked on one of the blankets with her back facing Caleb. Her arms were over the top of her head and she spoke in a language with elongated vowels and sharp consonants, which Caleb vaguely recognized. Daniel stood next to his mother, and was in the process of taking off his pants as Caleb entered the room. When he finished removing his lower garment, Daniel tossed the pants towards the other side of the room and, except for his cut, stood naked before his mother. The Church family was so close to one another that if Daniel thought of something pleasant they would surely touch.

Together, mother and son recited an incantation in a call and answer fashion, and even though Caleb didn't know the words that were being used, he did understand how grotesque they were. Behind the Church's, propped up against the far wall, was the bloodied and bruised Eddy. Other than a brief glance in Caleb's direction, the blonde Mariachi didn't move. He was barely conscious and hardly breathing.

As the flames from the fire danced along the floor, Caleb caught sight of a dark spot in the center of the room. It was a gruesome looking thing, like the open maw of a monstrous sandworm. The black hole pulsed against the light, giving no glimpse of what it contained, and in the quiet between the words Morrigan and Daniel spoke, Caleb almost thought he heard the Pit sing.

The Church family finished their incantations by blowing a kiss towards the cauldron and thanking someone named Dian Cécht. Morrigian reached underneath one of the blankets and brought out a long robe of black feathers, which she draped over herself. Daniel looked over her shoulder in an easy way that showed no concern for the short man in the entrance, nor the pistol Caleb was holding.

Calmly, Daniel said. "You should put that gun down little man, I wouldn't want you to hurt yourself."

Caleb tried to lift his hand and point the gun towards Daniel but couldn't. His head was still fuzzy from earlier, from when Morrigan had mentioned the snake in the tall grass, and the most he could manage was to wave the pistol in their direction.

"I SAID PUT THAT FUCKING GUN AWAY!" Daniel screamed.

The sudden burst of aggression grounded Caleb. Finally, he was able to aim the gun, but before he could fire, a lump of burning embers collided with his face. The Prospect had been so focused on Daniel that he neglected to keep an eye on Morrigan, and she had taken that opportunity to scoop up a smoldering pile of charcoal with her bare hands to fling into Caleb's eyes.

The attack sent Caleb stumbling backwards. He tripped over his own feet and fell onto the ground and lost his grip on the pistol. Immediately, Caleb felt the weight of Daniel's body crash into him. A hurricane of knuckles pummeled Caleb's face and his mouth exploded with the copper bright taste of blood. Caleb put both arms up in a feeble attempt to defend himself, but Daniel countered this by lacing his catcher's-mitt sized hands together, rearing back as far as he could, and bringing both fists down into the Prospect's chest.

It was like a sledgehammer had come down on Caleb. Air rushed out of the young man's lungs. A crunching snap shook the chamber, and an immense and immediate flash of white-hot pain sizzled through Caleb's body. Something was broken, something important. All the wannabe outlaw could do was go limp and sprawl out upon the floor.

Daniel stood. He grabbed Caleb by the ankle, dragged him across the ground, and threw him into the oil drum. A flash of light and then a curtain of stars blinded the Prospect. In his daze, Caleb felt tender fingers running through his hair, and had the vague understanding that Morrigan was kneeling beside him. For the first time, her stench reached Caleb's nose. It was a mixture of lavender and rancid meat, and it caused his stomach to roll.

"I don't know if you're the one that we have been waiting for," Morrigan sneered, "but one way or another you are going to scream my son's name tonight."

"He's not the one, I can promise you that." Daniel stepped closer and towered over everyone else in the room. Then, he kicked Caleb in the thigh hard enough to give him a charlie-horse. "You know who I am, don't you, little man? You're not a mouse, right? You didn't just happen to sneak into my chamber tonight?"

Caleb tried to wipe a dribble of blood away from his lips, but all he ended up doing was smushing the hot balaclava into his bleeding mouth. "I know who you are, you son of a bitch!"

"I resent that," said Morrigan flatly.

The king of the Scum Fucks reached down and grabbed Caleb by the scruff of his neck, but this time the Prospect was filled with survival and rage. He grabbed Daniel's wrist, kicked him square in the knee, and rolled. Danny-Boy hadn't anticipated the move, nor the strength contained within Caleb's small body and his eyes went wide with surprise as he was thrown onto the ground. Caleb turned until he was on top of Daniel, then stuck both thumbs into the Scum Fuck's eyes and dug in.

Daniel screamed and used his palm to push Caleb's face high into the air. This defense gave Daniel enough momentum to roll his opponent over, until he was able to gain control, and swat Caleb's hand away. Now on top, Daniel grabbed his opponent's throat with both hands and squeezed.

Tunnels of black crept into Caleb's vision framing Daniel and threatened to darken everything. He realized that if he passed out now, he would be dead for sure. With his remaining consciousness and strength, Caleb kicked off the ground and rolled the fighters one last time.

They tipped over the precipice of the pit and fell down a mud-slick wall until they landed hard in the cold earth at the bottom. Caleb ended up on top of Daniel and had the wherewithal to brace his fall by sticking out his elbow, digging it deep into Daniel's gut, and allowing all his weight to crash down at that singular point. The biker-king screamed as the air fled from his lungs Caleb hoisted himself into a mounted position on top of the man and began punching. Daniel reached up, trying to find something to hold onto, but only ended up yanking off Caleb's balaclava. On his next attempt, Danny-boy reached behind Caleb's head and was able to pull the young man down until they were face to face.

Even through the blood and mud, Daneil saw the youth that had pummeled him, and in his disbelief shouted, "Jesus Christ on a fucking cross, yer nothing but a boy!" Then, without warning, and with the speed of a venomous snake, Daniel lunged at Caleb's cheek and bit that part of his face clean off.

A sharp aching pain exploded across Caleb's cheek as Daniel's teeth slid underneath his skin and tore away that hunk of meat. The Prospect yelped like a kicked puppy. When he looked down, he saw that Church, who had a mouth painted bright crimson, had begun chewing.

Laughter, like a maniac caught in the thralls of a full moon, poured over the top of the pit and cascaded down the walls. At the precipice, Morrigan hopped up and down while clapping arrhythmically. Her face was a twisted snarl of bulging eyes and wicked teeth.

Caleb took in the horror show happening around him and his brain flooded with terror. There was no sanity left in the chamber, only madness, no humanity before him, only a pair of ghouls. The Prospect twisted his wrist free from Daniel's clutches and punched the Scum Fuck right in the face. But Daniel was quick. He grabbed Caleb's forearm with his bicep and locked it in place. The King Scum Fuck let out a demonic giggle to signal the pleasure he took for this minor victory, and as he opened wide, Caleb saw his own flesh bobble inside the fiend's throat.

Caleb rallied his strength, and with his other hand he punched Daniel hard in the face. But once more, the biker-king was able to grab the Prospect's hand and lock it in place with his massive bicep. Caleb tried to pull away, but he couldn't. He tried to stand, but Church pulled him back into his chest. Like a rat in a snare, Caleb thrashed from one side to the other and fought to gain some semblance of control over his own body, but he was given no quarter. Exhausted, Caleb paused his escape attempt and looked down at the man beneath him. Daniel stared at him with a look of pure ecstasy, all the while chewing on the young man's flesh.

The expression on Daniel's face sent a terrible surge of electricity through Caleb's body. Instinctually, the Prospect leaned back and using every bit of strength he had left, brought his forehead into Daniel's nose. Blood sprayed like an opened fire hydrant and Daniel screamed. Again, Caleb leaned back and then flung himself forward in Danny-Boy's face. This time he connected with Daniel's mouth and his teeth fluttered away. Caleb reared back again, and once again brought his face back down. Then he did it again, and again, and again, and again, and again, and again, and again.

With every head-butt, Caleb's strength seemed to grow, and his power intensified. In the middle of the assault, Daniel's screams changed from a grunting howl to a high-pitched shriek, like something straight from a b-horror movie. The cry was blood curdling and it echoed off the walls of the pit, causing mud to slide down to the bottom. Over and over and over again, Caleb brought his face into Daniel's, until finally the horrible high-pitched scream cut out, and the biker-king's tremendous arms loosened, then fell limply to his sides.

With his body prepared to shut down on him, and finally free of Daniel's clutches, Caleb leapt up almost to his feet and shouted,

"FUCK YOU DANIEL CHURCH AND FUCK YOUR GODDAMN MOTHE TOO!" and then brought the full weight of himself down in one final head-butt.

Caleb's forehead stayed in the warm embrace of Daniel's oozing face for a moment. Ribbons of skin, slushy chunks of muscle and fat, and jagged bone chips smeared across Caleb's face, decorating him in a grim mask of death. The biker's body was lifeless. There was no rise nor fall of the chest, no spasm nor tremble, only stillness and quiet. Within that silence, Caleb felt an intimacy that he had never experienced before. A calm washed over him, the animal part of his brain that craved carnage and wildness had been sated. Caleb was a new man, a more viscous beast than he had been before.

Suddenly, Morrigan fell into the pit. Caleb sat up, and as he looked over at the woman, pieces of Daniel fell down the sides of his face. At first, neither of them moved, both of them being concerned that the other would lash out with mortal fury. The witch's expression was wild, half murderous and half that of a fan-girl who had found their way backstage at the concert of their favorite singer. The black feather on her cloak stood at attention and her eyes glowed with intensity. In her hands, Morrigan carried the ember hot iron bowl that had been dangling above the fire when Caleb entered the chamber, and the smell of burning flesh joined her rancid flower scent.

"You really are magnificent aren't you!" she hissed. "Who would have guessed that such violence could exist inside someone so small?"

The faint sound of a door being kicked in bounced off the chamber walls, disrupting their moment. Morrigan put the cauldron to her lips and drank the contents of it greedily. When she was done, she tossed the cauldron to the ground, and Caleb saw that her palms were burned clean off. Morrigan's face went flush, and her eyes glassed over. She leaned over her son, flopped his head backwards, and opened his mouth with her fingers. Then she reached into her throat, and tickled something deep inside until a gurgling wretch happened. From her parted lips, a waterfall of stomach acid, rot-gut elixir, and putrid herbs poured into Daniel's mouth. Morrigan had become a satanic bird feeding her massacred chick.

"Hey, anybody down here?" came a floating voice from within

the first chamber. "If you're a Scum Fuck you better let us know right now! If you throw down your weapons, we'll let you live. I promise!"

A guttural rumble, half bear half raptor, came from Morrigan's throat. She looked at Caleb one last time, with those glowing eyes of hers, then scurried up the wall like a spider and disappeared.

Blood dripped off the tip of Caleb's nose and fell right into Daniel's mouth. The Scum Fuck king's vocal chords vibrated, but only as a reflex. The sound that escaped Daniel was a death rattle, a low humming shockwave emitted as the final neurons ceased firing. It was a hauntingly peaceful moment for Caleb, and he was so adrift in this grim catharsis that he almost allowed himself to remain silent as the Dead Mariachis entered the chamber.

"I… I'm here…," he called out, meekly. "I'm in the pit!"

"FUCKING PROSPECT? Hey man that you? Your voice sounds fucked up. You okay?"

Caleb simply nodded to himself, failing to realize that no one could see him do so. The footsteps got closer and someone dropped down beside him.

"Holy shit kid!" The man standing beside Caleb stopped moving as soon as he realized the scene he had come across. "Hey, hey! The Prospect killed Church!"

"What?" exclaimed another voice, which belonged to someone standing outside of Caleb's field of vision, by the opening of the pit. "Get the fuck out of here!"

"No, it's true. Church is dead. Little buddy fucked him up, but good. He's like a pile of hamburger meat down here."

The Dead Mariachi who had jumped into the pit leaned down and looked Caleb in the eyes. The man seemed vaguely familiar, but in the state he was in, Caleb couldn't put enough of the pieces together to figure out who was looking at him. The dark-skinned man hugged Caleb by the waist and lifted him to his feet. Two other sets of hands grabbed the Prospect by the armpits, and lifted him out of the pit.

"Jesus!" said one of the Dead Mariachi's who had helped lift Caleb out. "Would you look at this kid's face? It's a fucking death-mask.

Absently, Caleb touched his chin, and felt his finger slip against the slick blood that covered him. When he pulled his hand away, the Prospect saw red smears of shredded flesh and flecks of white bone on his fingertips.

"Rosey, you sure that's Church down there?" asked one of the other Mariachis.

"Yeah, I'm sure," said the man in the pit. "This fella is wearing Church's cut, and I recognize those damn apple tree tattoos on his arms, and the bird on his chest."

One of the men holding Caleb nodded. "Alright then. Take that bastard's cut from him, and let's get the fuck out of here boys. The fucking pigs will be here any minute."

CHAPTER 18

————┼————

Just before midnight, the bikers finally reached the basin of Sharbot Lake. Caleb led them along the top of a granite cliff, on a private road that was separated from the edge by deep woods, and down a curving hill until finally they reached a quaint looking cottage by the water's edge. The place was whitewashed with green trim and twice the size of Hellbilly's childhood home, which still made it on the smaller side as far cottages in the area went. The driveway leading towards the place was long, and it bordered a forested incline that eventually turned into the steep rock face of the cliff. Squished between that rock face and the cottage was a massive pile of broken and jagged debris, made mostly of wood, from an old structure that had probably been taken down at the end of the last season and left to decay over the winter. The pile was covered in snow and it gave the property a gothic feeling.

A breeze came off the lake, giving the bikers one final chill as they stopped their motorcycles in front of the woodpile and lowered their kickstands into place. Death Mask immediately went about the task of searching for a way inside, while Hellbilly held Oscar tightly in his bundle of sleeping bags and rubbed the child's arms. It took a few devastating minutes, but eventually Caleb knocked over a planter and a key fell onto the deck.

The inside of the cottage was as cold as the outside was, but there was no wind and that instantly warmed the travelers. Death Mask saw a small wood stove in a tiled corner of the living room and began searching for kindling and matches. Meanwhile, Bill raided the bedrooms for new clothing to wear. Hellbilly found dark coloured sweat-pants, hoodies, and t-shirts that were big enough for him, but Death Mask was resigned to a pink and purple sweatsuit that clearly belonged to the lady of the house. Caleb didn't care though. after such an intensely cold ride, warmth was all that mattered to him. For Oscar, Hellbilly found a trove of children's clothing, and he layered the boy as generously as he could. When he was finally dressed, Oscar looked like he was three times his actual size. There was no food left, and the only jug of water was frozen solid, but once the fire was going, Death Mask was able to melt some of the ice and give everyone a few mouthfuls to drink. Hellbilly found a small stash of booze inside a China cabinet, and he pulled out a bottle of rye whiskey. Each biker took a swig to warm their belly, and with their chores completed, the three amigos sat down on the couches and chairs that circled the wood stove and rested.

The flames warmed the small den quickly, and in only a few minutes the place was toasty. Shadows danced around the room, playfully hiding the secret spaces that lined the walls, and except for the occasional swish of liquor being tossed down someone's gullet everyone was silent. Oscar and Hellbilly nestled together on the couch with the boy resting his head against the big guy's shoulder and Bill stroking the child's hair tenderly. Within minutes, Oscar began blinking in long and heavy intervals, and each time his eyes shut it took more effort for him to open them than it had the time before. Eventually, the boy closed his eyes one last time, and they didn't open again.

Hours passed, and though it went unsaid, at some point the notion that Eddy had taken too long in reaching their location crept into the minds of both Dead Mariachis. Eventually, the room stopped feeling warm, and the shadows were no longer pleasant.

As much to break the rising anxiety as anything else, Death Mask asked, "Any idea what time it is?"

"Clock in the bedroom said eleven forty-five, but that was when we first got here. It's probably after two by now," answered Hellbilly.

Caleb watched his friend stare blankly into the fire and realized that Oscar was not the only road-weary member of their group. "How are you doing, Hellbilly?"

Bill shrugged and continued to look into the flames without emotion.

"I'm sorry about your old man."

"He died fightin'," Hellbilly said with a subtle nod. "I hope he realized that, even if just for a moment. If he did, a part of him woulda died happy. He would have liked knowing that he met his end with his boots on like that."

An immense sadness entered Caleb's chest, and he was unable to find any comforting words for his friend, so instead he said, "I don't know what to make of those things that attacked your house, man. I been trying to figure out what they were, what I even saw out that back window, and while we were running away, but I can't wrap my damn head around it. They were like something out of a zombie movie."

"One of 'em was Olivia Renaud."

Death Mask shook his head, unable to comprehend what his partner had just told him.

"Rotting faced, foaming at the mouth, looking like she wanted to eat me alive, and my father blew her head clean off. I'd have killed him for it too, but I could barely move. I was so scared." Hellbilly's voice was monochromatic and sterile.

Death Mask picked up the bottle of rye beside him and gave it to his partner. "I'm sorry, Bill."

Hellbilly tilted the bottle and took a gentle swig. "I never did right by her. Could have. I could have left her alone, but I stepped in and messed up her whole life just so I could say I had. As much because I wanted her, as because I wanted to know I could get Paulo's future wife. I think Paulo found out about us. I think that's why Liv is dead."

"It's not your fault, what happened to Olivia. It's Paulo's."

Hellbilly shook his head, and in a voice that remained all shades of gray, he said, "I killed her a long time ago. Just like I killed Gloria and my boy."

Death Mask sucked his teeth. "Bill, I'm sure they're fine. No one is gonna go after them. They'll be safe."

"I don't mean it like that." A single tear rolled down William's cheek. "Hell, you grew up without a father. You know how that absence hurts. Hurts more than any smack in the mouth ever could. My boy has probably spent his whole life wondering why I picked being an outlaw over him. And Gloria has no one to help her, no one to shoulder the burden of being a parent with, or celebrate it with. How hard do you think your mother had to work to raise you all by herself? How long do you think those nights were when you were sick and she had no one to help? Or those days when you were a wily and angry young buck, and there was no one besides her to reign you in?"

Caleb looked down at the floor. He knew exactly what Bill was saying. Now that he was getting older, Caleb often wondered how much of his mother's troubles stemmed from raising a child all by herself. He saw her drinking less as a weakness these days, and more as the only comfort she had on those long lonely nights that Bill spoke of.

"Sure, my family is walking and talking and living the best lives they can, but no matter how good things are for them, they have a hole that can't be filled. A hole I left in them." Bill reached into his hoodie, and pulled out the picture of his son, which he had taken from his father's workbench. "I wanna see my boy again, Caleb. I wanna know who he is. I want him to know who I am."

"You will," Caleb said, eagerly. "He will."

Bill nodded. "I hope so."

The stillness of the moment waned Caleb's desire to press the matter of the people at the house, but there was still a long time before dawn and Death Mask knew that he had to return to the subject of the dead, and explain their connection to the horrible day they just had.

"I need to tell you something about the Scum Fucks."

Hellbilly looked over at his partner for the first time since they had arrived at the cottage, and Caleb took that as a cue to continue.

"The night of the raid, me and Eddy got separated from our group. We ended up fighting Danny-Boy, his mother, and I guess that red-headed goon from your dad's place. They took Eddy, and I followed them, alone, into some chamber deep underground. When I got down there, Church and his mother were performing some kind of… ceremony or ritual, I guess that's what it was. I fought Danny-Boy, and me and him fell into a pit, that I think they made. We scratched and cut and bled on one another. He gave me this," Claeb pointed to the scar on his cheek. "Anyway, he got me all wrapped up at one point, like I told you earlier. It was just like people say, I beat him to death with my own face, but when it was over, something strange happened. His mother jumped down into the pit with us. I thought she was gonna try and kill me, but that's not what she did. She had something in her mouth and she puked it into Danny-Boy's mouth. Then she looked at me like she was half angry and half excited, and called me magnificent. The boys came then, so she ran away, like a fucking bug. They dragged me and Eddy out of that pit, and out of that chamber, but the look on that woman's face, her eyes, it stuck with me. It was like she had a terrible job to do, but she was thrilled to be the one doing it. I know it sounds like I've gone off the deep end, but I think she was trying to bring her son back from the dead. Maybe… maybe she eventually figured out how to actually do that."

Hellbilly stared at his partner and said nothing.

"I know how it sounds." Caleb shook his head and felt suddenly vulnerable. "It sounds like I'm the one who's strange."

"Bunch of zombies ate my dad tonight," said Hellbilly flatly. "One of those zombies was a woman who I've been in love with since I was young. I'm so far beyond giving a shit about strange. I mean hell, that old bitch probably did figure out how to bring people back from the dead. Olivia sure looked like a corpse."

Death Mask spat into the flames and felt a renewed connection to his partner. "God damn Paulo. Set us up to die and be labeled as child killing goofs at the same time. Leader of the Dead Mariachis indeed. Our *bastard* king."

"He ain't my king," Hellbilly shook his head with a look of disgust on his face. "As soon as this rotten day is over I'm going back to my clubhouse, I'm getting my cut, and then I'm gonna slit Paulo's fucking throat and stick his head on a pike. I'm gonna make sure everyone knows that he betrayed his brothers, and gave his wife over to the enemy, so they could use some black-cult magic to turn her into a rabid dog."

"Amen to that."

"Paulo don't get to take our club from us. If he thinks we're gonna roll over and let him have us buried as traitors, with the ashes of our cuts sprinkled over our graves and our headstones pissed on, well FUCK THAT! I was raised to raise hell and I aim to do some more hell raisin' before they bury me."

Death Mask chuckled in solidarity. "Yes, sir!"

The flaming shadows in the living room were washed out by an amber light. Something with an engine approached. Death Mask and Hellbilly looked over their shoulders, but neither man could make out what was happening outside. The sudden change in the situation filled the biker's veins with ice water and turned them back into the outlaws they were.

"You got anything left in that Baretta of yours?" asked Death Mask.

Hellbilly shook his head. "I dropped that back in the basement, but the Peacemaker still has a few rounds."

That seemed to satisfy Death Mask, who stood up and peeked out the window. "I can't see anything out there, just light."

"You think it's Eddy?"

"It ain't cops. They'd be giving us orders by now, or knocking down the doors."

"Unless they just wanna kill us."

"If they were murderous cops we'd probably be taking fire by now. Them bastards don't have a lot of stealth."

"That better be Eddy," Hellbilly said, as he eased his way from underneath the sleeping Oscar. "I'm not up for any more surprises tonight."

The bikers converged by the front entrance and waited. Finally, they heard a clunking sound, like a car door was opening, and then…

"Caleb! Bill! It's me! Come on out, I need some help with all this shit!"

The brothers smiled at each other. The sound of Fast-Eddy's voice couldn't have been any sweeter. It brought a promise with it that the dreadfulness of the night was finally over. Excitedly, the bikers raced out of the cottage, but as soon as they were outside, they knew that they had been deceived. Whatever sound they thought they had heard, it didn't belong to a car door. The only other vehicle in the driveway besides their own was another motorcycle, and the voice they heard was certainly not Eddy's.

There was a chopper in front of them. It was long and muscled, and painted with green and brown sparkling flakes which dazzled in the moonlight. Tied to the front of that bike was a naked Eddy. His skin was the color of lace and his fingers and toes were blackened from frostbite. The blonde Mariachi twitched and convulsed, his eyes rolled into the back of his skull, and he foamed at the mouth. Before Eddy stood a gargantuan man, who used a hunting knife to cut the leather straps that held the Dead Mariachi to the Chopper's handlebars. When the last tie was cut, Eddy crumpled to the snow covered ground and lay motionless.

Slowly, the fiendish giant turned to face Death Mask and Hellbilly. A bald head and devilish goatee were the only parts of the brute's face that looked human. Truly, he was a jigsaw puzzle made of leather, a smashed mound of flesh coloured playdough. Around his arms and shoulders was an intricate web of spiraling tattoos in geometric shapes. His arms were peppered with tiny red apples, and a large black bird reached out from his chest towards his shoulders. The man stepped forward, becoming silhouetted by the headlight of the chopper, and Death Mask realized he was wearing the same brown leather cut that had been gifted to him when he killed the President of the Scum Fucks Motorcycle Club a decade earlier. The same cut that he had asked Eddy to retrieve from his mother's apartment, where it had been hiding all these years.

"Damn cold night, isn't it?" said a woman.

Caleb and William looked beside the motorcycle and registered Morrigan's presence for the first time. She was draped in a long silk nightgown, which offered no protection from the cold. She stood with her bare feet against the snow, but looked as comfortable as if she were on an exotic beach.

Hellbilly raised the peacemaker and cocked the hammer back. "Leave Eddy where he is and get the fuck out of here, or I'll blow your god damn brains out!"

Morrigan's eyes became serious, but her son just laughed. It was a wet and awful bellow.

"Hell of a welcome," said the shattered man standing in front of the chopper. Daniel Church did a playful little hop and grabbed his vest like he was a fashion model on a runway. "Awfully nice of you to keep my cut safe for me D-D-D-Death Mask. Seems like you took good care of it, too."

"I killed you…" was the only thing Death Mask could think to say.

Daniel nodded, and the bones in his neck cracked. "Why yes you did. Don't let this moment take that away from you."

"You can't have the boy!" Hellbilly exclaimed.

"Okay then." Daniel smirked.

Morrigan stepped towards the pair of bikers and Hellbilly aimed the Peacemaker at her. "You must be the Thunderbird. I always wondered where you were hiding. Guess it just wasn't time for your lines yet." A curtain of black hair fell over Morrigan's face and when she brushed it aside, her attention was on Caleb. "You look so much stronger now, little man. Older though, but that suits you."

Hellbilly stepped forward, but Death Mask grabbed his hand and prevented him from going further.

"Smart boy," said the witch with a pleased smile.

Daniel's eyes glistened with mischief. He walked over to Fast-Eddy and picked up the biker by the scruff of the neck. Then, like a striking rattlesnake, he thrust his teeth into Eddy's throat and began drinking.

The Peacemaker cracked and thundered through the forest, causing all the snow-covered birds to take flight. The bullet collided with Daniel's chest, but the Scum Fuck only rocked backwards a little. Daniel opened his mouth to giggle, and blood gushed from the sides of his maw, speckling the snow at his feet.

The sight of a dead man laughing off a .45 slug to the chest froze Hellbilly and Death Mask in place. Above all the horrors they had seen that day, this was by far the most terrifying. Before his demise, Daniel Church had been a man of infamy, and now here he was before them, unfettered by pain, unrestrained by life, and uninhibited by God himself.

Something brushed against Hellbilly's leg, and the biker nearly fired his gun again from the startle. Oscar had come up beside him and Hellbilly stole a glance at the boy.

"We have to get away from her," Oscar said in a worried voice.

Hellbilly looked at Morrigan, then back at the boy. "From who? That woman? I think you got your wires crossed kid, that man there is Daniel Church, he's a walking god damn corpse and he means us all kinds of harm."

Daniel finished drinking, tossed Eddy to the ground, and slowly uncoiled himself until he stood magnificently tall.

"No," said Oscar, while shaking his head. "The crow is the dangerous one. She plays with magic that she doesn't understand."

"HA!" Morrigan laughed. "The nerve…"

Oscar scowled, then darted off the front porch, across the lawn, and into the woods beside the cottage.

Daniel hopped up and down with excitement, leapt onto his chopper, revved the engine high and tore back down the driveway in hot pursuit of the boy.

"He's gonna cut him off at the top of the hill," Hellbilly shouted. "Go get Oscar. I'll help Eddy."

Death Mask nodded, then pounced on the Harley, fired up the bike with a single try and took off after Daniel.

In the dust-up, Hellbilly walked towards Morrigan with his pistol aimed at her chest. "Listen lady, I don't like hittin' women and I never killed one before, but I'll do what I need to do to protect that boy. YOU HEAR ME BITCH?"

Morrigan glared at the approaching outlaw, and with a smile she hissed the words, "Sssshhhhhhriveled Tooooooonnnnnnnnguuue."

Immediately, Bill's mouth began to dry. His tongue squeezed itself like a sponge being wrung out. A moment later, all the moisture was gone. He ran his dried tongue against the top of his pallet and it felt like two pieces of sandpaper being rubbed together. The sensation reverberated through Bill's skull. It brought him unwillingly to his knees, and it hurt. It hurt worse than anything the biker had ever felt in his life. Panicked, Bill reached into his mouth. He felt something like a sundried tomato inside and probed the shriveled appendage. Then, to his horror, Bill's tongue slipped out from between his lips and plopped on the ground between his knees.

Morrigan sauntered across the front lawn and stepped over Bill as she passed. She patted the Dead Mariachi twice on his head, like he was a dog, and walked towards the place in the woods where Oscar had fled.

As the witch disappeared from his sight, Bill was finally able to scream.

C H A P T E R   1 9

The forest screamed with the sound of engines. Death Mask followed the cherry red glow of Danny-Boy's taillight up the steep incline of the ice-covered cottage road. They bopped and bounced over the rough terrain, and with his deformed face, Daniel kept stealing glances of Death Mask from over his shoulder. Taunting the Dead Mariachi with a shattered grin. When they reached the top of the hill, the Scum Fuck suddenly veered into the woods and disappeared between the snow-covered trees.

Death Mask kicked out his back tire, skidded to a halt, then pulled back on the throttle and bound across the ditch into the forest. He found himself dodging evergreens and boulders and tearing through the wilderness like a sprinting wolf. Daniel was a few car lengths to Caleb's right, and he rolled through the brush like it was his home. The bikers bounced over branches and hopped across valleys, they slid over ice patches, and muscled out of snowdrifts. Their arms and legs became extensions of their bikes, stabilizing turns and pushing them forward when needed.

Even though Daniel was making a b-line for the top of the hill, where Oscar was likely to emerge, Death Mask refused to push the Ultra-Limited past the steady pace he had established. It took every ounce of personal discipline he had not to open the throttle in full, but to falter now would mean the bike would spin-out and Death Mask would lose the precious ground he had gained.

Halfway to the cliff, Caleb's front tire came in line with the back of Danny-Boy's chopper. He knew that he needed to pressure his rival into making a mistake, so Death Mask veered to the side and collided with Danny-Boy. The chopper wavered and Death Mask was able to pull forward. Now, both men rode shoulder to shoulder, eye to eye, axel to axel. Daniel drew a blade from inside his cut, the same one that he used to cut Eddy down from the front of his bike earlier, and slashed. An electric bright sting radiated up Caleb's forearm, and he suddenly felt wind on the inside of his flesh. The cut was deep, and the blood it unleashed splattered on the snow with a "glopping" sound.

Daniel laughed into the moonlight with his head tilted backwards and his eyes ablaze. Caleb pulled his arm up and growled at his opponent. The top of the hill approached them, and Caleb knew he only had a few more moments to disrupt Danny-Boy's plans. He veered away, establishing a few feet of clearance, and then turned, hard, back towards Daniel's chopper.

The dead man went flying. His chopper tumbled through the snow, and Danny-Boy came down on a nearby stump with both feet planted. As Death Mask rode past, the Scum Fuck leapt into the air and pounced the back of the Harley. The Ultra-Limited wobbled, but Death Mask was able to keep the bike upright. Daniel crawled over the top box attached to the back seat. As Danny-Boy approached the front, Death Mask swung his fist like a hammer and caught Daniel in the temple. The dead man shirked the punch and slashed Caleb's back with a clawed hand. Danny-Boy's fingers easily tore through Caleb's pink sweater and raked through his skin like freshly tilled soil.

Death Mask shot upright. The Harley entered the open space in front of the cliff, and acting on instinct, Caleb jumped up onto the Ultra-Limited's seat, then placed one foot on the gas tank. He looked back at the monster approaching. Danny-Boy had himself all the way onto the back seat now, with both knees cradled there. The pair locked eyes. Then, with the strength of an Olympic snowboarder, Caleb turned the bike until it was parallel to the cliff. Death Mask and Danny-Boy both leapt off the Harley as it toppled over the side of the cliff and crashed down the rock face.

When Death Mask landed from his heroic jump, he came down hard and the whole world turned off.

Oscar heard the sound of snow crunching beneath Morrigan's feet and knew she was allowing that sound to happen on purpose, just to scare him.

He dodged branches and rocks as he climbed the gentle slope beside the rock face. He only looked forward, refusing to look back and give more power to the abomination that followed him. In the distance he heard engines, then a crash. He saw a motorcycle topple over the cliff and fall down the rockface. Then the woods were silent again.

Oscar slipped on a patch of ice and fell into the cold snow, which washed over him like a terrible bath. The witch crunched the snow again and her footstep was close. Oscar feared that if he looked in her direction he would find Morrigan standing right beside him, grinning in her evil way. That fear ignited the embers of hope buried in Oscar's soul and propelled him back to his feet. A surge of energy tingled his muscles, and gave fresh power to his legs. Suddenly, the hill didn't seem so high and the snowdrifts weren't so daunting. Instead of trudging through the muck, Oscar bound up the hill like a graceful deer.

Behind him, the witch cackled.

The shriveled tongue mocked Hellbilly. Bill had trouble comprehending the immense tragedy he was looking at. It didn't seem real that such an important part of him would be lying at his knees, outside of his body. Hot tickling pin pricks walked up his face, like a thousand razor sharp spider's feet, and squeezed his chest. A moment before his panic consumed him, Hellbilly heard Morrigan cackle. The shrieking laughter reminded Bill that Oscar was in danger.

William closed his eyes, and for four seconds, took a deep breath. Then, he held that breath for four seconds, and finally allowed that air to escape him in a slow and controlled manner. He did this three more times and concentrated on pushing back the pinpricks of panic that threatened to overtake him.

As he finished his final cycle of breath, Bill opened his eyes and saw Eddy move. The blonde man stirred only a little, but it was enough to catch Bill's attention. Hellbilly looked up from the raisined muscle between his knees to his brother beside the bike, then in the direction Morrigan and Oscar had lit out in. He could no longer see either the witch nor the boy, and the thought of Oscar being alone in the woods with that terrible creature filled William with fright. Bill stumbled to his feet and in a series of awkward and disorganized steps, ran to Eddy. The blonde Mariachi's eyelids fluttered, but his face was devoid of color and the spot on his neck where Daniel Church had latched himself seeped blood. Bill smacked his friend firmly in the face twice, and Eddy's eyes opened.

"Billy?"

"Geh hup!" Bill attempted to say, but the words came out sounding like he was retching.

"My hands. My feet. I… I can't feel them."

Bill lifted Eddy to his feet, took off his hoodie, and placed it on the naked man. Hellbilly felt a sudden and blinding need to bring Eddy along with him, as if leaving his friend behind now would mean he would never leave this horrible place. With Eddy draped over his shoulder, Bill headed into the forest and up the hill.

Caleb woke up by the edge of the rock face, buried in the snow. Another few feet and he would have tumbled over the edge and fallen into the splintered woodpile below. His back ached, his ribs did too, but they were nothing compared to his arm. Caleb sat on his knees and rolled back the long sleeve of his sweater. The gash that Church had inflicted on him was the size of a tortilla. Just as floppy and both pink muscle and glistening red bone could be seen. The edges of the wound were a mess. Clearly, it had been torn open further during the crash. With his clutch hand down and his torso feeling like a bomb had gone off beside him, Caleb tried to regroup his brain and remember where he was. He stood, and the world spiraled. From the corner of his eyes, Death Mask saw someone looming tall and dark. He knew right away that it was the man he had killed ten years ago, and also knew, somehow, that Daniel had been observing him, waiting to see how well he recovered from the crash.

"You're not so tough," Danny-Boy said in an even tone.

Caleb's head refused to steady itself, and he stumbled to his left, and then to his right. The pain he felt trembled him, and Caleb worried that he didn't have enough strength to defend himself against the violent onslaught that was sure to come.

"You know, *Death Mask*, for years, I wallowed because of you," Daniel continued. "I expected to die fighting, but I couldn't reconcile that I had been murdered by a tiny little Prospect with bad teeth and a terrible attitude."

Caleb heard something coming up behind him, but the world fuzzed in and out of focus, so he couldn't figure out what he was hearing.

"And my face! I mean, *my god*, look what you did to my face!" Daniel laced his hands behind himself and began pacing on top of the snow, never sinking into the powder, almost like he weighed nothing at all. "I don't know why my injuries didn't heal. They should have. Something went wrong with the spell I guess. It was supposed to bring me back to life and make me stronger than I was. The peak version of myself. I am stronger, I think, but this is far from my peak. *You* mangled me."

Feet tromping through the snow was the sound Caleb was hearing. He recognized it just as Oscar reached him. The boy threw his arms around Death Mask and squeezed.

Daniel whistled at the sight of the boy. "Here he is! Little Mr. Bonus-Points."

Hellbilly and Eddy came over the ridge next, and Daniel began clapping. "The whole gang's here! I don't see ma-ma, but that just means it's my time to shine."

Hellbilly handed the half-naked Eddy over to Death Mask and stormed past his friends. Bill placed himself between the vampire and raised the Peacemaker until it was aimed directly at Daniel's head.

Daniel threw his hands up in mockery. "Don't shoot!" he laughed. "I wouldn't want you to waste another bullet, big-man."

Hellbilly cocked back the hammer of the revolver.

"You aint' taking the boy," Death Mask growled.

"I promise you, I have no intention of taking that child anywhere else today. He can die right here, with all of you," answered Church.

"You ain't killing him either!" shouted Eddy with his head still listless.

Daniel guffawed. "Hate to break it to you, but indeed I am. It's nothing personal, I'm sure he's a great little guy, but that boy needs to be taken care of. Should have been taken care of a long time ago if you ask me."

"You're a sick fuck!" Death Mask said.

"No sicker than you are."

Hellbilly shook his head and sneered.

"Bullshit!" spat Caleb. "Don't you try and compare yourself to us."

"Why not?" Daniel had a genuine look of confusion on his face. "We're built the same. We move through the world in the same ways."

Death Mask glared, "We're not the same."

"No?" said Church, with his head cocked to the side. "Let's inventory shall we. We're all bad ass sons-of-bitches who don't take shit from anyone. We like to ride, like to drink, I'm betting we all like to fuck incredible looking women." Daniel smirked, and pointed at Hellbilly. "I tasted you in the blood of Paulo's wife, you lingered in her. Means she loved you. Good looking woman, her. I bet she was as tasty to me as she was to you."

Hellbilly rocked on his feet, but stayed true, and remained on guard. Daniel beamed at the sight of Bill's discomfort.

"Look, we are all the type of man that needs something we are willing to die over, and we found that thing in a patch and a leather vest. My father was a Scum Fuck, did you know that? He led the charge into Ontario back in the eighties and nineties. He was a *real* man, tough as fucking nails. You didn't mess with Cormac Church, no goddamn way. But, he was a cruel man, devoid of love and compassion, and the day he died was the happiest day of my life. I didn't become a Scum Fuck *because* of him. No, I became a Scum Fuck *in-spite* of him. Because I was always going to be the man I am today. I was always gonna be an outlaw, just like you boys." Daniel grinned from damaged ear to damaged ear. "And do you know what I have come to realize in my old age?"

The Dead Mariachis all squirmed.

"The only real difference between you all and me? Is that when I was coming up, I was in an area with a bunch of Scum Fucks, and when you were coming up, you were in an area with Dead Mariachis. If you'd come up in my neck of the woods, you'd be a Scum Fuck. And if I'd come up where you were, I'd be a Dead Mariachi. And, if we'd all come up together, we'd be calling each other brother right now. Hell, maybe you'd even have the chance to see the night the same way I do. It's lovely. Anyways, that's it boys, the big difference between us all, just like in real estate, the only thing that matters; location, location, location."

"Fuck that!" Death Mask scowled. "You're a Nazi scumbag! You had Robbie Balls-Out killed for nothing. Raped his wife! TRIED TO KILL OLIVIA RENAUD ON HER FRONT PORCH!"

"Oh hell, you're bringing up the past, boy!" Daniel waved his hands in the air frantically and sunk an inch in the snow. "I was a different *thing* back then, filled with hubris! But you, little man, you gave me the greatest gift I have ever received. You humbled me. Beat me in combat, smashed me into the earth, shattered my face forever, and left me to die. In truth, I needed that. I had stood with my back straight for too long, it was a blessing to be reminded of what it meant to crawl. In that dark earth, with the taste of your flesh on my lips, and my mother's magic in my belly, I awoke. Shattered, yes, but born again by the grace of the great healer, Dian Cécht."

"You play with magic that wasn't given to you," said Oscar, meekly. "Your mother forced open a locked door and raped a god to get what she has."

Daniel glowered at the boy, and without humour said, "Imagine the balls it takes to do that?"

"You're a fucking goof!" shouted Death Mask. "No better than any other run of the mill child molester."

"Uh oh!" Daniel put a finger in the air like he was a school teacher. "That's too far, and it's wrong. I never hurt that kid. Not really. Did I boy?"

Death Mask felt Oscar pull on his sweater and bury his face into the biker's side.

"Sure… he saw me eating a time or two, but I never laid a hand on him."

Death Mask lost his patience. "YOU'VE BEEN TRYING TO KILL HIM ALL GOD DAMN DAY LONG!"

"No," Daniel said calmly, "he was supposed to be saved by the police. You were the only ones that were supposed to die in that shootout, and you couldn't even do that right."

"You abducted him."

Daniel shook his head. "You have this whole thing wrong. I didn't take him from that mall. That was your brother, your king, Paulo Renaud. I may be the boogie man, but Paulo is the thing that goes bump in the night."

The Dead Mariachis felt truly frozen for the first time in that long and horrible day. Death Mask looked down, saw that Oscar was quaking and knew right then that what Danny-Boy was saying was true.

Church saw the realization that had come upon the men, and sizzled with excitement. "Sorry to disappoint you gentlemen, but I really don't give a damn about that boy."

Death Mask squinted. "You're full of shit."

Daniel smiled. "You know that I'm not."

Caleb knew he wasn't. It all fit together. The entire miserable day had been one long ruse to hide the horrendous thing that Paulo had done. He abducted a child, did something unspeakable, but couldn't bring himself to murder Oscar and bury him in the woods. He needed help, and being the keen opportunist that he was, Paulo used it as a chance to get rid of some of his other dirty laundry as well. Maybe, in a moment of marital openness, Olivia had made the fatal mistake of telling her husband about her past indiscretion. Maybe Bill had told someone about it in a drunken stupor, or it could even be that Paulo had known all along. In any case, their transgression was the nail in the coffin for both Bill and Olivia. As for Caleb, Paulo simply saw him as a threat, but knew his legend was too valuable to the club to get rid of him. Being labeled a child molester though, that meant an immediate expulsion, even posthumously, and would evaporate the legend which Death Mask had carefully fostered for himself. It was a beautifully Machiavellian plot, perfectly Paulo.

"Now," Church continued. "I'm gonna do what Paulo didn't have the balls to do in the first place, and I *am* gonna kill that child. But, I promise I'll do it quick. The only one I really wanna make suffer is you Caleb Driscoll, Mr. Big-Shot *Death Mask*. You owe a debt to me. These woods are gonna hear you scream my name tonight."

Daniel took a step, and his foot sank to the ankle. In turn, Hellbilly advanced a single pace.

"Willbilly, Helliam, MOTHER FUCKER, whatever your name is," Daniel seemed vexed all of a sudden, "you can either step aside and walk your sorry ass out of these here woods, or stand in my way and die screaming, too. Either way, we are gonna find out what kind of man you are tonight."

Daniel crouched down like a panther and sprung towards Oscar and the Dead Mariachis. Bill looked past the barrel of his Peacemaker to the center of Daniel's chest, and envisioned his bullets passing through the vampire's ribcage. He saw the image of Pete McConnell's face as the basement door closed, and then, with his whole heart, William "Hellbilly" McConnell fired.

BOOM! BOOM! BOOM! went the Peacemaker, followed by the click of an empty cylinder.

Each bullet caused Danny-Boy to sink deeper into the snow. By the time he reached Hellbilly, Church was buried up to his knees. Still, he kept coming. William saw death in the Scum Fuck's eyes, and knew he only had one last chance to save his friends and the child he had sworn to protect. Hellbilly threw his gun into the snow, reached out and wrapped his arms around Daniel, then with an incredible burst of power he lifted the vampire king of the Scum Fucks high into the air. Daniel sank daggered fingernails into Bill's shoulder, opened his sharp mouth, and hissed. Bill twisted in the direction of the cliff, and the momentum of the turn carried both of them over the edge.

The rockface tore the men apart. Bill's good arm fractured against a rock, and his bad elbow cracked and burst through his skin. Both of Hellbilly's legs shattered against a slab of granite, and the skin in his back flayed completely. Near the bottom, Bill cartwheeled, and his skull cracked open against a boulder like a melon thrown onto a tiled floor.

When they finally came to a stop, it was in the jagged woodpile beside the cottage.

The pain Bill felt was blinding. His body didn't know how to process what hurt, because everything had been ripped open. So, Bill's mind short-circuited. There was a plopping sound in front of him, and when Bill looked up, he saw a bloody hand with the letters "MFFM" tattooed along the knuckles. He moved his left arm, but could only see his shoulder wiggle and realized that the hand in front of him was his own. Because his brain was so overloaded, the sight of his detached arm was only a point of interest, not the traumatic event that it should have been. Hellbilly looked down and felt a stick push against the bone in his cheek. He understood then that he had no flesh covering that part of his face, and that his exposed skull was grinding against the wooden stake.

Laying beneath him, smushed into the woodpile by Bill's incredible frame, was Daniel Church.

The Scum Fuck was as mangled and mashed as Hellbilly. A piece of wood had come straight through Danny-Boy's mouth and unhinged one side of his jawbone. Daniel's right shoulder had been obliterated, his legs were twisted and crumpled, and his eyes were glassy and clouded over like an old corpse. The biker-king shook violently and coughed blood onto Hellbilly's open face. Instinctively, Bill tried to look away and prevent the tainted blood from entering his open wounds. That's when he saw the pike. It was sharp, but rough, and it had come through the crow on Daniel's chest, exactly where the creature's heart should be. Still feeling disorganized from the shock, Bill looked from the pike to Daniel's face, and saw that the man was withered now. Slowly Danny-Boy's flesh crinkled into that of an old man, then it mushed like a rotten pear, and finally it licuified then melted away, leaving only Daniel's bones behind.

The pain came then. Bill felt the sear of his missing arm and the throb of his face. He felt all manner of sharpness, and a horrifically dull ache. His brain caught up with his body, and he understood that he was shaking, that he had been shaking this entire time. He drifted in and out of consciousness, through a sea of memories and images, and found one he wanted to hold on to.

Instead of Daniel's rotten skull in front of him, a curly haired little boy with a mischievous grin appeared. The child was as happy as any boy had ever been. Suddenly, Emmitt aged into a teenager with arms that were too long for his body and a bad piercing above his eyebrow. William laughed at the sight of the gangly looking kid, and the teenager looked at Hellbilly with a scowl that said, "don't look at me," then burst into the most beautifully warm and inviting smile Hellbilly had ever seen. The teenager changed into a man, strong and proud, and he held a child of his own in his hands which he presented to Bill. Hellbilly saw all of this and wanted so badly to reach out and touch his vision, to tell the boy that he loved him, that he was proud, but his remaining hand was caught in the wood, and he couldn't move.

As the dark encircled him, Bill allowed the warm thought of his son to guide him into nothingness, and eventually, without a sound, William let go.

CHAPTER 20

———————|———————

Morrigan's scream tore apart the remaining sanctity of the forest and carried with it the news that both Hellbilly and Danny-Boy were dead. Death Mask's bones electrified when he heard the anguished cry. The hatred of the sound pulled terror out of a hidden place in Caleb's mind, a spot that hadn't been touched since he was a little boy listening to the sound of trees scraping against his bedroom window during a storm. The biker moved as quickly as he could over the rocks and sticks that littered the forest floor, but he was weighed down by the empty Peacemaker which Hellbilly had dropped and he had retrieved. To make matters worse, Caleb was still groggy from the crash, so the going was slow.

It was Oscar who was in the lead now. The boy dragged Caleb forward by the sleeve of his hoodie and Death Mask pulled the nearly unconscious Eddy. The boy was filled with an unbridled energy. He Jeté'd over obstacles like a cougar and muscled his way through snow banks like a steam-powered locomotive.

Behind them, Morrigan continued to scream. A strange ripple accompanied her shouts. It shook the woods and sent a shiver of fear through Death Mask's spine. He was sure the other two felt the shiver as well, but Eddy was too beleaguered and Oscar too focused to show it.

"We have to go faster!" Oscar commanded.

Another shout ripped apart the night. Death Mask looked over his shoulder and, in the distance, saw Morrigan coming over the hill. Her eyes blazed with white lightning and saffron, her silk robe fluttered like the fins of a koi fish in a disturbed pond, and a cloud of dark smoke curled around her. She walked on all fours like an enraged mother bear and propelled herself forward like the hound of hell that she was.

The stupor Death Mask had been in the grips of evaporated at the sight of the devil racing towards them. He stopped for a moment, tucked Hellbilly's peacemaker into his front pocket, bent deeply at the knees, and threw Eddy over his shoulders.

"Run!" he shouted to Oscar. "I'm right behind you!"

The boy nodded and took off in the direction of the road. Death Mask used his renewed energy to bound through the bush, racing towards the open space ahead. Through the trees, a pair of headlights came into view. Caleb felt an instant surge of adrenaline and hope, and picked up his pace even more. Every time the biker took a step though, his foot touched a branch or rock and his ankle buckled. Perhaps it was the sound of the witch behind him, or the hope that came with the sight of the growing headlight, but something kept Caleb upright and moving forward. As the trio crashed through the tree line, the headlights reached their pinnacle and then screeched past them.

All hope, optimism, and faith drained from Caleb when he saw the vehicle the lights belonged to. It was the bus. The same damn bus that had been filled with ghouls when it arrived at the McConnell house hours earlier.

Death Mask stopped completely. He put Eddy on the ground and pushed Oscar behind him. Caleb took a series of short – but deep breaths, then took the Peacemaker out of his pocket, held the gun by the barrel, and lifted it over his shoulder like he was about to swing a hammer. His fingers were so cold that they could barely hold the pistol, but Death Mask settled into a feeble stance and readied himself for violence.

The door to the decrepit school bus opened, and Winston stormed out. The other vampire Scum Fucks followed closely behind. Winston glared at Caleb, then the boy, but when his eyes found Eddy, he exploded with jubilation. The red-headed beast pointed at the withered biker, whom he immediately recognized as the cause for his facial deformities, and laughed.

"This is a fucking gift! I am going to take my time with you pretty boy!"

Morrigan flew out of the woods just then, like a desperate wolf, and slid from one side of the road to the other. She crashed into the snowbank by the ditch, then regained her composure and stood like a wretched Goddess. Her face was twisted into a terrible maze of angry creases.

Caleb felt the gun in his hands shaking. He wondered how long it would take the monsters to tear him apart and then move onto the child. Then he heard the sound of crunching snow beside him. From the corner of his eye, he saw that a wobbling, weaponless, and naked from the waist down Fast-Eddy, was standing shoulder to shoulder with him. Then he saw Oscar fall in on his other side. The boy had picked up a rock the size of a baseball, and was mimicking Death Mask's stance. Together, the trio readied themselves for whatever hell was about to come.

Winston boomed past Morrigan, and was about to head straight for Eddy, when the witch whistled and screamed "HEEL!"

Like the dog he was, Winston returned to Morrigan's side.

For what seemed like an eternity, Morrigan stared at Caleb, looking him in the eyes, and peeking into what he had left for a soul. When she finally spoke, it was half whimper and half roar.

"When you took my son, I knew it was coming. I was prepared. But neither the tea leaves nor the ashes, warned me about your friend. I walk the earth now with HALF A SOUL! But, I swear to every god and every goddess that has ever been and ever will be, that I am going to skin you alive, Caleb Driscoll, and make a coat out of your flesh. I'll drain your blood, won't let none of these nightwalkers drink it, and let it go to waste, putrefied on the rotten ground! I'll bite you to death, and you will scream my name the whole GODDAMN time!"

"Lady!" Death Mask shouted, "I don't know what gods you pray to, but I don't think they give a FUCK about your bullshit."

Morrigan growled. Winston and the other Scum Fucks walked forward. Suddenly, they were washed out by a bright light. Death Mask was caught off guard and stole a quick glance over his shoulder, terrified that more fiendish horrors had arrived. Instead, he saw a convoy of cars and trucks that stretched back almost the entire length of the road. In the lead was a white Chevy Tahoe, with flashing lights that alternated between red and blue. The Tahoe's back passenger door opened before the vehicle came to a stop, and a statuesque woman jumped out.

"ISTÁ!" Oscar shouted.

The boy grabbed Death Mask by the hand and pulled him towards the convoy. Caleb grabbed Eddy and the pair slowly walked backwards towards the cars. Oscar reached his mother and hugged her with one arm as tightly as any child had ever hugged their parent, while still keeping his grip on Death Mask with the other hand.

A police officer holding a shotgun stepped out of the Tahoe next. He racked the gun and pointed it at the vampires. Other people got out of their cars, too. Men and women, a few teenagers even. Some had guns, but most of them had baseball bats, axes, machetes, or whatever else they had found that could be used as a weapon. Caleb even saw one fellow with a chainsaw standing next to a Kia Niro. The people lined the roadside, an entire community of defenders, ready to battle anyone who stood in the way of them reclaiming their lost child.

Finally, the passenger side door of the police car opened and an elderly woman stepped out. The Elder walked past Renee, past Oscar, past Eddy and Death Mask, past the police officer, until she was between Morrigan and everyone else. She stood as straight and tall as a pine tree and addressed the witch directly.

"You stay where you are. No need to try your luck any further tonight. You'll regret it."

"Get out of the way…" Morrigan said with absolute contempt. "That man right there owes me a debt and you have no idea what I will do to you if you try to stop me from collecting it."

Jean laughed. "You? Ohhhhh, you can't do anything to me. I know what you are." The old lady pointed past Morrigan to the Scum Fucks behind her. "I know what they are, too. You don't belong in these woods. Your kind are always lost on this side of the ocean. You've never really been able to get a footing over here. Like I said, stay where you are, let us leave in peace, and I won't trespass against you any further tonight. Unless I have to."

Morrigan paced to one side, and then came back to the spot where she had been standing. "You can have the boy. I just want the little man he's with. He killed my son."

Jean looked over her shoulder, right at Oscar. The pair locked eyes, and with that look she asked the boy what he thought of Morrigan's offer.

"No," said Oscar, as he squeezed Caleb's hand.

An explosion of heat came from that single word. It shook the woods and brought Morrigan to her knees. The other vampires wavered where they stood and had to grab the bus to steady themselves. When Morrigan looked back up at the crowd, she had aged terribly. No longer was she the vibrant woman who had given chase through the woods, instead she was a wrinkled old hag covered in sagging flops of skin, with liver spot decorations. Her teeth looked rotten, her spine was wrinkled, and her hips were withered. Only her hair remained full and lush.

"There you have it," said Jean. "You can stay in this place or leave, it makes no difference to me. But you *will* let us go first."

Slowly, Morrigan rose to her feet, but her back wouldn't straighten. Her hands were clawed with arthritis and she shook from the cold winds and the snow. With her teeth chattering, she hissed, "He owes a debt to me."

"That may be," Jean said, "but you don't have the strength to collect it tonight. Not from me, and apparently, not from the boy either." The woman smiled when she mentioned Oscar.

Death Mask felt a gentle pull on his sleeve. It was Renee. Oscar's mother led the rescuers towards the police car, and as they approached the Tahoe, someone gave both Eddy and Caleb elegant, black long coats to wear. Eddy was helped into the SUV first, Caleb followed next, but had a little difficulty getting into the vehicle with Oscar still clinging to him. Renee followed her son into the back seat. She held the child firmly against her bosom and bit her bottom lip until it was white.

The car was exquisitely warm, and as they nestled into their seats,

Caleb exhaled all of the terror he had been holding inside of himself. He let go of the face of Pete McConnell, of the sight of Oscar's curled and beaten body, and even of the charred remains of the married couple who had haunted his dreams from the war.

Behind them, car doors slammed shut and engines turned back on. The police officer backed away from the dead with his shotgun raised. When he reached the Tahoe, he slipped into the vehicle and positioned himself behind the wheel, ready to take off.

Jen the Elder stayed for a moment though. She said something to Morrigian, something that Caleb couldn't hear. The vampires grimaced when the Elder spoke, and Morrigian looked like she was about to be sick. Then, the old woman turned and presented her back to the fiends as if they posed no threat to her whatsoever. She walked back to the SUV, got in as spryly as anyone could, and closed her door.

"We can go now," she said. "We don't have anything to worry about from them. They understand their place."

The police officer threw the Tahoe into reverse and backed up. When he came to the first driveway, nearly a half a kilometer away, he performed a country turn, and sped off to join the rest of the convoy. As they made their way through the dark woods, Caleb watched quiet tears pour out of Renee Delaronde's eyes, savored the feeling of Oscar's fingers wrapped tightly around his hand, and listened to the gentle hum of the Chevy's engine.

EPILOGUE: WARMER IN QUEBEC

————————

It was warmer out. The snow banks lining the roads were dwindling and the breeze that fluttered through the Outaouais farmlands carried with it a hint of sunshine from the south. An ancient looking Oldsmobile pulled into a driveway outside of Gatineau Quebec, and slowly made its way down the slush filled mud path. The farm had once been alive with pigs and chickens, and back then the fields grew sweet hay and grain corn in the summer, but now the place was barren. As the car pulled into a spot in front of the house the bland baritone of Vince Harper drifted out of the speakers, a casualty of the syndicated radio station from Ontario which plagued southern Quebec.

"This morning, Ontario Provincial Police confirmed that human remains found near Sharbot Lake on Monday belong to William McConnell. Mr. McConnell, and his associate Caleb Driscoll, were the subjects of a nationwide man-hunt two weeks ago when police issued a warrant for their arrest in connection to the disappearance of Oscar Delaronde and for their involvement in the Brockville shootout with OPP missing persons detectives."

"Oscar, the eleven-year-old Tyendinaga resident, whose disappearance gripped the nation's attention last month, was returned to his community shortly after the shootout. Since then, Tyendinaga Police Services have refused to lay charges against either McConnell or Driscoll, and maintain that both men were instrumental in returning Oscar safely to his family. Despite Tyendinaga Police's stance on the suspects, a nation-wide warrant still exists for Caleb Driscoll, whose whereabouts remain unknown.

"The confirmation of William McConnell's death comes on the heels of an internal investigation that led the OPP to uncover several off-shore accounts linking the missing persons detectives involved in the Brockville shootout to senior officers in the Dead Mariachis Motorcycle Club, which both McConnell and Driscoll were members of."

"As part of this morning's press conference, OPP Superintendent Josh Harnbeck issued a warrant for the Dead Mariachis national president Paulo Renaud, who they believe is a key figure linking the offshore accounts to the deceased detectives from the shootout, and William McConnell."

Paulo turned off the radio and cut the Oldsmobile's engine. He scanned the tree line around his Great Aunt's house and studied the ground around her front door. There were no footprints, nor lurkers amidst the trees, so the portly biker unbuckled his seat belt and stepped out of the dilapidated land-yacht. He pulled out the groceries he had purchased two counties over and shuffled towards the house. He would have liked to have sent his Great Aunt out for the shopping, but she had taken ill since his arrival, and was in no shape to go out. Luckily, he had been able to hit the grocery store before the press conference and felt confident that he'd kept a low enough profile to not raise suspicions about his presence. Still, it would only be a matter of days before he would have to find a new hideout.

"TANTE!" Paulo called out as he closed the front door behind himself. "Je suis de retour!"

Paulo was already in the living room and heading for the kitchen when he realized that his aunt had not answered him. His next realization concerned the quietness of the house. Usually, he could hear his aunt's television set blaring at all hours of the day, but there were no daytime television sounds tumbling down from the second floor. Something about this situation was very wrong.

With fear beginning to set in, Paulo looked around. He scanned the room quickly, but his search stopped when he saw a black leather vest laying on the coffee table in the middle of his aunt's living room. The vest had a series of well-worn patches, all of them red fields with black horrorshow lettering. The name "Hellbilly" was stitched onto the left breast and on the right side, in inverse colours, were the numbers "1313."

CLICK… Paulo recognized the sound immediately. It was the tone of a revolver's hammer being cocked back.

Death Mask stood in the doorway to the kitchen. His face was bruised and scraped, but otherwise he looked strong. Caleb wore a long black coat, with his cut draped over top, and he aimed a .45 caliber revolver, which had once belonged to three generations of the McConnell family, directly at Paulo's fat head. The gun looked like something straight out of an old western movie.

"How in the hell did you find me?" Paulo asked.

By the front door, someone racked a shotgun. Slowly, Paulo looked over his other shoulder, just as Eddy came out from behind the hallway staircase. He held the shotgun with stubby and bandaged fingers, but seemed to have a firm grip on the weapon.

"We had help," Eddy growled.

"I'll bet you did by God's good Grace," Paulo sneered.

"It's funny, people won't do it themselves, but if you tell them you are going to kill someone who hurt a child, they will help you any way they can." Death Mask offered.

Paulo's lips curled. "You wouldn't understand what I am even if I told you."

"We know what you are, asshole," said Eddy.

Paulo licked his lips. His eyes darted from one side of the room to the other, trying to figure out if he had an exit strategy, but there was none. Death Mask and Fast-Eddy had gotten the drop on him. The President of the Dead Mariachis turned and faced Death Mask head on. As he did, the corner of his eye bulged and a centipede crawled out from beneath his lid. Caleb looked at the place where the centipede had crawled from and saw that underneath Paulo's eyelid was rotting gray flesh. It was almost like Paulo was a corpse wearing a human skin suit. The bug scurried down the side of Paulo's face and then nestled into his beard.

"Well I'll be damned," said Death Mask, "The boy said a monster took him. I knew that monster was you, but until this moment I didn't realize the kid actually meant what he was saying. What the *fuck* are you?"

A flashy smile came over Paulo, then he reached towards his belt. He got two fingers around his .38 before Death Mask and Eddy unleashed on him. The force of two opposing firearms sent Paulo spiraling backwards, into his great aunt's couch, over the back, and splashing through the front window.

The room filled with gun smoke, and the scent of smoldering flesh. Death Mask grabbed Hellbilly's cut and walked out the front door. Eddy followed.

On the front lawn, Paulo lay in a twisted wreck. His body was contorted and broken, and though smoke rose from the bullet holes in his chest, no blood seeped out. An odd smirk was plastered on his ugly face, giving him the appearance of the Cheshire Cat. But, the most horrific thing about his mangled body were the bugs. Maggots poured out of his mouth and crawled away from his eyes. Centipedes and beetles pushed open his fingernails and dropped onto the lawn like Paulo was giving birth to them. A moth fluttered out of his pant leg, and spiders came out of his shirt from the spot they had torn open by his belly button.

Caleb gagged and almost lost his composure. He felt a calming hand on his shoulder, and turned to look at his partner.

"We need to go," said Eddy.

"But what the fuck is he?" Death Mask asked.

Eddy shook his head. "I don't know man. A monster, I guess. Doesn't matter, we need to get the hell out of dodge, brother."

Death Mask nodded and walked away from the horror show on the front lawn. The bikers made their way through the desolate field and slipped through the tree line at the back corner of the property. They were less concerned about leaving footprints this time. Fifteen minutes later, they were in the clearing where they had left the truck Renee's uncle gave them. A curly haired woman with a lovely face waved at them, showing that it was okay for them to approach. Eddy got in first and hugged his wife. Death Mask hopped in next and patted

Judy on the shoulder, thanking her for waiting for them.

As they drove off, both Death Mask and Eddy kept their cuts on. Caleb's face was all over the news, so they figured that if they were spotted by law enforcement it really made no difference if they were showing their rockers or not. To make matters worse, every outlaw biker from Newfoundland to Mexico knew that both Death Mask and Fast-Eddy had a green light. Still, they had the open road ahead of them and there wasn't an indigenous person in the country that was going to report them to the police. They pulled onto a back road, and an hour later were on the Trans-Canada Highway, heading east. With a little luck, in fourteen hours they would be in Nova Scotia, ready to give Emmitt McConnell his father's cut, and tell the unbelievable story of how Bill died a hero.

Listen to The God Damn Dead playlist on Spotify

ABOUT THE AUTHOR

Colt Skinner is a typical Canadian dad who spends his days giving up his seat on the bus and holding open doors for strangers. However, while he's being polite he is also daydreaming about serial killers, eldritch monsters, and what it would feel like to be drawn and quartered. Inspired by his real-world experiences of being the lead singer of a punk rock band, nightclub bouncer, goat farmer, private investigator, and well-rounded degenerate, Colt's stories feature rich characters in down-to-earth situations highlighting that more often than not it is the people sitting next to us we should fear, not the creatures who go bump in the night.

Website: www.coltskinner.ca

Instagram: instagram.com/colt.skinner.author

TikTok: @colt.skinner.author

X (Formerly Twitter): @Scary_Skinner

ABOUT THE PUBLISHER/EDITOR

Dawn Shea is an author and half of the publishing team over at D&T Publishing. She lives with her family in Mississippi. Always an avid horror lover, she has moved forward with her dreams of writing and publishing those things she loves so much.

Follow her author page on Amazon for all publications she is featured in.

Follow D&T Publishing at their website, **www.dt-publishing.com**, or search for their Facebook Group

Or email here: dandtpublishing20@gmail.com

The God Damn Dead by Colt Skinner

Edited by Tasha Schiedel

Cover Art by Ash Ericmore

Formatting by Ash Ericmore